The Last Temptation

A novel by
GERALD K. MALCOM

Q-Boro Books
WWW.QBOROBOOKS.COM

Q-BORO BOOKS

Jamaica, Queens NY 11431

WWW.QBOROBOOKS.COM

(For store orders, author information and contact information, please Visit Our Website for the most up to date listing.)

ISBN 0-9753066-8-5

First Printing August 2005

Library of Congress Control Number: 2005904820

This is a work of fiction. It is not meant to depict, portray or represent any particular real persons. All the characters, incidents and dialogues are the products of the author's imagination and are not to be construed as real. Any references or similarities to actual events, entities, real people, living or dead, or to real locales are intended to give the novel a sense of reality. Any similarity in other names, characters, entities, places and incidents is entirely coincidental.

Cover Copyright © 2005 by Q-BORO BOOKS all rights reserved

Cover Layout & Design – Candace K. Cottrell

Editors – Shelley Rafferty, Melissa Forbes, Candace K. Cottrell

Printed in Canada

Dedication

Carmen and Bianca

Acknowledgments

To the man upstairs…thanks for giving me the courage and strength to continue to do what I do. Without our late night and early morning conversations, I would be a total loss. I would like to thank my children for allowing their precious "daddy time" so I could complete this book. To my children Warren, Davion, Denzel and the little princess Zoe…ice cream for everyone, but me. It's a lactose thing…ya'll wouldn't understand. You are my heart and soul. I would like to once again thank Mercedes by getting on my knees and kissing the ground she walks on. Fighting through the struggles and still giving head rubs, now that's love! To my immediate family; my mother Peggy, my brother EB, my sisters, Rochelle, Aqueelah and Bendelia. I'm trying to make the doughnuts. To my other moms, Joyce and Alma, thanks for supporting me as though I was your own.

Now for the book world and those who have helped me through this rough process. Echo Soul. Thank you Kim for supporting me from day one. I love you. I can never leave home. Or you can never get rid of me. It's the same thing. Echosoul.com.

My sister and homegirl, Jamise L. Dames. I love that we can talk about everything. Keep hitting those best selling charts. My other sister, Nakea. Philly? What? I love you guys. Can't forget about our traveling voice and fellow night-on-the-town girl, LaShon.

Q-Boro Books, what can a brotha say? I would like to thank Mark Anthony for taking a chance and bringing me out to the party. So this is how it looks? LOL Candace…thanks for helping me not go crazy and with your editing.

To my silent group of friends that are the voices for some of the craziest characters around. My brothas from the heart, J-Cob, Court, Juan, K-Will and EB.

I would like to thank Saundra for being an ear, a friend and a great listener.

Super shouts to Glinessa and Ty for taking care of my woman.

To the few authors that I've met and were so gracious to give me a little time and information about the biz...Eric Jerome Dickey, Jamise L. Dames, Shannon Holmes, Terri Woods, Timm McCann, Angie Daniels, Brenda Jackson, Beverly Jenkins, Tony Cheathem, Zane, Marlon Green, Trustice Gentiles, Doreen Rainey, Michael Pressley, Iyalna Vanzant, Gayle Jackson Sloan, Will Cooper and any other author I may have forgotten in my quest to give thanks.

I cannot forget Janice Aaron from Odysseys Book Network in California. I appreciate your raw opinion of the book when it was in its rawest form.

Super shouts to my editor Shelley Rafferty for teaching me once again all about the literary world. I've learned so much from you over the past few books and I love that you are not afraid to tell me that something is not my best work.

Shouts to Kenny Braswell with Urban Voices. Soul Kitchen for providing me that poetic food. My other brothers, Aaron, Morgan and Jordan. To Mantic Records, Angel, Wakalak, J Swan, Matthew and all the others who continue to work from the ground up.

It's been two long years since this book was supposed to be released, but because of things out of my control, it wasn't. It was a blessing in disguise. I wasn't ready to give the world what I was blessed with.

To all of my readers that stuck with me throughout the rewrites...thanks for the support. Way to stay hungry for my words and accepting of my stories. To those who are forgotten...you truly are not. It's been hard, but worth it. I struggle to find my voice at times, but I am steadily recording so I can perfect the pitch. I am here world, I am here!

Gerald K. Malcom

Prologue

TWO DAYS AGO...

*S*irens blared.

Men yelled.

Women shrieked.

"Jump!"

Traci cowered against the wall, not knowing where to go. As the red flames turned blue, her life flashed before her eyes. Thirty-something years went by in thirty-something seconds.

Her mind drew vivid pictures of Jordan, her mother, BET, pregnancy, her first doll, Jamaica, Solomon, pretzels, Sharlana, elephants, and a few other things she couldn't quite catch.

Her bedroom door crumbled and in its place appeared a barrage of fire engine red flames that fought their way through. Perspiration trickled from her wrinkled brow as she pressed her knees tighter against her chest and rocked back and forth. Ever since she could remember, her mother's steady rocking had always calmed her nerves.

More voices shouted, "C'mon."

As the red flames screamed and reached for her, she kept rocking. Her right hand shielded her mouth while the left fanned away thick gray D.C. smog that found its way into the heart of her apartment. She inhaled once and tasted charcoal. Two quick gasps allowed sooty residue to infiltrate her lungs, but not before staining her tongue with an unfamiliar taste. Death called fifteen feet away. It wasn't her turn to answer, so she continued to rock.

She rocked herself like her mom used to rock her when she was younger.

She rocked herself like Coretta rocked Martin.

Like Betty rocked Malcolm.

Like Jacqueline rocked John.

Like Harriet rocked freedom.

Like Jordan rocked her.

Ten feet away, her walls sweated like she did, even got darker like she was. Voices from outside continued to shout, and the heat continued to reach, only her arms weren't extended to meet it.

She continued to rock as she cowered deeper into the corner. She watched the flames change from red to blue and the walls change from white to black.

She called for Jordan, but he couldn't hear. She apologized for being so difficult, she cried for not being so honest, and she begged for another chance to make it right.

In her moment of despair, when her life was on the line, it was Jordan who mattered most.

More voices were followed by more vivid pictures, which were followed by the taste of more charcoal and more apologies.

The reds turned to blue, charred white walls bubbled, gray smog lingered, and suddenly everything went black.

Chapter 1

TRACI

"Get me extension 534, please," Traci said. As she listened to a jazz rendition of "Don't Worry, Be Happy," she turned her attention to the black pad on the edge of her cherry wood desk. After repeatedly poking the pad with her pen, she threw her head back and let out a long exhausted sigh.

The operator interrupted the music to which Traci had unknowingly begun to sway her head. "I'm sorry, but Ms. Braxton seems to have stepped out. Would you like to leave a message?"

"No. I'll try back later," Traci muttered hastily, not waiting for an answer as she slammed the phone down.

She leaned back, and before getting totally comfortable, she called her receptionist and informed her to hold all her calls, except for Jordan's. She knew that at any time, staff could come in and act like they never saw a child catch a cold. The work wasn't physically challenging, but mentally, to run a daycare she needed all of her faculties. Every once in awhile, she took a much needed break. She kicked off her black Manolo Blahnick's and rested her feet on a pile of papers that were going to do exactly as she was-- sit for the day. She rocked in her chair as she thought about how lucky she was to have a man like Jordan. He had his faults, but he was a blessing compared to the others. Traci shook her head and marveled at how long she had put up with the likes of Solomon, the thug wanna-be; Bashawn, the fake Muslim that cheated on her with a white woman; and who could forget Tiny, who was...well, the name speaks for itself.

Maybe I need to cut Jordan some slack, she thought. But that thought faded quickly. It never failed. The moment she slacked up, he'd slip up.

The crease that separated her forehead in half was soon replaced with smoothness as she smiled thinking about the time she was stranded at work for the day. She was waiting on Child Protective Services to file a report on a parent that never came to pick up her child, when Jordan showed up.

Traci looked shocked as Jordan pushed his way through her door with roses and dinner in tow.

"I thought you were supposed to be going to a basketball game today?" she asked.

"You didn't think I was going to let you starve," he said grinning, showing off the dimples that were deeply embedded into his rich, mud-colored skin.

Conscious of her current environment, Traci got up and showed him some restrained affection. "You are so special," she said.

She wanted to show him how much she really appreciated his gesture, but instead she resorted to a peck on the cheek, as little Jessica, the abandoned child, watched every move they made.

Jordan playfully plucked the little girl's ponytail. "How are you doing, Jessica?"

Jessica giggled, put her head down, and retreated behind Traci's leg. Jordan reached into the white bag, pulled out a Happy Meal, and held it out to the little girl. An unexpected warmth surged through Traci.

A cocky smile replaced his easy grin.

Traci ushered Jessica in front of Jordan so she could accept the bag. "Can you say thank you to Mr. Styles?"

Her voice was soft, barely audible. "Thank you, Mr. Styles."

Jordan extended his hand. "No problem." Jessica placed her tiny hand inside his and he led her to the miniature table across from Traci's desk.

Traci watched in amazement at how macho, yet gentle, Jordan was. He had told Traci he was on his way to a game, but when she called to let him know what was going on with her day, he rushed her off the phone. She guessed that the game wasn't that important because he decided to spend the evening with her and Jessica instead. That was just one of the many reasons she had fallen in love with him.

****

In between these thoughts, the door swung open quickly.

Sharlana burst through. "Are you all right?"

Traci quickly jumped to her feet and assumed a defensive stance. "Girl, you almost got knocked out," she joked.

"Whatever," Sharlana said, bypassing Traci's feeble attempt at a punch. "My mom just told me what happened."

Traci sat back down, and threw her feet back onto the desk. "I'm fine. It was just a little fire."

Sharlana sat on the edge of Traci's desk, wide-eyed. Sharlana was five-two and one hundred forty-five pounds with an auburn weave that fell to the middle of her back. Her dark-skinned complexion enhanced her high cheekbones and full lips, and whenever they went out, she would get most of the attention. Not that the tight jeans she wore to accent her perfectly rounded ass did much to deter most, not even the white guys. Traci often wore heels to stay a full head and shoulder above Sharlana. Her style was classic with earth tones to match her cappuchino complexion. Sharlana loved the weaves, while Traci choose the Halle haircuts. Traci had beauty reminiscent of Dandridge, and Horne. Sharlana was impressed with fashion of the moment. Her friends joked that she had that special something that attracted everyone. Only Sharlana didn't understand why white guys also felt comfortable approaching her. "That's embarrassing," she always told her friends.

"There is no such thing as a little fire. Are you sure you're okay? I had to leave work early."

Sharlana was always finding reasons to leave work early. She worked at one of the biggest telemarketing agencies in the city selling headstones, of all things. As much as she talked, it was a wonder she didn't sell out of the headstones. Who in the hell wanted to talk about the possibility of dying over the phone? Traci was convinced that people often bought the headstones just to get Sharlana to shut up. But if anyone could sell a microwave to the devil, it was Sharlana.

"Damn, Lana. I'm glad the whole house didn't burn down, because you would've taken off the rest of the year."

They laughed.

"You're lucky I came to support your evil ass. Have you spoken to Jordan?"

"I left a message. He hasn't returned my call yet."

Sharlana pursed her lips. "He's probably at somebody's-"

"Lana, don't start. Not today." As a matter of fact, Traci was getting tired of Sharlana's snide remarks about Jordan. Sharlana just couldn't see what Traci saw in him. Between her two best friends, Sharlana and Yana, neither one of them had ever forgiven Jordan for the night that they both had met him. Even though Traci and Jordan hadn't been going out at the time, it did look kinda funny for the three women to walk up on him as he escorted a strange drunken woman out of the bar. But it wasn't for them to judge.

Sharlana shrugged off Traci's remark. "You know I'm just joking. You always get stank when someone brings up that tired Negro."

Traci shook her head disapprovingly.

Sharlana knew when to back off. "I was just coming to let you know that you can stay with me if you want. My man won't mind a little company," she joked.

Traci smiled. In the twenty years she'd known Sharlana, there'd been only two men in her life, and neither one of them was there now. She was the type of woman who would rent three Julia Roberts movies, sit by herself, and eat Cherry Garcia ice cream until her stomach was on the verge of exploding. Traci knew Sharlana had good intentions, but Traci wondered if she could put up with Sharlana's crap for a month. This fire had set her back. It seemed like whenever she finally got into a schedule, shit happened. Normally for Traci, it was Cardio Kickboxing on Mondays and Wednesdays, graduate school at Georgetown on

Tuesdays, Jordan's house on Thursdays and Saturdays, and the girl's night out every other Friday.

"I'm fine at the hotel I stayed in last night."

Sharlana sighed.

"Alright, I'll stay for the week," Traci conceded.

Sharlana jumped up and gave her a hug. "You won't be disappointed. We can go rent some movies and-"

"And if you're not going to give me any privacy, then maybe it's not a good idea," Traci warned.

Sharlana's smile was without malice, almost apologetic. "I'm sorry. You know I've always wanted a little sister."

Traci remembered all the hard times Sharlana went through during her childhood. Between the divorce of her parents and the molestation from Uncle Jimmy, she definitely could've used more family.

"All right. Tonight, just one video and then you know I've got to study."

"That's fine." Sharlana headed toward the door. "Give me a call and let me know when you're coming."

Traci sat back down at her desk, ready to get something done. She smiled and yelled, "I'll call you later, Sis."

Talking to Sharlana always made Traci reflect on her own childhood. Like Sharlana, Traci had no brothers or sisters. Her mother was half white and half black, while her father was half absent and half gone. She wouldn't know him if he walked up to her and begged for a dollar. But that never stopped her mother from demanding the best from her daughter. Growing up as a latchkey kid, Traci learned how to survive on microwave dinners and sandwiches because her mother never allowed her to touch the stove.

Traci picked up the phone and decided to give State Farm one more chance before calling the higher authority to pitch a bitch. She hated to be like that, but she knew it was always the squeaky wheel that got the oil.

She got the operator again and by this time she was seething. She left a message for Ms. Braxton to contact her on her cell phone by eight that night. The fire had all but taken the wind out of her sails.

Exhausted from the day's events, she decided to clock out early. She locked her office door and headed to her car. She wanted to go to Jordan's, but he had never returned her call. Instead, she opted for the bar.

Chapter 2

JORDAN

Deanna's head slid through the crack in my door. "Mr. Styles, Traci Johnson called about two hours ago."

She must've noticed my mood swing because she quickly followed with, "I'm sorry, Mr. Styles. I answered the phone, then I went to lunch, and by the time I returned, I had totally forgotten."

If she weren't the boss' niece, I would've gotten rid of her "amnesia ass" a month ago. "That's okay, Deanna."

Deanna, who was from Kentucky, was like the fine and friendly southern girls I had always heard about. But for her, they should add another F for forgetful. She needed a job after college, so she called on old Uncle Willy. I remembered the conversation as if it was yesterday.

****

Mr. Amsterdam barged into my office and pushed aside some papers so he could sit in the seat across from my desk. "You need someone to help you get your shit together."

I completed the paragraph I was working on and then stared at him intently. "I don't need anyone. This is a controlled mess," I said, grabbing the papers from him and putting them inside my desk. "If someone came in here messing around, I wouldn't know where to find anything."

He coughed up what sounded like two lungs, swirled it around, and gulped it back down with a frown. "I'm from the old school and I say you need a woman to come and help you get your shit together, and that's that!"

I hated when he interfered. I knew when I needed some help. But by the twinkle in his eyes, and the slow swirl of his cigar, I knew he was up to something.

I waved my white flag in defeat. "Alright, we'll place an ad in the paper tomorrow."

He laughed to himself. When William F. Amsterdam was a young man, he came from Kentucky with two things: good credit and a dream. He and his wife of twenty-four years started this computer business from scratch. He hired me because he said that I had the same fire in my eyes that he used to have. His eyes didn't possess that flame anymore. With his wavy hair split neatly down the middle, he reminded me of the fast talking street guys hanging in the D.C. bars looking for young love. He wasn't very tall -- five feet six inches-- and he weighed about one hundred and eighty pounds, with a love for racquetball and a good Scotch. I watched him as he cut the butt of his cigar and searched for his lighter. What the hell is this, his victory cigar? He rocked back in his seat and eyed me curiously. After lighting the cigar, he blew three perfect halos in the air. I could smell the familiar scent of old black wood, reminiscent of my grandfather's cigars.

"I'm glad that you agree with me Jaw-don," he drawled. I tried correcting him before but it never sunk in. "I have the perfect person for you." He gave me a relaxed smile showing his beige and orange colored teeth.

"Who?"

"My niece!" He paused and waited for some type of confirmation from me.

I can't even pick my own damn... "Alright, Mr. Amsterdam. Is it okay if I meet her before you hire her?" I knew it was a bad move, but I was willing to try anything to get a jump up on the competition for the new promotion. I'll be nice and see what happens.

He got up, walked toward the door, spun around, and blew another perfect halo. "It's too late. She'll be here tomorrow."

****

At this moment, I turned my attention back to Deanna as she searched for a pen to take dictation. She was the same height as Mr. Amsterdam, but her weight was distributed quite differently. His weight was all in his mid-section, while hers was equally proportioned. Her oval face was caramel with a chocolate mole on the right side of her lips. She was attractive, but not too attractive. Her smile more than compensated her attitude. Her cleavage merged in the middle of her chest and seemed to discuss ways to break free. Her breasts greeted me every morning and shouted, "Help! We're overcrowded." I couldn't do a damn thing for them.

As I finished my last sentence, her pen dropped. "Did you get all of that, Deanna?"

She walked over and playfully chided me.

"I don't want Uncle Willy Wonka coming down on me for calling you, Deanna."

She giggled and slid back into the chair across from me. She was wearing a beige two-piece business suit that clung to her like static cling to a college kid's laundry. Licking her lips, she invited me into places I didn't want to go. I shook the thought away because in Traci I had finally found a woman that made me happy. I was content, even though she withheld sex like it was a prize.

"That'll be it for right now," I said sternly.

Deanna got up and sashayed seductively to her desk. A slight scent of perfume followed her from my office.

I gave Traci a call.

Her voice was calm. "Where were you last night, Jordan?"

"Had a late night. Had to drive Tony to Delaware to pick up a used car. Why?"

Silence. She sniffled.

"What's wrong, sweetheart?"

"My house caught on fire," she explained weakly.

Oh shit! I shot up and began to pace the room as far as my little black phone cord would allow. "Oh my, God! Are you alright?"

Her voice was shaky. "I'm fine. I called you last night and left a few messages for you to call."

"Damn, I'm sorry. I didn't know."

"I know. It's not your fault."

"Where did you stay last night?"

"Hotel."

"By yourself?"

"Yeah."

"Where was the fire?"

"In the bedroom."

"Were you in the house when it happened?"

"Yeah."

My heart raced as I continued to probe. "Were you in the bedroom?"

"Yes."

"What happened? How did you get out?"

Traci broke down and started crying. "The firemen were telling me to jump out the window," she said in between sniffles, "but I couldn't."

"That's okay, baby. As long as you're alright," I consoled. I wish I could've jumped through the phone and been there to comfort her. She continued to explain how three firemen burst through her door and carried her out through the smoke-filled room. She didn't remember much except that everyone stood outside and clapped as she was carried out.

"Don't move, baby. I'm coming to pick you up, okay?"

"That's okay. I still have a few things to do before I leave. Are you off early today?"

"No. Same time as usual, but I can leave."

She politely declined again and we agreed to meet at Friday's to finish the conversation.

I rushed through the rest of my paperwork and hurried to the restaurant.

Chapter 3

TRACI

$\mathcal{T}$raci rolled over and slammed her hand against the alarm clock. She was glad that Friday had arrived. Ms. Braxton had finally done her job and gotten Traci into a hotel after three sleepless nights at Sharlana's. She also informed Traci that her house was going to take about three weeks to complete. Traci and Ms. Braxton mixed like oil and water.

"Good morning," Sharlana yelled through the thick oak doors. Sharlana lived in the Georgetown area, not too far from where Traci went to school. Traci had wanted to live in that area for as long as she could remember. Her aunt used to own a nice little studio in the heart of Georgetown, while Sharlana went for more lavish surroundings: a large two-bedroom with all the fixings. She gave Traci the bedroom that was near the workout room. Because of the high ceilings, cool air traveled quickly through the house, so Traci pulled the thick, royal blue Afghan up to her ears, attempting to block out the world.

"Morning, Lana," Traci yelled back, hoping Sharlana would keep moving. Traci wasn't a morning person, and she hated to be interrupted while trying to get up. She took a whiff of the hazelnut scent that snuck underneath the door.

"Do you need anything? I made coffee."

Though the scent was appealing, Traci declined and rolled back over.

****

After leaving work, Traci grabbed all of her things from Sharlana's and headed for the Marriott. Downstairs they were having a happy hour, but she wasn't in the mood to be around a bunch of people she didn't know, so she purchased a Diet Coke from the soda machine, went upstairs to her suite, and got comfortable on the lounge chair. She surfed the cable channels before pausing at *Road Rules.* This show pissed her off, but enticed her at the same time. It was about a bunch of young people traveling across the country without a care in the world. For some reason, she couldn't keep away from the channel. She loved to see people who didn't have a care in the world bitch about stupid stuff.

The phone rang in the midst of the show.

"Hello?"

"Hello, Ms. Johnson. How are you?"

Traci tried to catch the voice, but couldn't. The silence annoyed her. "Fine."

The voice was baritone and heavy. "You don't even know who this is, do you?"

The anticipation was nerve-wracking. "No!" Traci was becoming irritated at the little game someone was playing. She sucked her teeth before emptying her lungs with a loud hum. "Who is this?"

Sensing her sudden mood swing, he hurriedly answered, "I'll give you a hint."

Silence filled the air.

Traci shouted into the phone, "Hello! Hello! Hello!"

There was shuffling on the other end of the phone and then music played. Traci's generic receiver became Teddy's silky voice and sang to her, "Turn out the lights and light a candle…"

The voice returned a little deeper and huskier. "You remember this?"

Traci threw her head back and swallowed the memory of the song…whole. Mr. Solomon Jackson. The girls around the way called him AJ, for Action Jackson. His body was like his name: strong, powerful, and large. Solomon was the only man that made Traci cum with only a kiss. He was six feet, seven inches and black. He was so black that you didn't know where his hairline started and his forehead began. He was the shiny black that many women dream of. He was also from an island. Staten Island. Like the movie, *Baby Boy*, he was there to serve, lick and protect. Traci reminisced on how they met.

She was having a party for one of her girlfriends at her house and everyone and their momma was invited. Traci had gone to the store to get some ice when Solomon arrived. They both stood in front of the door waiting for the other to make a move.

His eyes told hers that she was beautiful. His eyes slid down her neck and carefully licked her nipples, showing each that they were special. Her jeans were next on the list. He paused at her zipper and nodded with a slick grin. His voice was confident, yet humble. "You're dripping."

"Excuse me?"

"The ice," he replied. The twinkle in his eyes didn't fit his thugged out persona. He stood with his legs spread shoulder length apart like he had the best shit known to women.

Sharlana rushed outside to check on Traci. "What took you so-" Her voice trailed off and squinted at Solomon and then at Traci. "I see you've met Mr. Solomon Jackson," she said with a smirk. She drew Traci close and playfully warned, "Don't look into his eyes girl."

Traci looked at Sharlana and informed her that it was too late. As she walked by Solomon, a hint of his sweet cologne caressed her nostrils. A young lady behind him yelled for him to wait up.

The rest of the evening was filled with drinks and stares. Mentally, Traci made love to him every time she looked in his direction. She loved when a man was a man. She loved the smell of work, the dirty nails, and the grungy beard. All of her life, she was attracted to men she could never bring home. Why should tonight be any different even though her friends had informed her that Solomon was there with Patricia?

While Solomon, Patricia, and another couple socialized in the kitchen area, Traci, Mona, Sharlana, and Celeste sat on the sofa drinking beer.

Mona, who was an average height, light-skinned, slim honey with a ghetto ass, jumped off the couch and peeked into the kitchen like she was a member of the S.W.A.T. team. She came back, slid between Celeste and Traci, and whispered in her thick Jamaican accent, "I know he's fucking her."

Celeste, the six feet, sable colored model with flamingo legs and a killer instinct, added, "That bitch walks around like she's the shit, too."

Traci didn't like to start any shit, especially in her own house. "Leave it alone."

Everyone stared.

Celeste wouldn't let it go. "You're the one that's been staring at his broke ass all night long."

"No I haven't," Traci denied vehemently, slamming down her half-emptied bottle, missing the coaster.

"And who cares if he's broke anyway?" Traci had her share of busted men with good jobs. If you weren't going to take their money, why should you care how much money they had? Celeste and Mona were the takers. If a man flashed money in front of them, they made sure he got their number that evening. Traci wasn't into the competition. And anyway, those two were the same women that talked shit about a man, but when the coast was clear, they would be the ones on the attack. When it came to men, Sharlana and Traci were alike: if it happened, it happened. "I don't need no twenty-something rent-a-thug anyway," Traci unsuccessfully tried to convince them.

"I saw the way you were staring at him outside," Sharlana added. "If you want the man, don't be scared to go for yours. This is your house," she reminded Traci.

Relenting under peer pressure, Traci looked at her half-emptied bottle of beer and decided that it was time to make her move. She guzzled the rest and waved the empty bottle in the air. "Anybody else want something to drink?"

Celeste gave a little smirk. "I'm good. Go get your rent-a-thug."

They all laughed and gave high-fives.

Ignoring their comments and laughter, Traci wheeled around and began walking slowly toward the kitchen. On her way, she kept reminding herself that she really was thirsty. As she neared, everything seemed to get foggy. Her thoughts weren't clear like they were moments ago. She put her hand on her shirt, checked her heart rate, and held her breath as she placed her hand on the door.

Just as she applied pressure to the door, Celeste bumped into her. "Excuse me, Traci."

Traci grabbed Celeste by the arm. "What are you doing?"

Celeste shook her arm free and whispered, "Just trying to get this bitch out of your way."

Solomon and Patricia were standing toward the back of the kitchen, while the other couple stood near the refrigerator, each making their own party. From his position, Solomon couldn't see Traci and Celeste arguing about what move to make. Without warning, Celeste bolted past the first couple and headed directly toward Patricia. "Excuse me, Pat, I think you left your lights on."

Patricia thanked Celeste for being so nice and left to get her keys. Celeste followed her into the living room.

Solomon sat on the counter drinking a beer, waiting patiently for Traci to invade his personal space. She laughed to herself at the nerve he had to be sitting his ass on her counter. She had consumed only two beers, but it seemed as though she couldn't walk without instructions. Her feet were like her emotions: tangled and confused. On her eighth step she realized she was still a foot away. He didn't get up to greet her, but instead remained on the counter waiting for her to finish her approach. At that point, nerves made her not want to continue, but there was no other reason for her to be heading his way.

She finally arrived and stood in front of her Ebony Prince whose crown was tilted to the side. "Hello, Solomon."

He lifted his head up slightly and jumped down, landing in front of her with a loud thud. She was so close that she could see every hair on his chin. His skin emitted a peculiar scent that turned her on.

"What's up, Ms. Johnson?" He gave her the smile that had many women opening up everything from their legs to their bank accounts. His lips were large, dark, full, and inviting.

To Traci's dismay, her nipples greeted him before she had a chance to. She toyed with her empty bottle, searching for a purpose for her hands. "I'm fine, Solomon." Unconsciously she stared at every curly follicle sticking out of his white wife-beater. It was tacky, but sexy. "Are you having fun?"

He nodded. "I'm chillin'. I forgot to thank Mona for inviting us."

Traci remembered Patricia was there with him. "I told her to invite some people she knew. We really like Patricia."

Solomon's eyes closed, his head dropped and swung slowly from left to right before he let out five seconds of frustrated air.

Traci's eyebrows furled and tried to meet in the middle. "Aren't you-"

He tilted his head and moved closer. "Aren't we what?"

Traci backed up, slightly uncomfortable with the closeness. "Um..."

"Did you want to ask if we're together?"

"I g-g-guess." The air between them was thick and the smell of stale beer and his Obsession cologne lingered. Her nerves were shot as her heart decided to run a race that her legs couldn't keep up with.

He bent to pick up a bottle cap. As he rose, he slightly brushed against her breasts. Looking down at her nipples that were still erect, he smiled. "Cold? I could turn up the heat for you," he said, inching closer with an underhanded smile.

Traci marveled at his level of cockiness. He was probably just a good lay. She wondered what would make him think she would even want him. They were on two different levels. She had just finished two commercials for BET, and who was he? Up close, she realized he was a gorgeous chocolate brother that attempted to hide his natural beauty by thuggin' himself out. Beneath the grungy beard she noticed smooth black skin, and underneath his nappy Afro she saw a fine grade of hair that would look nice with a good haircut. Regardless of the way he tried to portray himself, her intuition told her differently. He just seemed a little lost.

Solomon looked around and extended his hand. "Can we go somewhere where we can talk?"

Traci, without thinking, accepted his soft, large hand and led him to the sitting room that was located near her bedroom. She walked him through the back of the kitchen because she didn't want her friends thinking she was falling for any of his bullshit.

Traci's sitting room comfortably fit a desk, chair, a couple of bookshelves, and small couch. The walls were off-white with an African border. She used the room to do work she brought home and to occasionally have drinks and conversation with company. Solomon found his way to the burgundy leather couch, sat down on the edge, and pulled her close. Traci was now in the arms of a man whom she had only spoken to twice. She didn't want to be there, but she needed him for some reason. Maybe it was because she was tired of the married but single executives trying to push up on her, and she needed a strong man to take her.

He rose, grabbed her hand, and drew her near as they began dancing to the music that played in the distance. As Traci's heart thumped faster, his movements against her became more aggressive. She looked around and was happy that no one could see where she was and what she was doing. She felt content in his arms as she rested her head on his shoulder and slid her hand around his waist. Her breasts were firmly fixed on his stomach and she could feel the separation of each of his abdominal muscles. The small of his back was powerful and his whole body felt like it was sculpted from granite.

Solomon's hand massaged her lower back as he backed her up against the wall. She could hear light chatter in the background and wanted him to take her anywhere. Solomon sensed that all the fight had left her body as she succumbed to his will. His hands found their way to her firm butt and he cupped each cheek. Her head fell into the hollow crease that separated his chest in half, and she inhaled the strong scent of his body. It was a sweet musky smell that sent her eyes to the back of her head. She was happy he wasn't feeding her any corny lines, but instead taking her as if he had always known her. Always known her spots. Always fed her cravings.

Solomon pinned Traci's hands above her head and leaned all his weight against her, and she felt what women screamed about. His sledgehammer pressed into the pit of her stomach and she let out a silent sigh.

For a minute, they rocked so close, so slow that she could feel every pulsating throb of his Mandingo.

As she continued to inhale his essence and feel his power, her mind traveled to Jamaica. They were no longer against the wall, but instead she lay on her back with her legs pressed firmly against her breasts as Solomon panted above her on the beach. Against the wall, he placed wet kisses on her neck. But on the beach, the wet kisses blessed her nipples. He caressed and stimulated each nipple, going back and forth so each had equal time. She opened her legs wide, took whiffs of the salt water, and heard the birds call her name.

Against the wall, he nuzzled her ear with muggy licks. But on the beach, his tongue found her navel. His tongue lightly penetrated her bellybutton before continuing its southern journey.

Solomon placed Traci's face inside his large hands and introduced his tongue to hers. In Jamaica, his probing tongue found her clitoris. Seconds later, she came.

****

Solomon cleared his throat.

The phone suddenly seemed like an uncomfortable tool pressed against her ear. She couldn't remember what they were talking about. It had been at least a month since she and Jordan were intimate, and her body longed for the physical. Her legs shifted from left to right as she felt heat on her thighs and a throbbing sensation on her spot.

"What were you saying?"

Solomon's voice dropped to Barry White range. "Just playing a song for you."

"Why?"

"I know that you're feeling bad about the fire."

Her tone was defensive. "How did you know where I was?" Even though he couldn't see her, she quickly closed her blouse to hide her aroused nipples.

"It's not that hard to find out." He paused. "Your mom told me where you were staying."

Traci's mom was a pain in her ass when it came to Solomon. Her mom didn't like Jordan too much because she said that her left hand told her that he was a player. If her third eye really worked, she would've known that Solomon was no good. Traci just never told her mom about him because her mom would've dogged her out for getting involved with someone so soon. She was so afraid of Traci being with a white man, she wanted her to find the blackest man alive.

"I told her about doing that," Traci huffed.

"It's not her fault. She knows that I have good intentions." He laughed. If he was sitting beside her, a comment like that and his smile would've made Traci smile, but he wasn't.

"Why are you calling me?" It had been at least a year since she last spoke to him. During that time, there were no calls, no return calls, no letters, no mail...nothing.

"I was just checking to see if you were okay."

Emotions ran high. Why did he wait over a year to find out if everything was okay, Traci wondered. This inconsiderate bastard didn't return any of her calls and left her to deal with life and their failed relationship on her own. Traci was annoyed at the fact that he still had an effect on her. He still made her mind race and insides tingle.

"I gotta go."

"Before you go, how are you and Jordan Stales doing?"

"It's Styles, and if you can't show him the proper respect then maybe you shouldn't be talking to me."

"Okay. You got it."

He told her that her Mom loved him and said that they spoke about various things from time to time. He asked if she had decided to give acting another shot. She expressed her contentment with leaving show business alone entirely because the thought of traveling back and forth to L.A. and N.Y. for auditions that never came to fruition had been too much for her.

She said it reminded her of him: too many broken promises and shattered dreams.

Her mother always pressed the issue of having something to fall back on, which was one of the major reasons she had stayed in school and got her degree in child psychology. She loved going where people were real and where the kids didn't judge her on how many commercials she did or didn't do. Solomon, on the other hand, was supposedly getting his life together. He owned his own business near the White House, which was bringing him major paper. He was always a schemer looking for the quick dough, so Traci didn't bother to ask about his new business. Instead she opted to let him know she and Jordan were working out wonderfully. Even though she and Jordan had a few problems, she couldn't let Solomon think there was an opening.

Chapter 4

JORDAN

For the past six months I'd been working at Marigold Industries and had grown to enjoy the switch in my career. Prior to Marigold, I spent three years at a computer firm before being let go. I wasn't bringing home the same type of money, but at least I enjoyed going to work now. As director of a new Marigold project, Computers for Change, it was my job to get companies to upgrade their computer systems and receive software training. The fringe benefits were great: I was able to take potential clients to dinners, get a few tailor-made suits, and I had a huge office with a view of downtown D.C. I was never into the big swivel chair with my feet up thing, but I figured you couldn't knock it until you tried it.

Deanna yelled through the intercom, "We're ordering Chinese food, would you like to order, Mr. Styles?"

I spun around in my seat to answer, in the process knocking over a piping hot cup of coffee.

"Shit!" I attempted to shake french vanilla off my latest proposal.

Deanna rushed in. "Are you okay?" She grabbed the handful of papers and began smearing the proposal with her hands: blending my vowels with my consonants.

"Just leave it!" I barked.

Deanna put the papers down and backed up toward the door with a frown. She buttoned up the top two buttons of her shirt as if to insinuate that I didn't deserve to see her cinnamon cleavage.

I turned my attention to my drenched proposal and tried to salvage what I could. Coffee was everywhere. My new suit was stained, and my desk was a mess.

While I cleaned, Deanna buzzed me to let me know that Traci was on the other line. I snatched up the phone, my voice matching my pissed-off mood. "What's up?"

"You don't sound too good. Everything all right?"

I fell deep into my chair, swung around to face the window and blocked out everything except for the skyline and my woman. At that moment, a cluster of clouds covered the sun, blocking the warmth that had beaten on my back earlier. The sun always made me feel good. My mother told me when I was younger that the sun was God's hand following me everywhere.

"Everything is all right. I just spilled coffee on all the work I just completed." I knew her next question.

In a motherly tone, she asked, "You saved it on disc, right?"

I shook my head at her predictability. "You know I can't write on the computer. I have to see it in front of me. Actually, I was about to enter it on the computer when Deanna yelled through the intercom about some damn Chinese food!"

"Your temp from hell, right?"

I reminded Traci that she was the boss' niece and there was nothing *temp* about that.

"I didn't call to irritate you, Jordan. I was just calling to let you know I really enjoyed the other evening we spent together."

My mind raced back to the other night. Traci was like an animal. We've had some beautiful sex before, but the other night was different. Something must've come over her. "I remember. I don't know what got into you," I said with a smile she could probably see over the phone.

"Was it a problem?"

Hell, no! "Hell, no!" I didn't know where the newfound Traci had come from, but I was going to cash in on this sexier model. "What are you wearing?" I asked.

"Huh?"

"Huh, hell. What are you wearing?" I repeated firmly.

"C'mon, Jordan. You know I'm at work."

I leaned back and loosened my pink paisley tie. "Do I ask for much?"

Traci paused. "Let me get up and close the door."

"That's my girl," I whispered. I propped my feet on the window sill, put my hands behind my head and leaned back, watching the clouds slowly disperse from the sun. A beam of sun shot through the sky and onto my leg. I watched little particles of dust fly in and out of the beam while I awaited her return. *This is going to be good, Styles.*

Traci picked up the phone and hastily replied, "A red suit with a cream blouse."

"Not like that. Go a little slower. Kinda like you did the other night when you wanted to tear my ass up!"

Embarrassment filled her voice, "Jordan."

"Let's start over. What are you wearing?"

Traci spoke slowly as if she had just turned her sexual meter from a one to a seven. "I'm wearing a crimson colored top with a matching skirt."

Like a little kid, I responded, "Yeah?" I positioned Sambuca, the name I affectionately dubbed my penis, to the left. He yawned.

She continued, "I'm also wearing a cum colored silk blouse."

Damn! Level eight came quickly. I shot up, becoming instantly excited at the sudden nastiness of my queen. "What color did you say?"

She giggled, "I meant to say that I was wearing a cream colored blouse. What did I say?"

You know you just said cum colored blouse! Sambuca flickered. "I don't know what you said."

"I just opened my blouse, Mr. Styles. I know you didn't tell me to do that, but I'm just trying to make you happy. Am I being a good girl?"

I didn't want to let her know that she was driving me crazy so I joked, "You're on level nine."

"Huh?"

"Never mind. You're doing good. Keep going."

"I'm putting my hands on my breasts, but it seems as though my bra is getting in the way. Do you want Ms. Johnson to undo her bra?"

I didn't know if I liked her sudden aggressiveness or if I was aroused by the thought of her talking dirty. Regardless, Sambuca was enjoying the show. "Keep going."

"Keep going, what?" she said.

Huh? She was making me work? Wasn't I supposed to be the one giving the instructions? "Go ahead and take it off."

Her voice became more professional. "Take it off, who?"

"Huh?"

"Huh, hell! Who do you want to take the bra off?"

I was confused at what she wanted. As I sat back, rubbing my hair for answers, I watched the clouds part, allowing my body total warmth. I spun around and leaned on the desk, waiting for the warmth to envelop my back. "You. I want Traci to take it off."

"I kicked Traci's ass out," she responded quickly. "Ms. Johnson is taking over. Now, who do you want to take it off?"

My tone reached a higher octave. "You, Ms. Johnson." She was trying to mess with my manhood. If she was doing it on purpose, she was succeeding.

"Ms. Johnson is playing with her nipples. Would you like to taste?"

Would I like to taste? "Yeah."

"Where are your hands, Mr. Styles?"

"One is on the phone and the other is resting on the desk."

"You don't need both of those hands. Unzip your pants and rub Sambuca until he comes to life," she directed.

I was starting to feel awkward, but beginning to enjoy myself at the same time. *Go ahead, Styles.* "I can do this," I assured her. "Keep going."

She moaned. "I think I'm wet, Mr. Styles."

Code Red! "Touch yourself, Tra- I mean, Ms. Johnson," I commanded. I had to regain control of my fantasy.

A few seconds later, her voice returned. "Like this?"

"Like what? I can't hear you. Taste your fingers," I ordered.

She moaned and began slurping noisily on her fingers. "Like this?"

I draped my arm across the desk, using it as a pillow while envisioning her slurping on everything from her fingers to Sambuca.

My imagination ran wild. I knew exactly where she was located. She was sitting behind her peanut-colored thick desk, a few feet away from the door. Her head was leaning on the desk while she bent over so no one could hear. They had thin walls and nosy women. She had two pictures on her desk: one of her mother, and the other was of us at the beach. There was a computer to the right, and above her head, on the wall, was a picture that I bought for her of two people straddling each other at the park. The picture was made up of deep browns, golden yellows, and bright purples. There was a huge window on the left that let in the same warmth I felt.

"Mr. Styles?"

"Yeah?"

"Pull Sambuca out."

Pull him out where? Even though I knew I was alone, I gave my office a once over. I unzipped my pants and slowly dug Sambuca out of my black and white striped boxers as though I was freeing him from jail. He yawned again and stretched out. Against my leg, he looked like a smaller extension of my thick brown thigh. Not even fully erect, he was at a size Traci always said most men would be proud of.

"I want you to rub yourself while I touch myself," Traci added. She was giving out more directions than a short order cook.

Obeying her wishes, my left hand lightly grazed the side of my growing penis. Within seconds, by stroking and listening to her panting, I was at full strength. Blood rushed and Sambuca throbbed inside my palm. It felt like warm kielbasa inside a piece of thin bread. "I'm rubbing, Ms. Johnson. Are you still lightly touching yourself?"

She let out a bevy of moans. "Can't you tell?"

"I wish I was there, I want to-"

"Shhh," she whispered. "Recite some of that poetry I love while you stroke yourself and think about me circling my spot with my fingers."

I began slowly pumping Sambuca and thinking about Traci's finger tap dancing across her spot. Her moans were more intense with each passing minute. As I pumped, she moaned. We harmonized.

My voice was deep and slow:

"Damn Sweetheart, I like this

Because your finger becomes my lips as I begin to kiss

You until you become wet, sticky and moist

I'm on my knees with my hands under you as I hoist

that fine, brown, sexy soft ass in the air.

Do you care

if I indulge?

Don't ask if I'm enjoying myself, Girl I know you see the bulge.

But this feels like Christmas & your sweet love box got to be the Grinch

Because you stole my cum and my man Sambuca, inch by inch.

I'm on my knees & it feels like we're miles apart, as if I was out of town

but I'm like Mary J. Blige's song because," I paused and sang, "I'm going down!"

Traci's phone dropped and I heard her whisper, "I'm cuming."

That momentarily stopped my flow. Just hearing that my baby was cuming sent me over the edge. My right hand methodically shook my shaft as I listened to her panting subside.

There was a rustling on the other end before she asked, "Jordan, are you there?"

"I'm here, sweetheart. Did you cum for me?"

"I did," she admitted. "Now it's your turn. Are you still pumping Sambuca?"

"Yeah."

She continued, "I'm lifting my skirt up, Mr. Styles."

Just the thought of my baby straddling me like the picture I had bought for her, had me going nuts. I have been asking her to come over and bless me one day. Until today, I thought it had never entered her mind.

While she spoke, I caught a good brain-freeze from something hot.

"I'm in front of your desk, facing the door and lifting up my skirt. I don't have on any panties either."

I was seeing everything as she spoke. "I'm looking directly at you and you're right, you don't have on any panties."

"Stroke yourself while you bend me over your desk and have a little taste."

Mentally, I threw Traci over my desk, pried her cheeks open and introduced my tongue to her. Her back buckled.

She smelled like rose petals and tasted sweet.

My tongue did the electric slide over her spot as our juices slow danced.

"How do I taste?" she asked seductively.

"Like sweet potato pie."

"I'm getting ready to sit down on you now, Jordan. Are you ready?"

My heart raced as my hand shifted to a faster motion. I could feel myself about to explode.

"C'mon, Jordan. Let Ms. Johnson ride it out of you. Do you feel me Jordan?"

Houston, we have a problem! "Yes." My hand started to cramp, but I didn't want to switch hands and change the feeling. Disrupt the mood. "Traci?"

"Yes?"

"I'm...I'm...I'm..."

"Yes?"

"Cuming!"

My door flew open and Deanna barged in. "Did you say, 'come in.'"

Chapter 5

TRACI

Traci sat in her hotel room, waiting for Sharlana. It was Wednesday and they were supposed to grab something to eat from Tiptons, a new restaurant downtown. So much had happened in the last week that she couldn't make sense of it all. She looked around the hotel room and wondered how she had gone from a two-bedroom flat to this. It wasn't that bad, but it wasn't her cup of tea. Maids that she didn't know were coming in, cleaning her room, and picking her stuff up off the floor. She threw herself on the queen-sized bed and stared at a dark spot on the ceiling. She wasn't sure whether or not to change out of her work clothes. She had worn the brown silk dress with tan flowers that her mother had bought her for her thirtieth birthday. Since then, she had pushed the hips of the dress out a little bit. To Jordan, she wasn't an oversized, middle-aged chick, but a fine queen that finally grew into her shape. She liked the way he always found the positive in something that she thought was negative. After deciding on some old jeans and a sweater, the bed looked very inviting.

As soon as her head hit the pillow, Sharlana knocked on the door and shouted, "Are you ready?"

Traci peeled herself off the bed and opened the door. "What's up, Lana?"

Sharlana threw herself onto the recliner, kicked her feet up, and muttered, "Tired."

"Me, too."

"Why don't we just get room service and order a movie?"

"If I would've known that, I would've just stayed in the bed."

Sharlana got up, stretched, and they headed for the restaurant.

"Are we taking my car or yours?" Sharlana asked as they approached her 2001 black Honda Accord.

Traci wanted to drive, but she wanted to have a drink or two, so she walked to the passenger's side of Sharlana's car, jumped in, and adjusted her seat belt so she could face Sharlana. It was a fifteen-minute drive to Tiptons and Traci dreaded bringing up the subject, but she had to tell someone.

"Guess who called me?"

Sharlana pulled off and popped in an old slow jam mix CD that blared, "Let's Get it On" by Marvin Gaye. "Who?"

Humiliation crept across Traci's face as she turned away. "AJ!"

Sharlana quit smacking her gum and quickly turned the music down. "AJ, who?"

All the energy Traci had, suddenly left her body. "Forget it. I really don't want to get into it right now," Traci said, turning the music back up.

They stopped at a red light and Sharlana wouldn't let it rest, slapping Traci's hand from the radio.

"What did he say?"

Traci shook her head. "He called me at the hotel and-"

Ignoring the green light, Sharlana continued to stare at Traci. "He called you at the hotel? How did he know you were there?"

Traci rolled the window down and spat out the piece of Wrigley's that had worked her jaw. "Who do you think told him?"

A horn informed Sharlana it was time to drive. She peeled off, letting out a I-feel-sorry-for-you chuckle. "Your mom, huh?"

"You got it," Traci said. "I don't know why she gave him my number. Anyway, let's just forget about it."

"Let's not forget about it because I know that I'll be the one hearing about this for the next two weeks, so you might as well get it over with."

Traci paused. "Solomon called me the other day and played a slow jam over the phone."

Sharlana shook her head with disgust.

Traci's head followed suit, but in the back of her mind she was flattered that he remembered their song. "Anyway, he played the song and then started asking about Jordan. The thought of Jordan must intimidate him."

Sharlana sarcastically chuckled. "Probably because Jordan has a fucking job. Not to mention, Jordan doesn't have kids running all over the city, or at least I think he doesn't. Girl, I told you to get him checked out."

"Anyway, I told him I really couldn't talk."

"Why didn't you tell him you didn't want to talk at all?"

"I don't know. It's not like he was bothering me. Hell, it wasn't like he said that he would call back either. I think he got the hint," Traci explained, trying to convince Sharlana and herself. Marvin Gaye faded and the Isley Brothers blended in smoothly with "Between the Sheets." For some reason, she couldn't get Solomon out of her system. It was sickening, because she didn't understand the hold he had over her.

"I know you're not thinking about seeing him again," Sharlana snarled. With every hard shift in gear, Sharlana let out a distraught sigh. "It's not like I care much for Jordan, but when it comes to those two, Jordan wins hands down. As a matter of fact, has Solomon ever taken you anywhere?" The faster she talked, the faster she drove. Sharlana pointed to herself as she continued her tirade. "I was the one that had to hear you bitch and moan about AJ. I had to listen to you complain that he wouldn't pay you back the money that he owed you. I was there last year when-"

"Hold up," Traci interjected. "I told you that I loaned him the money and he bought me something of equal value in return."

Sharlana snickered and eased the car into first gear as they approached the restaurant. "So, he bought you a gift with your own money?"

"No. He-" Traci stopped in mid-breath. Why was she defending him anyway? Solomon was like soda: quenching the immediate thirst, but leaving you thirstier for something healthier. "I don't want to talk about him anymore," Traci said, turning off the slow jams.

They remained silent as the radio played. Sharlana pulled into the lot and shifted nervously in her seat. "I forgot to tell you something, T."

Traci's expression told it all as her eyes rolled to the back of her head as if she had the lead role in *The Exorcist*. "What?"

Sharlana fumbled with her thoughts and her keys. Once the car no longer hummed, Sharlana's jingling keys informed Traci of trouble. "I kinda forgot to tell you that someone was joining us."

"Who?"

Still staring into the windshield, Sharlana blurted, "Celeste."

Traci's head whipped around, with her body following seconds later. "I know you didn't invite her to eat with us!" She was so mad that tears began to well in her eyes. Traci hated the fact that every time she got angry, she cried. People associated crying with being weak. It was a little flaw she couldn't correct.

"Calm down," Sharlana pleaded. "She called me out of the blue a few hours ago because she's going through some things, and I couldn't turn her down."

Traci wasn't giving Celeste any sympathy, not after the shit she had pulled. Even though six years had passed, Traci could never forgive or forget. Traci had done a few commercials for BET and she was in a position to help people out with the little change that she got. Celeste had been her friend for a few years prior and asked if she could stay with Traci for a while. Traci didn't mind, so she let Celeste stay in her guestroom for a few months. That summer, Traci had to go to South Carolina to visit her ailing grandmother and left the apartment to Celeste to look after until she returned. "Help yourself to whatever," she told Celeste before leaving. Boy, did Celeste help herself to her stuff. It turned out that Celeste had intercepted a phone call intended for Traci. Traci had an interview with BET to act in an upcoming pilot about a single man that had to marry a woman within a year to get some inheritance. The script sounded terrible, but that should've been her call. Not only did Celeste not call and tell her about it, she went on the interview in Traci's place. Traci returned to find out that Celeste had moved into a place of her own with an advance she had gotten on her newfound acting career. It wasn't until a month into Traci's return that she found out that Celeste had gotten a part in a similar sitcom, due to meeting the producer during what should have been Traci's interview.

Because Traci didn't know any of this, she had gone to the set to surprise Celeste with a bouquet of flowers for good luck. The director came to her and asked, "With all that beauty, why didn't you show up for the interview? This part would've been perfect for you." He proceeded to tell Traci about the events that led up to the new sitcom, and too mad to answer, Traci stormed off the set, and had not spoken to Celeste since.

Traci pulled down the overhead mirror. I look simply beautiful, she thought. Her voice became unbelievably pleasant. "Okay, let's go."

Sharlana got out of the car and rested her hands on the hood. A thin breeze provided temporary relief from the heat. "Look, Traci. There ain't gonna be no shit, is there?"

Traci flashed her trademark fake George Foreman smile and asked calmly, "Do I look like someone that would start trouble in a public place?"

"Let's hope we can act like adults," Sharlana replied.

She has some nerve. She's lucky she isn't going to get a mouthful for even inviting Celeste to come out with us.

Traci stormed through the front door, only to be stopped by the hostess.

"Table for two?" she asked.

Traci held up three fingers and smiled. Her smile vanished as she scanned the room intently. The restaurant was nicer than she had anticipated. She was expecting something small, but looked around and saw that it stretched to about fifty feet and was expertly decorated with vibrant paintings of jazz greats that breathed life into the place. In front, couples held hands across tables tastefully decorated in lavender and cream with matching candles burning in the center. Dizzy and Ella hung from the walls, watching the people who knew them. Cigarette and cigar smoke hung heavily near the front of the restaurant with the mixture traveling toward the back. In the rear, a young Miles Davis smoked his own cigarette while people of all nationalities noisily socialized and drank at the bar.

Like the Secret Service, Sharlana led the way through the crowd to where Celeste stood talking to a group of men. She doesn't look like a damn damsel in distress, Traci thought. Celeste had not changed a bit in six years. She just seemed a little taller as she towered over two of the guys that strained their necks to see her cleavage. She wore a leopard skin Prada jumpsuit, and even though it was dark inside, she sported shades.

Traci figured Sharlana and Celeste must have been keeping in touch with one another for her to be able to call her on short notice to meet. Regardless, as long as Sharlana kept the news of their friendship between them, Traci was fine. Celeste spotted Sharlana and waved for her to come over. Everyone exchanged pleasantries except Traci and Celeste. All felt the tension, or so Traci thought.

Sharlana pulled Celeste to the side and whispered something in her ear. They both looked back at the men and laughed.

Traci's heart flinched and her nails dug into her palm as she made a weapon. Traci pretended to look the other way when Celeste looked her way. This was going to be a little harder than she had thought. She trailed Celeste and Sharlana to the table, all along cursing herself for even walking inside the restaurant.

Once they were seated, Celeste extended her hand. "Hello, Traci."

Traci accepted her hand and maintained her firm grip a few seconds longer than necessary. She wanted Celeste to know that she was not to be messed with anymore.

"How's everything?" Traci asked.

The next half hour was spent with Traci at the bar, trying to stay away from Celeste and her sneaky ass. She was cornered by a guy she knew from college. Traci used the guy with the wrinkled shirt as a smoke screen to get a better view of Sharlana and Celeste laughing like old war buddies. Part of her was angry that Sharlana maintained their relationship, completely ignoring the loyalty between real friends. The other part of her wanted to go over and strangle that heifer, Celeste.

Wrinkled Shirt placed his hands atop hers and smiled confidently. "Would you like something else to drink, Traci?"

"I'm fine. Look, I'm not trying to be rude, but I'm waiting on someone." Usually she would come right out and tell a guy the truth, but she was trying to be nice tonight. She didn't want to take her anger out on the wrong guy.

"That's cool," he said. "I was just going to ask you who that tall female you were with was. She seems to have a lot of flare and with us going to school together, I thought maybe you could put a good-"

Before he finished his sentence, Traci was off to the bathroom. She stood in front of the mirror and looked herself over. *What the hell was she doing at Tipton's with Sharlana and that bitch, anyway*, she asked herself. She took out a tube of lipstick and refilled her lips. She couldn't go back to that basic lipstick. MAC made her lips look simply irresistible. That's one thing Jordan said drove him crazy. He was into this lips and hips stuff.

"You look beautiful," a voice chirped from behind.

Traci's eyes made a beeline from her lips to the spot where Celeste stood a few feet away. She ignored Celeste and continued to coat her lips.

"I said, you look beautiful," Celeste repeated.

Without acknowledging her presence with eye contact, Traci responded, "I know I do. I don't need some low-life bitch to tell me I look good."

Celeste let out a nervous chuckle. Her soft facial expression showed she was unfazed, but her shifting posture expressed otherwise.

An older blonde haired, heavyset, black woman strolled by, entered the middle stall with a huff, and slammed it shut.

"Look, I didn't come in here to hear this bullshit! I came in to apologize for any wrong that I've done, but obviously you aren't ready to hear what I have to say," Celeste explained.

Traci bent down close to the sink to gather herself. She could feel the tension building in her shoulders. She counted to ten, slowly.

Celeste took her glasses off, propped them on the edge of her shirt, and stood with her arms folded, awaiting a response.

Blondie let out a bevy of grunts before blessing the air with a mixture of old greens and eggs.

Celeste and Traci both covered their noses simultaneously.

Once Traci collected her thoughts, she turned around to face Celeste. She walked over and got so close that she could feel Celeste's hot breath on her forehead. Up close, Celeste wasn't the beauty queen that she was from afar. She had on enough make-up for two "Thriller" videos.

"First of all," Traci started. "I don't know why Sharlana even invited you to hang out with us. Obviously there is no love lost between us. It's been what," Traci said, attempting to count in her head even though she knew exactly how much time had passed, "five or six years since we've spoken?"

Grunt.

In a cold tone, Celeste responded, "Something like that."

"Well, I've since moved on. Past the bullshit that I went through with you. You didn't even try to explain to me what happened back then. You just let it ride. So if you think about it, why should I have anything to say to you?"

Grunt. Grunt.

Celeste clasped her hands together in mock prayer and pleaded, "Can you hear me out?"

Traci's arm shot straight ahead and returned to a ninety-degree angle as she stared at her gold Movado. "You've got a minute."

Relieved, Celeste exhaled and wiped her sweaty palms on the thighs of her jumpsuit. "First of all, you weren't going to be able to make it back anyway."

Memories of that time brought back feelings that Traci had thought she put away forever, but here she was about to let Celeste open up that Pandora's box. She was beginning to wonder if it was really worth it.

"I should've been the one that made that call. It was my life. I make my own decisions," Traci yelled. Her heart sent a rush of cold venom through her veins. Traci took a few steps back and leaned against the sink.

Celeste walked toward her in prayer again, pleading. "I'm sorry, but what would you have done in my shoes?"

Grunt. Grunt.

"Not what you did." Traci stood up and looked Celeste directly in her eyes. "Look, no disrespect, but I am not ready to talk to you. I went through a lot of shit behind what you did."

Blondie flushed and sprinted by them without washing her hands.

A tear crept from the corner of Celeste's eye. "If it means anything to you, I have thought about you often and I'm upset about the falling out we had."

Traci thought that if she were really upset, it wouldn't have taken her six years to finally speak up. She was up to something, but Traci couldn't quite put a finger on it. Traci bolted from the bathroom and informed Sharlana that she had enough of their little family reunion.

Chapter 6

JORDAN

I shouted a weak, "Hello," into the phone. Whoever it was better have a good excuse.

Traci began yelling about some psycho woman, and that she was on her way over.

I realized that it was only ten thirty, but it felt later. My boy, Tony, had worked everything from my abs to my back, not missing any part.

Five minutes later, I greeted her with a yawn. She greeted me with the third-cousin hug I hated before heading to the couch.

"Jordan, do you know who Sharlana had the nerve to bring to dinner with us?"

I knew where this conversation was headed, so I sat down next to her on the couch and turned on *Sports Center*. The Vikings were playing the Bears and the Vikings were getting mauled.

"That's bullshit!" I shouted as I watched the Bears score a touchdown.

"I didn't tell you who showed up yet," Traci screamed, pulling my chin toward her so I could give her eye contact.

I gave her a complimentary kiss on the cheek and turned my full attention to her. "I was saying that it's bullshit the way your girls treat you." Another yawn escaped from the side of my balled fist. "Who showed up, baby?"

Traci smiled half-heartedly, content with the sympathy I showed. "Celeste!"

"Who?"

"Celeste," she repeated.

I didn't know who she was talking about. "I don't know Celeste."

Traci grabbed my arm as if that would jog my memory. "You remember that female I told you about that stayed in my house and took my role for the sitcom back in the day?"

"Oh, yeah. Now I remember. Why did Sharlana bring her to dinner?"

"I don't have a clue. I can't believe she would invite her to hang out with us, especially after knowing our history."

Here we go, Styles. I knew that when Traci got this emotional, it would prove to be a long evening. Mentally I prepared for her emotional marathon. I wanted to prepare physically as well by getting myself a drink.

She reached for my arm. "Where are you going?"

To get a beer! "Nowhere," I said, retreating back to the couch. I sat back, laid her head on my chest and massaged the back of her neck. "Just relax, baby."

"I'm pissed. I thought the feelings had subsided, but just the mention of her name had me in an uproar."

As I applied deeper pressure, her body began to loosen. "You didn't do anything stupid, did you?"

She snatched her head up. "What do you mean, anything stupid?"

Way to go Styles. Real smooth! "I'm sorry. I didn't mean it like that. I meant, what did you do?"

Traci returned to my chest, wrapped her arm around my waist and slowly explained how Celeste followed her to the bathroom and tried to make up with her. After her explanation, I got up to get her a glass of wine. My phone rang three steps into my quest.

"Hello, Mr. Styles. I didn't mean to call you at home, but I had to call you before I left," Deanna yelled frantically.

I continued toward the kitchen to pour the drinks while listening to Deanna cry hysterically on the phone.

"What's going on? Are you okay?" I asked.

"I-I-I-" The phone line went dead.

After three quick taps on the flash button and a few hellos, I hung up.

Deanna never called me this late. I left the bottle of Chardonnay on the counter and retrieved my Palm Pilot from the bedroom. As I perused my numbers, the phone rang.

"Deanna?"

"I'm sorry, Mr. Styles. I just don't know where to turn."

Panic set in. "What's wrong? Did you call Mr. Amsterdam?"

She began sobbing even harder. "I tried, but I can't seem to get him."

"Do you need me to do anything?" During the months that Deanna worked for me, I found out from her that all she knew were me and Mr. Amsterdam. I felt inclined to offer my services. "You need to come over and talk?"

"I couldn't impose on you like that," she said in between a cough and a sniffle.

"It's nothing," I explained. As the words left my mouth, I remembered Traci was in the other room going through her own problems. *She'll understand, Styles. Let her lie down in the bedroom until Deanna leaves.* I gave her my address.

Between sniffles she recited my address and said that it would take her about twenty minutes to reach my house. I hung up and finished pouring Traci a glass of Chardonnay.

Traci took the glass of wine and sipped. "Who was that?"

"Deanna," I replied nonchalantly. I switched the channel back to the football game.

She reached for the remote. "I was watching that," she said. Then she thought for a second and suddenly gave up the fight for the remote. "Why is she calling you this late? Is everything alright?"

"I don't know. She was crying hysterically and I told her to come over before she left."

Traci's forehead wrinkled. "Left?"

My eyes remained glued to the television. "Yeah. She said she was leaving for a few weeks," I lied. I didn't want Traci thinking Deanna came over for bullshit. *Way to get out of that one, Styles.*

"Weeks?"

"That's what she said. I don't know what's going on. I told her to stop by for a second."

Traci raised her eyebrow and threw her head back. "I didn't know you guys were that cool for her to call you when she had problems."

"It's not like that," I said, attempting to pull her closer. "As a matter of fact, we'll only be talking for about fifteen minutes at the most and you can get some well needed rest in the bedroom."

Traci shot up. *Why in the hell did you have to say that shit, Styles?*

She cocked her head to the side. Her hands held her hips while her neck snapped and popped. "Why do I have to go into the bedroom?" She didn't wait for me to answer. "If you need privacy then I'll see you another time." She rushed toward the closet to get her jacket.

Don't start this shit! "Hold up," I screamed. She was pissing me off with her bullshit attitude. Everything had to revolve around her and her problems. "As a matter of fact," I said in a calm tone, "if you want to leave, then leave." I cleared a path to the door with my hand.

Traci whirled around, stunned. "You gonna just let me leave?"

"Look, you're the one getting upset because my secretary called me!" I walked over to the closet, stood in front of her and put my face close to hers. I could smell cigarette smoke in her hair and wine on her breath. "Right?"

"No!" She grabbed her jacket out of the closet and shoved her arms through. "That's not why I'm getting mad. I'm getting mad because I was here to talk to you."

"Well, I can't help it she called me, too. Do you think I called her and said, 'Traci's here, so please give me a call?' No, I didn't. Do you think I would've acted that way if a male friend of yours called?"

Her chuckle was full of sarcasm. "I don't have male friends calling me, anymore."

Yeah, right. And I don't have nuts! "Yeah, okay!"

"I cut off my male friends when we started getting serious."

"Why would you cut off your friends when we started dating?"

"I knew what most of them wanted."

"Which is?"

"They didn't want to be my friends."

"If you weren't giving it to them, then what's the problem?"

"That's why all that stuff happened with you and your little friend Monica. You thought passing notes and e-mails was cute, but apparently she had different ideas about what was going on. You men play stupid, and then when stuff goes down you say you never saw it coming."

I scratched my head. "So, you're gonna stand here and tell me that since we've been together you've never had a man call you?"

"No, I haven't." She paused and seemed like she was wrestling with a thought. "As a matter of fact, someone called me the other day," she conceded.

"I knew it."

"And what is that supposed to mean?"

"I know that as social as you are, men call you. Who was it?" *Don't ask questions you don't want her asking you, Styles!* I didn't care.

She didn't answer. Her weight shifted from left to right.

"Hello? Who called you? A blast from the past?"

"For your information, it was a friend."

"A boyfriend?"

"I just said a friend, didn't I?"

"He called you at work?"

"The hotel."

"How did he know you were at the hotel?"

Traci took a deep breath and revealed, "My mom told him."

Relieved, I said, "So, he's a friend of the family."

"I guess you could say that."

The doorbell rang and Traci gave me another generic hug. "I'll stop by later on." With that, she opened the door, exchanged pleasantries with Deanna, and left.

Deanna looked like she had been through hell. She had on a furrowed powder blue sweat suit with her hair pulled back in a ponytail. Her eyes were swollen and the whites were replaced with a dull redness.

I gave her a hug and showed her to the couch.

"Thank you so much. I hope I didn't interrupt anything," she said softly.

You did, but fuck it! "You didn't. Traci was going home to do some work." I sat down next to Deanna on the couch, leaned back, and turned the TV off. "Want something to drink?"

"What do you have?"

"Depends. What do you have a taste for?"

Deanna sighed. "All the wrong things."

"Meaning?"

She shook her head. "I seem to want things I can't have."

I patted her knee. "Well, you can have anything you want here. My house is your house."

She smiled. "Thank you so much, Mr. Styles."

"And enough with that Mr. Styles stuff outside of work." I stood up. "You make me feel like I'm fifty-years-old."

"I'm sorry," she paused, "Jordan."

I smiled. "That's better. Let me get you something to drink. The remote is on the coffee table."

She declined, stating that all she wanted was to talk and have a drink. I made her a rum and Coke, and when I returned she was sprawled out on the couch, eyes closed, and head snapped back.

I placed the cold glass against her unsuspecting arm. Startled, she sat up and let out a long sigh.

"Okay, what's the problem?"

"It's embarrassing."

I took a sip of wine. "Try me. I'm sure I've heard worse."

She shook her head again, swallowed two gulps of her drink, and began. "It's about a guy I'm seeing." She took a few breaths and continued, "I'll just say that his wife doesn't like the fact that we're seeing each other."

Wine traveled down the wrong tube. "His who?"

Embarrassed, Deanna put her drink down and stood up. "I told you it was a little bit of drama."

I grabbed her hand and gently pulled her back to the couch. "It's okay. You just caught me by surprise." I sipped my drink slowly, encouraging her to continue.

"Like I was saying, the man I'm seeing has a wife."

I studied Deanna as she explained how she and her lover met when she was in college. Without exposing it all, she told me about a few encounters between them during the last year. She didn't seem like the kind of woman that dated married men. It's not like I actually knew what a woman that dates married men looked like. Regardless, I would've pictured her with a pretty boy. Hell, she was fine with no kids and she seemed to have a good head on her shoulders

She continued, "I know I shouldn't be involved with him, but when I met him they weren't together."

"Is that a fact or is that what he told you?"

"He said it was a fact."

"Why did he go back?"

"Financial reasons. All I know is that she called my house. The only good thing is that she has my name wrong. She kept calling me Dana."

Her story had more action than a hooker's mouth. I shook my head in astonishment because I knew she could have anyone she wanted. I was confused at why she wanted a married man.

"What did his wife say?"

"She called my house and said she would do whatever it took to keep her man." Deanna finished the last of the rum and Coke and asked for another. I got up to head to the kitchen and invited her to follow.

A few steps behind me, she continued, "Like I was saying, she called me and said she would come over my house if she had to. She's crazy, Jordan."

She accepted the drink and followed me back into the living room. She took her seat opposite me, took a large gulp and gave a fake smile.

"What happened after you told her that you didn't know what she was talking about?"

"She didn't believe me. She kept saying, 'It's not that hard to find you, Dana.'"

"Is this the first time you had an encounter with her?"

Deanna nodded.

"I hope you're going to quit dealing with him now," I said with a fatherly tone.

"It's not that easy. I wish I could, but we have so much history. I mean he helped me a lot in getting where I am now. This man helped me financially to get through my last year of school and everything."

"Well, I should've tried to kick it to him, too. These student loans are killing me," I joked.

A genuine smile spread across her face.

"See, that's the Deanna I know. It's not that bad. Just lay low for a while. As a matter of fact, you can chill here for the night because I'm going over to Traci's hotel anyway." I kicked myself after the words left my mouth. Part of me felt like it was my civic duty, while the other part clamored for points toward a promotion. Kissing ass wasn't my style, but if it was ass with some pants on, then maybe it really wasn't kissing ass. Either way, her smile showed acceptance of my invitation.

She looked at me with admiration. "You really love her, huh?"

I reflected on my relationship with Traci. We've had our arguments, but I wouldn't trade her for anyone. "Yeah. I really do love her."

"That's what I need," she said.

"What? Some real love?"

"No. Someone like you."

The air was thick and my collar got hot. My eyebrows reached for my hairline and my mouth popped open. "Oh."

She threw her hand at me playfully. "Don't mind me."

I laughed it off. "I wasn't."

"But if you weren't-" She shrugged her shoulders, got up, and gave me a hug. I could smell her sweet scent as she embraced me much longer than a co-worker should. "Thanks so much. I thought I was going to lose my mind."

I walked to the back, returned to the living room, and threw her a T-shirt. I told her that I made up the futon in the spare room.

"You can get some sleep. I'm going to jump in the shower before I head over to Traci's. You'll probably be asleep when I leave, so just pull the door shut behind you in the morning, and we'll finish this conversation another time."

With the T-shirt in hand, she smiled as she headed for the guestroom. "I owe you."

Chapter 7

TRACI

Traci sat in her car and thought about going back. She thought about what Jordan and Deanna were doing. As she slid her key into the ignition, she pondered her next move before easing the key back out. *Why should I have to leave? Jordan was right. I could've just slept in the room until that damn Deanna left anyway.*

Her period was coming any day and maybe that's why she was so edgy. Anyway, she just wanted to get rid of his secretary and snuggle against Jordan's chest until she fell asleep.

She looked at her watch and realized she had only been gone for about fifteen minutes and they probably needed a little more time. Quickly she revved her engine and raced to the grocery store to purchase whipped cream and chocolate syrup.

Ten minutes later she was at Jordan's door, bag in tow. After knocking twice, there was no answer. She remembered seeing his car outside so she knew he was still home. She knocked again and there was still no answer. She hurriedly called him on her cell phone. Thoughts flew through her mind when Jordan picked up on the sixth ring.

"Hello, Jordan," she said cautiously.

"Hey, sweetheart, I was just thinking about you."

She listened carefully and could hear running water in the background. "Were you?"

"Hold up. I got soap in my eye."

Traci began expecting the worse. "I've been ringing the bell for a few minutes."

"I didn't hear it. I'll open the door for you in a second."

Jordan didn't act like he was trying to hide anything. When he came to the door with a towel on, it only reaffirmed her paranoia. As his drenched lips touched hers, she continued to peer in back of him looking for something.

He hesitantly relinquished his lip lock and smiled. "You must've read my mind. I was just on my way over to your spot."

"Were you?"

"Yeah." He led Traci to the living room. "What's with all the questions?"

Her left eye probed each of his words as they exited. She paid special attention to his body language and surroundings. "Oh, nothing," she said, taking a seat on the couch.

"I'll be out in a minute, Detective Johnson," he yelled, running back into the bathroom.

Traci looked around and noticed two glasses on the coffee table. She picked up the one with lipstick on the rim and took a whiff. The strong smell of rum overpowered the small drop of soda that remained. After quickly scanning the room, she noticed Jordan's bedroom door was closed. She waited until she heard him turn the shower back on before slowly tiptoeing toward his door.

It was dark in the room and it took a minute for her eyes to adjust. Her heart thumped like Jamaican bongos. The first thing she noticed was that his bed was extremely lumpy. Cautiously, she approached the bed.

"Looking for something?" Jordan asked, nearly scaring her to death.

Her body froze in the heated room. "Huh?"

"Are you looking for something?"

Embarrassed, she turned to face him and smiled nervously. "No."

The light from the hallway temporarily blinded her. Seconds later, she saw his large silhouette standing in the doorway with steam rising from his broad shoulders.

"Why are you being so quiet? Usually I can hear you a mile away. And why didn't you turn on any lights?"

"I don't know. I guess I was trying to surprise you," she said.

Jordan smiled and pulled her close. "Surprise me with what?"

"If I told you, then it wouldn't be a surprise, now would it."

Content with the answer, he turned on the nightlight, threw his towel to the floor and sat on the bed, legs spread eagle. "I'm ready for my surprise."

Traci looked at him, smiled, and wondered why she had doubted him anyway. She gave him his fair share of shit and he was still here. When they were dating, she could remember a time when he wanted to take things to the next level. He had prepared a nice dinner and even had his boy serve the food, but at that time she was still confused. She still had not gotten over Solomon. They were still doing their thing, somewhat. Needless to say, she declined his invitation to move things along. But he still stuck around.

Now Traci strolled over, clicked the night light off, and straddled his wet body.

Remembering the whip cream and the chocolate in the living room, she jumped up. "I'll be right back. Don't move."

Throwing his head back, he yelled, "Holla."

A few seconds passed before Jordan remembered that Deanna was in the other room sleeping.

Traci reached for the bag and heard a frantic Jordan yelling. "Traci, I forgot-"

Jordan stopped short of the door. Traci stood in shock as she watched Deanna come out of the bathroom with Jordan's T-shirt on.

Chapter 8

JORDAN

"To tell you that..." *Holy Shit!*

Traci and Deanna stood in front of each other and stared for what seemed like hours as sweat began dripping down my previously dry back. Neither one moved.

I had to clear my head because it really wasn't the way it looked. I glanced into the dining room mirror and noticed I still had my towel wrapped around my waist. I quickly excused myself to change. I rushed back in with shorts and a T-shirt on, and a tickle in my throat.

"Traci, I forgot to tell you that Deanna was going to stay here while I came to your place."

Traci looked at me and then back at Deanna. Still too stunned to say a word, she stood in cement filled shoes while her neck swiveled back and forth between Deanna and myself as though we were involved in an intense tennis match. Deanna, on the other hand, eyed Traci and then me, unsure of what to say about any of this.

Deanna pulled her T-shirt down to cover herself as much as the triple large Georgetown shirt she wore would allow. She took a step back and explained, "It isn't what it seems like, Traci."

Traci's hands clenched tightly into a fist as she took a step closer to Deanna, "What do you think it looks like, Donna?"

"It's Deanna," she corrected. "And I know what it looks like, but honestly, it isn't. I just came here to speak to Jordan about some problems I was having, and to tell him I might have to leave town for a bit."

"Oh, we are calling him Jordan now instead of Mr. Styles, huh?" Traci snarled. "It doesn't look to me like you're leaving to go anywhere. It looks like you're getting mighty comfortable." Traci turned to me, scratched her head and pointed to Deanna. "As a matter of fact, Jordan, isn't that the T-shirt I bought for you from my school?"

The thought had never crossed my mind. I was starting to get a headache and wanted out. *Tell everybody to get the hell out of the house, Styles!* I couldn't do that. Kicking people out would be like admitting guilt. "I guess it's the shirt you bought for me. How am I supposed to know that when I'm just throwing her a shirt?"

"Because you shouldn't have been throwing her any shirt. What am I supposed to think?"

I looked at the situation again and tried to put myself in her shoes. But then I quickly took off her Payless pumps and put my Nikes back on. "I know it looks crazy, but why would I plan on doing something stupid when I was coming to see you?"

Traci quickly folded her arms and cocked her eyebrow. "When I came here it didn't look like you were coming to see me. And why couldn't you hear the doorbell? You hear it any other time."

"I was in the shower with the music up. Would I be that stupid to have someone over here right after you left?"

"Would it be okay if it wasn't right after I left?"

What the hell? "I wouldn't do that anyway." I went over to Traci and tried to console her, but she shook free.

"I don't know what you would do," Traci snipped.

Tightlipped, Deanna stood, watching the whole episode. She could've jumped in anytime she wanted because I was sinking.

"Look, let me get dressed and we'll talk about it," I calmly said to Traci.

Deanna put her head down and spoke almost silently. "I'm sorry, Jordan. I should just leave."

"Perhaps you should just leave," Traci instructed calmly.

I stepped between them. "Hell, no!" It was about time I put my foot down. "There's nothing going on here. If you need some place to stay, Deanna, then you can stay here. I'm not going to let you go back home and get yourself in trouble because my woman doesn't trust me. Just go back in the room and get some rest while we get out of here and have a much-needed talk. We are long overdue."

Traci looked at me like I had five eyeballs. I went back into the room to put some pants on, leaving Traci to look stupid by herself.

Three minutes later I was fully dressed and standing over Traci. She was sitting on the edge of the couch clutching the glass partially covered with burgundy lipstick.

"It doesn't look like you two were having a life or death conversation."

Don't start! "Are you going to start again?"

Traci thrust the glass into my face. "Is this what you call life or death?"

"What the hell are you talking about?" I snatched the glass from her. Soda splashed the carpet. I grabbed Traci's hand, attempting to lead her to the door. "Let's go. You've done enough damage for today."

She pulled away. "I'm not going anywhere until you tell me what's going on with you two. First the Monica chick, and now I have to deal with another one."

"Why do you think something's going on with us?" I was tired of her insinuations. I knew what was going on and what wasn't.

Traci walked toward the room Deanna was in. My first reaction was to stop her, but if she wanted to find out what was going on, I had nothing to hide.

Traci slammed her hand against the frail wood that shielded Deanna from her. "Open the door!"

While she waited for Deanna to appear, I stood and watched her tap her foot, rapidly wearing out a portion of my sandy brown rug. The room was deathly still. No clock ticked, no television played, no music blared, and my heart didn't thump as loud as it should have.

Deanna came out of the bedroom fully clothed with the T-shirt in hand. "I really don't want to get into an argument, Traci. I'm having my own problems and I don't need to get involved in yours," she explained, handing her the shirt.

Traci snatched the shirt and blocked the bedroom door with her body so Deanna couldn't get out. "Well, you should've been thinking about that before coming to my man's house and getting naked."

Deanna started to respond, but decided against it.

"You're not saying anything, so maybe you did have other plans," Traci said, attempting to bait Deanna into an argument.

Deanna remained motionless, watching the ceiling fan oscillate.

Traci, becoming more agitated with Deanna's silence, moved her arm from the door and came toward me. "I'm going to leave! Don't follow me," she spat.

Follow you to where, the nut house? I let Traci walk to the door and exit without incident. I was embarrassed for her. All this bullshit, and I was actually going to see her.

Deanna eased toward me and rested her calm hand on my shoulder. "Maybe you need a drink now." She smiled, left, and came back with a tall glass of wine.

"Thank you." After a few sips, I turned to her and explained how embarrassed I was. She told me that she could actually understand where Traci was coming from and that I should go after her. I knew right then that I would never understand women for as long as I lived. The woman that just got screamed on told me that I should go after the other one. It boggles my mind the way they stick together, even if they don't like each other.

****

The next day at work, I didn't know what to expect. I had no doubt that Deanna would act weird.

I came in five minutes before my nine o'clock meeting and breezed through it. After the meeting I was sitting at my desk scanning proposals when Mario came in with the mail.

"What's going down, Jordan?" He gave me a high-five and the knuckle knock.

Mario was our Chinese mail courier that operated out of the basement. He said that his main reason for coming to the States was to act in a movie opposite Sanaa Lathan. This job was temporary until he got into the movies. Mario, who took his name from an actor that played in his favorite movie, *Posse*, was about five-five and solid. He lifted weights and was pretty diesel to be so small. He also sported a blond-colored goatee that hung a few inches below his chin. He claimed it was his flavor saver.

"What's up, Mario?"

He shuffled through some mail and handed me two pieces. He put the rest back into his silver rollaway cart and sat on the edge of my desk. "Why don't that fine honey at the desk give a Chinese brotha no play?"

My twisted lip expressed my view about him being completely crazy. "Who are you talking about...Deanna?"

His face lit up. "Yeah."

I didn't make it a habit of fraternizing with staff, but for some reason I took a liking to Mario. I decided that after three months of bothering me about her, it was time to school him on a few things.

"Have you ever said anything to her?"

All of his energy seemed to leave his body. "No. When I bring her mail, she don't even try to peep a vanilla brotha out. I don't know what's wrong with her."

I laughed and invited him to sit. "Do you think a woman like that talks to anybody?"

He thought about it for a second and shrugged his shoulders.

"There you go. First of all," I said, pointing to his shirt, "a fine woman like that wouldn't talk to anyone with a football jersey on."

He stood up and pulled his shirt out as though he was seeing it for the first time. "There's nothing wrong with my jersey. Women say they want a little thug in their life. So, why not have a tiny thug in their panties," he joked.

I laughed. "I can see why she doesn't give you the time of day."

Mario's smile disappeared. "Why?"

"Because you've got to come at her correct."

"I don't lie to her."

"Not correct like that, but correct like, with your stuff together."

He shook his head. "I got it. Next time, I'm gonna walk up and say, 'You got a fatty girl.' Word."

I started laughing so hard that my stomach hurt. "You need to find you a nice Oriental chick and get down with her," I said, returning to my work.

"They don't understand the hood."

I looked up. "And you do?"

"I know the hood. Who else do you know that got game like me?"

"Nobody. As a matter of fact, what are you and your game doing this weekend?"

Mario grabbed his cart and began pushing it toward the door. "Nothing, why?"

"Me and my boy are going out. Wanna come?"

A smile replaced his puzzled look. "Indeed. That's gonna be jiggy?"

"That's gonna be-" I started. I thought about correcting his slang, but decided against it. I didn't want him to have new words to talk to me with. He was better off with that old school slang. *Be nice, Styles. Don't let him hang himself. If you're at the club and the chicks won't talk to him, he'll be talking to you.* I continued, "When you say it's going to be something, you finish it with things like it's off the hook, off the meat rack or off the heezie."

He covered his mouth and bobbed his head, "Word. I see what you're saying. I like that heezie shit."

Chapter 9

TRACI

Jordan is a certified dickhead, Traci thought as she left Georgetown's campus. He didn't even follow her out the door last night. No telling what him and his dickretary did when she left. All she knew was that she wasn't about to look stupid for anybody.

She got into her car and headed for McDonald's to grab a bite. Whenever tension became unbearable, a Big Mac and fries would always cure her. In the middle of her order, her cell phone rang.

"Hello, Traci."

"Hold up," she yelled into the phone, stunned. She returned to the intercom and ordered a Whopper with cheese.

"You're at McDonald's, Miss," the lady shouted through the intercom.

Too embarrassed to finish the order, she pulled off. As if the person on the phone could see her mouthing the words, she pressed the phone onto her leg and mouthed, "I'm an idiot."

She let out a long sigh before returning to the phone. "Hi, Solomon."

"Hey, love. How are you?"

"Fine, and you?"

There was an awkward pause.

"Just a little tired, that's all."

"Working hard?"

"Studying actually."

Traci had never thought of Solomon as the studying type. And what exactly was he studying for?

She pulled into a parking spot, intrigued. "What are you studying?"

"Business management."

"That's nice," she said. A light breeze tickled her skin, giving her goose bumps as she sought for a follow-up to his answer. After searching for a comeback, she realized that she shouldn't have been speaking to him about anything. Solomon's M.O. was to chase a woman down, get her to chase him, and then walk.

"Let's cut the formalities, Traci. I just left class and I'm starving. Do you want to grab a bite? I see that you were at Burger Donald's anyway," he snickered.

Without thinking, Traci blurted, "Yes." Guilt was soon replaced with renewed vigor when she thought about Jordan, Deanna and Monica. Just like Sharlana said, how can he just let you walk out the door without coming after you, let alone without calling you? Sharlana seemed to enjoy when Jordan fucked up. It was only a bite to eat, she told herself.

Solomon wanted to meet at Tipton's, but Traci had had enough of that place, so they agreed to go to a restaurant near the college. Her ride to the restaurant was filled with many thoughts. It was like they were destined to meet again. Who would have

ever thought that Solomon would go to college? Definitely not
Traci. As a matter of fact, they hadn't seen each other since a few
months after she had met Jordan. Solomon and Traci were off
and on for at least seven years. Solomon would always casually
creep in and out of her life. Sharlana would always tell her that he
wasn't to blame because he only did what she allowed him to do.
Traci paused for a minute, thinking about whether to continue
onward to the restaurant, but the thought of Jordan and Deanna
together quickly had her revving up her engine. If he could talk to
his friends, so could she. It wasn't like she was going to sleep with
Solomon or anything. She just needed closure.

She got out of her car and slowly approached the restaurant
with some fear of seeing Solomon for the first time in almost a
year. She looked herself over and was satisfied with how her blue
jeans clung to her shapely thighs and her white sweater made her
36 Cs look like DDs. She wanted Solomon to realize that he had
messed up, and she wanted to make him deal with the fact that
he couldn't have her even if he wanted to. It wasn't enough to tell
him on the phone. She wanted him to come back crawling so she
could look down on him, show a little sympathy, and stick her
classic black Ferragamo shoe in his classic black ass.

Traci stepped into the dimly lit restaurant and searched for
Solomon. Not finding him, she walked to the bar alone. She
found an empty stool and ordered a drink. The restaurant was
filled to capacity as people occupied most of the twenty-five
tables scattered amongst the huge room, while the bar
entertained more than fifty people.

"Can I pay for that drink?"

Without turning around, she knew it was Solomon. The
stuffy air at the bar blended in with a hint of Obsession cologne.

Whenever she smelled that particular cologne, she thought of him.

Solomon smiled and stepped back so Traci could admire him from a distance. "Oh, now you don't know me?"

Damn! Not only did he wear black slacks with a cream mock neck that fit snug to his deeply defined chest, but he also had the nerve to have on black Kenneth Cole casuals. He was definitely stepping up his game. And for what?

Traci threw her head back to allow more distance so her eyes could record the whole picture. "I didn't know it was you." She shook her head and returned to her drink to gather her thoughts.

Solomon threw his hands in the air and laughed. "What, no hug, kiss on the cheek, or high-five? You sure know how to treat a brotha."

She got up and hesitantly gave him a hug. Her body shuddered and she immediately let go. "Better?"

Appeased, he smiled. "Yeah." He pulled up a stool next to hers and pointed to a table in the back toward the left side. "That's our table over there. I arrived a little early and by the time I got back from the bathroom, I spotted you walking toward the bar. I wanted to come right over to you, but I couldn't, so I just watched you for a while. I couldn't help but notice how good you're looking, Ms. Traci." He reached underneath her stool and spun her around to face him. "Seems like you're being well taken care of."

"As a matter of fact, I am," she responded coldly. Why would he even bring up her being taken care of? That only made her wonder why she was here and not where she should've been.

He placed his hands on hers and reassured her with a look that everything would be okay. "I'm sorry, Traci. Can we at least have a bite to eat and chat?"

The contact felt so comfortable. So real. A guilty feeling started to build, but she quickly dismissed it.

Traci grabbed her drink and the two headed for the table.

Solomon pulled the chair out for her. She continued to sip on her drink and get acclimated with her surroundings while a tall blonde waitress poured their water. Traci ordered a chicken salad and watched Solomon watch her.

The waitress turned to Solomon, who continued to stare at Traci and asked, "And what would you like, sir?"

Solomon looked at the waitress and then at Traci. "I want Traci to marry me."

Water flew from Traci's mouth onto the back of the man's suit jacket seated across from them. Embarrassed, she quickly ran to the table with a napkin in hand. The old man with the curled mustard moustache told her not to bother as he shooed her away and cursed under his breath.

Solomon rushed to the table and offered his hand to the man. "I'm sorry. I just asked my lady to marry me and she got excited." He looked at the older lady that was the man's dinner companion. "Miss, you can understand how she must feel." He pointed to her large diamond ring and asked, "How did you feel when he popped the question?"

The lady smiled.

Solomon reached into his pocket and pulled out a fifty-dollar bill. "For the inconvenience, let me at least pay for your dinner?" The lady, who resembled Lena Horne, politely declined, but the man took the bill and mumbled a thank you.

Traci attempted to hide her face from all the stares. Solomon came back, sat down, and told the waitress to give them a few moments.

When the waitress left, Traci quietly yelled, "Your lady?"

"I know you're kinda in shock, but I can make things right for you," Solomon tried to explain. He reached into his pocket, pulled out a wad of money and waved it in the air as though he was fanning away poverty. "Money isn't an issue anymore. I can take care of you." Without waiting for a response, he quickly finished. "I'm tired of playing the games, Traci. Don't you still love me?"

Traci couldn't figure out what part of, "she didn't want him," he didn't understand. He thought he could walk back into her life, flash a wad of money, and have her run back to him. "I love you like a friend. I love you because we've got history together. I love you because you were my first love. But I don't love you because I want to be with you. As a matter of fact, if you loved me so much, why weren't you there for me when I really needed you?"

Solomon dropped his perfectly oiled bald head and began massaging it from front to back.

"I called you repeatedly and you never returned any of my calls," she continued.

"I was going through some bullshit and it was a tough period for me. Can we talk now? What's up?"

Traci covered her face with her hands and began crying. "I was pregnant." Streams of tears dripped down her cheeks and fell to the table. She didn't bother to wipe them away. She wanted him to see her pain. She quickly collected herself and with a hoarse voice said, "I was three months pregnant and did you even care to call me back? I left message after message for you to call me."

Solomon sat there, aware of the stares, and said nothing. He wanted to wipe away her anguish. Throughout their relationship, Solomon had provided the shoulder to cry on, he was the one that she cried about, and the one to wipe away her tears. This time, he knew it was different.

Traci lifted her head. With every bit of information she screamed, a new tear hit the cream tablecloth that was now scattered with dark drops. "Did you call me? No, you didn't. I had just met someone that seemed to care about me when I was pregnant. Where were you? Where were you when I was one and a half months pregnant and scared? Do you know who consoled me when I was scared?"

Solomon remained silent.

"Jordan. He came over and showed me affection when you didn't."

The pit of Solomon's stomach churned as he began processing all of Traci's information. "So, you were sleeping with him while you carried my seed?"

"He never knew." Traci shook her head in disbelief. She wondered if he even had a clue. "No, I wasn't sleeping with him while I was pregnant. I cried for you many nights, and where were you? Where were you when I was all alone? Where were you when I had to make a life or death decision? I made a choice that will haunt me for the rest of my life. My first child will never be able to walk and talk, and you have the gall to ask me whether I was sleeping with Jordan when I was carrying your seed?"

Stunned, his voice shifted to a softer tone. "I didn't know, Traci."

"Why didn't you call me back after I left all those messages?"

Solomon reached for her hands. She instinctively pulled away.

"I thought you were just telling me stuff to get me to come back."

"Don't flatter yourself," Traci spat with venom. She looked for the waitress so she could cancel her order. Suddenly, she didn't feel like eating. After trying unsuccessfully to locate a waitress, she glared at Solomon and said, "I've gotta get going. Cancel my order!"

As she stood up to leave, Solomon grabbed her hand. "Please sit down for a second." Traci's hesitation let him know she still cared. "Give me two minutes of your time?"

Her brain told her no, but her heart was driving her to wherever Solomon wanted to go. "You've got two minutes." She sat back down and leaned back in her chair, ready for anything.

Solomon took two long sips of water and cleared his throat. "First of all, I'm sorry about the whole situation. I was going through a lot of shit at the time and I just thought that you were trying to scare me." Traci lifted up in her seat and opened her mouth, but Solomon got closer and gave her an apology with his expression. "You said I have two minutes, right?" She eased back and he continued. "Like I was saying, I know I fucked up, but I want to make it up to you. Didn't I tell you that I was in school now?"

The waitress came back to the table and Solomon waved her away without looking in her direction. "I'm taking business management classes. I've got a business that I'm running." Confidence took over his shaky voice. "Shit, I'm doing good for myself. Money isn't an issue now. Let me take care of you?" he pleaded.

"Enough of the bullshit, Solomon! Tell me the truth. Why weren't you around? Was it drugs, another woman, or did you just get tired of me?"

Solomon fidgeted. "It wasn't any of that, baby. I just had to find myself."

Traci couldn't take the generic answers. She wanted to know the truth, and she wasn't going to say another word until he decided to tell her the real reason. Her strumming fingers told him she wasn't buying it.

He scooted closer. "Okay." He continued to massage his head. "It was drugs," he mumbled.

"What?"

"Drugs!"

"Using or selling?"

"Neither. I got popped in a deal that went bad."

Traci shook her head.

Solomon continued, "But I wasn't selling anything. I did seven months because I was the driver. I needed to get some money in my pocket to start my business. My friend said all I had to do was drive them and a package to Virginia Beach and they would hit me off with five to six grand."

Traci sat back and wondered why he didn't tell her these things a year ago. This was one of the main reasons she gave Jordan so much crap in the beginning. She was not going to ever open up to a man like she had with Solomon. She could not, and would not, trust a man again.

"So, what am I supposed to do? Drop everything and everybody because you're back?"

Solomon reached over, put his hand on top of hers, and smiled. "That would be a start."

Traci snatched her hand away. "I've been happy for quite some time now, and I can't even believe that you would dare ask me to come back to you."

Solomon stood up and pulled Traci's chair out for her. "Well, I know deep down inside, you haven't given up on me."

Traci stood up and mumbled, "Whatever." She walked toward the door and heard her name being shouted a few tables away.

"Traci," the voice repeated from behind.

Traci turned around and saw Tony waving.

Chapter 10

JORDAN

Tony was waiting for me as soon as I walked through the front door of the Zanzaa Bar.

I have only two good friends in this world: Tony and Dallas. Last year, Dallas decided to move out of state with my sister, Renee. I had known Dallas longer than I had known Tony, but we didn't have a lot in common. Tony was the one I went to for the heart-to-heart talks. Confusion set in when Dallas got with my sister, but Tony was the one that talked me out of the major attitude I had. He said that if Dallas treated her right, why should I be concerned. I was excited that I no longer had to worry about a man putting his hands on her again.

Friday night was always the day to be at the Zanzaa. All the fine Black women of D.C. came with co-workers to get a drink after a long, hard week of work.

When Mario returned from the coat check, I introduced him to Tony. "Tone, this is Mario. A friend from work."

Mario slapped hands with Tony and looked around admiringly. Luckily for me, he had exchanged his sports gear in favor of a pretty nice two-piece casual blue collarless suit. "This is fly, J."

While Mario admired the ladies, Tony nodded toward him and then back at me. "Who the hell is J?"

I shrugged my shoulders.

Tony pulled me to the side. "Styles, I got some shit to tell you."

Mario followed. "What's going down, Big T?"

Tony gave Mario a look of unfamiliarity.

All three of us walked further from the dance floor toward the bar located near the lounge area.

"What's up, Tone?"

He took a sip of his beer and looked around to see if anyone else was listening. His big ass was always talking like his information was top of the line security. For someone who was six foot, five inches and two hundred eighty pounds, he always seemed a little paranoid. Who in their right mind was going to walk up to him and start trouble?

"I saw your old lady."

Ah, shit! "Where? In here?"

"No. I saw her at this little restaurant near the campus last night."

Phew! "A little restaurant?"

"Yeah. That's not the half of it though."

I spoke to Traci last night and she didn't mention anything about going out. *You gotta watch her ass too, Styles.* "What's the other half?"

"She was with this dude."

"A who?"

"Some guy," Tony said, finishing his beer.

Mario heard every word and shook his head. "That's some foul shit! Your chick is off the heezie!"

"Shut the hell up," I yelled over the loud music that seemed to follow us. "Tone, let's go over there for a second." I led him toward the bathrooms. "You can stay right here, Jackie Chan."

Tony laughed and repeated, "Yeah, Jackie Chan."

Mario looked Tony up and down and waved his hand in front of him. "All right, Biggie Smalls."

My heart beat through my shirt. My breathing was short, my hands cried, and tears of anger pressed, but determination fought them off.

"What's the deal? Where'd you see her?"

"Hold your horses, let me get it out." Tony called a barmaid over. "First I gotta get me some water."

The waiting allowed shorter breaths, more wailing from my palms, and a fistfight between tear ducts and manhood. Tony got his bottled water, cracked it open and sipped slowly.

"Like I was saying, I saw her at this restaurant last night and she was screaming at some guy."

A thick-assed shorty with hazel eyes quickly stole Tony's attention. A sharp punch to the shoulder brought him back.

"Screaming?"

"Yeah, screaming. That's not all. She spit on some man and then her and the guy got a little closer and spoke briefly."

Spitting! Traci didn't have the guts to tell me that she was seeing somebody else? "Where's your cell phone?"

Tony gave me his phone. I left three messages for her to call me ASAP. My mind drifted while my eyes searched for answers in a few passing tight fitting skirts and jeans.

Mario wandered near us. "You okay, J?"

I shook off the bullshit and focused on the crowd. "I'm cool."

Tony left to talk to a female he knew, while Mario stood like he was the man, whistling at some of the chicks that strolled by. My pager chimed. I pulled out Tony's cell and rushed to the back.

"Someone just call me?"

"Jordan, is that you?"

"Who is this?" The bass line bounced off the wall and drove me deeper into the back.

"Deanna."

"What's up, Deanna?"

"Nothing, Jordan. I was just wondering if we could talk."

She's getting a little comfortable with your numbers, Styles! It's not like she was bothering me, besides she was kind of cool to talk to. "You can come to the club if you want to. I'm not going to be here long though. Maybe another hour."

I told her where the place was and she said it would take her about thirty minutes to get there. Tony walked over and I threw him his phone.

"Why you looking stupid?" Tony asked, snatching the phone out the air.

"Stupid?"

"Yeah, stupid," Tony repeated.

"Right. So, back to Traci," I said. "Did you see them hugging or something?" *Stop asking questions like a woman, Styles!* Why did she have me acting like this?

"I told you, she was just talking to the guy. Why are you getting all stressed out?"

"I'm just trying to make sure I'm not making a mistake," I said. I didn't want him thinking that I was insecure. *Who cares what he thinks anyway?* I had a right to think whatever I wanted, without him judging me. I didn't know why I cared so much. This macho shit was wearing on a brotha.

"You don't have to lie to me," Tony said. "Why are you so jumpy, anyway?"

"My secretary is coming," I mumbled, almost incoherently.

"Coming where?"

"Here."

"Why is your secretary coming here?"

"She wants to talk, I guess." I made sure I kept my voice down because Mario wouldn't know what to do if he knew she was coming. "Ain't nothing wrong with talking, is it?" I asked, knowing his answer would be condescending.

"I guess if there was a problem with talking, you would be acting crazier than you are about Traci talking to a friend," he replied with a smirk.

Funny! Tony sure knew how to stick it to me every chance he got. "Go ahead and pour it on," I snapped. I knew exactly what he was getting at. "The only thing is that I wasn't acting like that."

"You don't have to defend yourself to me." He laughed again.

I walked away because I didn't feel like hearing Tony preach the good word to me. I sat at the bar for about twenty minutes enjoying my freedom before a tap on my shoulder brought me back to reality.

I turned around to see Deanna standing behind me. *What the hell is going on, Styles? Look at...and...*

"Hello, Deanna." I couldn't take my eyes off her.

She gave me a hug and a kiss on the cheek. Her scent was tempting. "Hi, Jordan. I'm really sorry to bother you tonight."

"That's alright. You want a drink?"

"I don't know. I'm trying to watch my figure," she smiled as her hands seductively glided down her black skirt.

Well, who in the hell is watching the kids? I looked her up and down and smiled. "You dance?"

She smirked. "You breathe?"

"Let's go." I grabbed her hand and led her toward the crowd. We squeezed our way into the heart of the dance floor. The DJ went from House Music to Hip-Hop. Deanna didn't play on the dance floor. She had her dance face on and she had more hips and ass flying than a fire at Jenny Craig's.

She took a step back and admired my moves. I decided to hit her with the Running Man. She doubled over and laughed hysterically. She pointed at my feet as she continued to do the two-step. "What the hell is that?"

I froze in the middle of a move. "Maybe you can't hang." I went from fifteen to eighty miles an hour on the dance floor.

Deanna looked around to see if anyone was looking before she started doing the Cabbage Patch. "Didn't think I knew any of your dances, did you?" she teased.

Damn, Styles. You got your work cut out for you on the dance floor. "That's a small time move, let's go back a little further." She smiled as I broke my neck doing the Wop. "Didn't think I had it in me, did you, youngster?"

We moved closer. My left foot led while her right foot followed. For three minutes we created our own soul music. My hand cradled the small of her back and she moved closer as many songs played in my head. Even though she was younger than me, she made me hear Jackie Wilson, the Temptations, Smokey, and the rest of Motown. Our legs continued to move in harmony to that old music with the new jack lyrics. Our eyes dated and found out that it couldn't, wouldn't, and shouldn't work.

Deanna grabbed my arm. "Hold up, I'm not done yet, Old Man." She began swaying her hips as she did the electric slide across the floor. I looked around and apparently some people were enjoying our old dances and had joined in. As if on cue, the DJ put on the "Cha Cha Slide."

I wiped the sweat off my brow, took Deanna by the arm, and led her off the dance floor. We stood by the edge and watched people listen to the instructions of the song. "Just when I learned the electric slide, they go and switch it to the new 'Cha Cha Slide!'"

Deanna laughed and pointed to the dance floor, surprised. "Is that Mario out there doing the *Cha Cha Slide?*"

I turned to my left and couldn't believe my eyes. Mario was out there doing his thing. *That's some embarrassing shit, Styles. Don't worry about it. They probably do the Cha Cha all the time over in China.* "I guess that is Mario." I shook my head in astonishment and walked back to the bar. "I taught him everything he knows."

In silence, we stood side by side watching Mario glide across the floor with three older black women. Usually Deanna had on tight fitting blouses and skirts, but tonight she had on a simple black dress that showed no cleavage. I was amazed at how mature she looked to be so young. I opened my mouth and turned toward her to ask her what she had come to talk about, but she seemed like she had forgotten about it and was just having fun.

A tall suave brotha approached Deanna. He was far from corporate with a cream colored suit and a black wide collared shirt that showed off a tiny gold chain and nappy chest hairs. I guess it didn't look like we were there together as he slid between us.

His voice was confident. "What's up, sexy?"

Deanna kept nodding her head to the beat and without hesitation, responded, "Nothing much. You looking for something casual?"

Tiny Chain seemed taken aback by her question. "Yes. Wait, no." He hesitated and shook his head. "I don't know. I'm just out here relaxing."

"Just joking. Where are you from?"

He smiled. "New York." Happy that she was joking, he inched closer. "I'm not used to this shit. I like when it's all about black."

Deanna put her drink down, turned her head, and glared toward the stranger. "What do you mean, all about black?"

"C'mon, Sista. Take a look out there."

"And?"

"Look at those black women over there dancing with that Chinese guy."

Her eyes followed his.

"If I were out there dancing with a white chick y'all would be all over me. Hell, if we were in China, I bet I wouldn't get any play from their women, right?"

"I don't know. Never been to China."

He didn't like the answer he got, so he went with a more direct approach. "What's your story, sweetheart?"

"My story is that the Chinese guy you were talking about," she paused and bit back a smile before finishing with a straight face, "is my boyfriend."

Tiny Chain's jaw dropped as he let out a nervous laugh. "You're bullshitting."

The "Cha Cha Slide" had just ended and Mario was on his way over to the bar. This was building up to be some funny shit. I pulled up a stool and watched the sitcom unfold.

Mario spotted Deanna and his face lit up. "What's up, baby?"

To his surprise, she ran toward him and gave him a big hug. "Hey, sweetheart."

I almost spilled my drink because that wasn't in the script. The guy at the bar quickly sized up Mario and then looked at me like it was all a dream. While Mario stood about 5 feet, five inches, this guy towered over him at six feet, four inches. He wasn't as thick as Mario was, but it looked like he could hold his own if shit went down in the club. He looked like a tall Wesley Snipes.

Mario couldn't believe the reception he was getting from Deanna. He stroked his goatee as he strolled my way.

"See, Styles. Chicks are digging the Asian invasion," he said with a new hitch in his step.

"You got it, Mario," I admitted as I slapped him five.

"You damn right I got it. Were you doubting the Chinese Playa from the Himalayas?"

"You watch too much TV."

"You're just mad that you couldn't get her if you wanted."

I didn't want to touch that statement and ruin his mood.

The guy looked at Mario and shook his head in disgust before walking away. As soon as he left, Deanna walked toward us with a huge smile.

Mario stepped in front of me and greeted her again, this time with a little more confidence. "What's up? I didn't know you were digging a brotha."

"I wasn't," she snapped back sarcastically. Confused, Mario shook his head and mumbled something about never understanding the black woman before heading toward the restroom.

"You handled yourself pretty well," I admitted.

"I had to. You never came and saved me."

"Saved you?"

"You couldn't tell I needed help?"

My twisted lips and raised eyebrows let her know how I felt. "You got to be more direct. I can't read minds," I said. "He looked like your type, anyway."

Deanna whirled around in her seat to face me. "And what is that supposed to mean?"

Don't go there, Styles. "Forget it. I don't want to get into your business like that."

She had a devilish grin on her face as she continued to sip on her drink while never taking her eyes off me. It seemed like the more she drank, the more comfortable she got with the conversation.

"Don't get scared now, Jordan."

Scared? She had no idea. I pointed to the brown leather couches near the pool tables. "Let's sit down."

Her black dress caressed her thighs as she strutted across the floor with an overabundance of raw sexuality. I slid onto the couch, got the barmaid's attention and ordered another drink while Deanna watched Mario try to kick it to a female by the bathroom. After ordering her drink, she inched closer. Uneasiness crept in. We never got this personal.

The barmaid returned with our drinks and before I could take out money, Deanna reached into her purse and pulled out a twenty. I insisted. She resisted my chivalry. I thanked her in between swigs.

Her words slurred. "I want to thank you for the other day."

"Don't you think you've had enough to drink?"

She pulled down her skirt that had never risen. "I can handle my liquor. I'm a big girl, right?"

Watch yourself, Styles! I looked her over. "From what I can see you seem to be a pretty big girl."

"And from what I saw, you're a pretty big man." She began laughing hysterically.

"What are you talking about?"

She continued to snicker. "C'mon, Jordan. You're not stupid."

I looked toward my zipper to see if anything was sticking out. Everything seemed to be safely contained. "What are you talking about?"

Deanna attempted to sip on her drink but couldn't get the straw in her mouth because she was laughing so hard. "I'm talking about that day in the office when you yelled for me to come in."

Damn, Styles. I thought I had put everything away. I had forgotten all about that incident. I guess I would have to try and play this one off.

"What are you talking about?"

Deanna jumped up, stood in front of me, and straightened her face. "Forget it, Jordan."

I rose quickly and stood an inch away from her face. "Let's not forget about it. As a matter of fact, what do you think you saw?"

"I don't think I saw anything. I know I saw something." She paused and reached for her drink. It gave her more confidence. She continued with a lower voice, "I saw you sitting behind your desk with your thing out."

Oh, shit! Quick. Think, Styles! You weren't pulling it out! I didn't know what to say, but my mind began racing to find an answer.

"I wasn't pulling anything out," I snapped. "What I was actually doing was-" I paused and looked around. "Let's sit back down."

Deanna looked at the couch, then back at me and smirked as she sat down. All this looking and laughing allowed me precious minutes to think. I ordered two bottles of water, brushed off my black slacks, and began again, "Me and my girl were play fighting that morning and she accidentally kneed me in my groin."

Her laughter relayed her disbelief.

I paid no attention to her sarcasm and continued, "I was on the phone speaking to her and I was explaining to her about the pain in my loins. She told me to see if they were swollen. So, that's when I unzipped my pants and took it out."

Her foot tapped the stained tan carpet rapidly as her eyes rolled to the back of her head. "Go ahead, finish."

She doesn't miss a beat! I put my water down and scratched my head. "Where was I?"

She quickly informed me, "You were unzipping your pants."

I didn't know whether she just wanted to know because she was curious, or whether all this talk was exciting her. I felt slightly uncomfortable discussing such a sexual matter with my secretary.

She nudged my arm. "Hello!"

"I'm sorry. Back to the story." I paused to gather my thoughts. "Like I was saying, I was unzipping my pants and then someone beeped in on the other line. I clicked over and it was Tony shouting because he didn't know whether I was going to meet him at the club. That's when I shouted, 'I'm coming,' and then you walked in." *Good going Styles!* It sounded like bullshit, but it could've happened.

She grabbed her water, took a few sips, and searched for the lie in my eyes. She let out a few um-hums and then a long-winded, "Oh!"

I wasn't sure where to take the conversation. I fidgeted like a high schooler.

She cracked a smile.

I decided to change directions. "So, enough about me. What's going on with you and your married friend?"

She folded her legs and spoke quietly. "I'm still seeing him."

I wasn't going to let up. It was my turn to play detective. "I thought you had enough of him. He got you confused like that?" I chastised with a chuckle.

"It's not funny. I don't know what to do. I love him, but I'm not in love with him anymore."

I decided to ease up a little. Her wounds didn't have time to develop a good scab yet. "Has his wife called or come back over to your spot?"

"No. I think she got the hint from the last time."

"Did you tell him about it?"

She bit the insides of her cheek and put her head down. "I did, and he wasn't too happy with his wife."

I inched closer and put my arm around her shoulders. "Can I give you some advice?"

"Please?"

"If you don't love him like that, then you gotta leave. Don't look back. Why be with someone that you can't have? If he's threatening you with taking away money that he's giving you, tell him to kiss your ass because you've got a job now. You don't need a man holding money over your head."

The DJ's voice blared across the microphone informing everyone that it was the last call for alcohol.

Deanna stood up and looked at herself in the long lounge mirrors that were adjacent to the sofas. "It's not as easy as that."

Tony and Mario walked toward us laughing. They looked like two cops in a new movie starring Jackie Chan and Biggie Smalls.

"What's up, Tango and Ass?" I greeted.

Mario looked at me and shook his head. "Why'd you front on a brotha? You were gone damn near all night."

Tony added, "Yeah, where'd you disappear to?"

I escorted Tony away from Deanna. "I was chillin' with the secretary."

Tony looked over my shoulder and stared at Deanna with his mouth wide open. "Shit!"

We walked over to Deanna and I introduced her to Tony. Halfway to the door, Deanna pulled me to the side and whispered, "Thanks for the talk."

"No problem. Anytime." I gave her a hug and as I went to kiss her on her cheek, she turned her head slightly and kissed the corner of my mouth.

As she buttoned up her jacket, she blurted, "And this will be our little secret."

A look of bewilderment crossed my face. "What?"

She came closer, pulled my head down and whispered in my ear. "Your pinstriped boxers and all that-" her voice trailed off as she let out a loud chuckle.

Chapter 11

TRACI

$\mathcal{T}$raci was livid. It had been over three weeks, and in spite of the quick insurance settlement, it seemed as though nothing was being done. She walked around her house, taking note of everything that didn't appear to have been touched. The living room was the only room completely redone. She dropped to one knee and thoroughly inspected the hardwood floor before letting out a sigh. It was as smooth as a baby's bottom.

"Looks good, huh?"

The voice from behind startled her. Traci stood, whirled around, and brushed dust off her pants. "It does look very nice. My name is-" she started.

The tall husky black man in paint-splattered overalls interrupted, "Ms. Johnson, right?"

"Yes." She accepted his large crusted hand. His callouses pressed against her palm.

"The name is Larry. Let me show you what we're doing with the house. I know it looks a mess right now."

Mentally, Traci let out a loud hmmm.

Larry led her toward the kitchen and began explaining what was being done. He bent to show her the new black and white floor tiles and as he pointed out the different colors, the crack of his ass became exposed. Traci guffawed.

He immediately stood up, pulled his shirt down, and led her to the bedroom where the most damage had been done. He pointed to the wall where the fire had taken out a huge chunk.

"This was sheet rocked a few days ago." He ran his hand up and down the white and gray striped wall. "We're going to paint over the walls tomorrow."

Traci followed and felt the smooth wall. It intrigued her how these men could replace things and make it look as if nothing had ever happened. Memories were replaced. No longer could she see dents and bruises that represented history. She rested on the little ladder that sat in the middle of the floor and realized that while the downstairs looked a mess, the real mess was being taken care of. Hopefully it wouldn't take much longer.

"So, when do you think the place will be completed?"

Larry scratched his chin. "The boss says that he'll be here to do the major work on the outside of the house sometime this weekend."

"How come the boss is never here?"

"He's got a lot of contracts to do, so what he does is hire us out to do the painting, taping, and tiling, then he comes in and does the big stuff. It's kinda like we're the prep cooks. We do the grocery shopping, dice the onions, cut the peppers, and then he comes in, cooks the meal and gets all the glory."

"Well, I appreciate the work you're doing here," she said, winking at him.

Larry ushered her toward the front room and explained that it would probably be about a week and a half before she could move back. He also explained that she could come and check whenever she wanted.

She thanked him and walked out the door.

Larry rushed to the door and yelled, "Is there anything special you want done before we complete the job?"

"Just hurry up," she said before turning and laughing to herself. "And you can get rid of all that old furniture."

****

Instead of staying inside the office to have lunch, Traci and Sharlana walked to the park a few blocks away. Leaves blew by and pigeons flew down to pick up scraps of bread that someone had laid for them earlier. For it to be the beginning of April, it was a beautiful day as the sun snuck behind clouds every few minutes and the humidity hugged the few strangers that ate lunch a few feet to their left. The homeless stayed away during the day, but flocked to find a bench to sleep on as soon as the streetlights dimmed in this antique park. Everything from the benches to the trees seemed to have been there since the beginning of time.

Sharlana covered up her sandwich and shooed away a few pigeons that walked too close. "What's been eating you, Traci?"

"What do you mean, what's eating me?"

"You've been real bitchy lately," Sharlana snapped, shaking free from her shoes. She found a bottle of clear nail polish in her jacket pocket.

Traci moved her food close. "Don't take those tired ass toes out while I'm eating. If I wanted to see toes like that, we would've went to the zoo," she snickered.

Sharlana ignored her and searched for the run in her stockings.

Traci sat back on the bench and watched Sharlana go through hell over a three-dollar pair of stockings. She told her about buying those cheap ass Hanes Her Way stockings. Traci shook free from her vanilla blazer, rested it across the back of the bench, stretched her arms, and let out an "I've been working hard all day" yawn.

After a few dabs, Sharlana put the polish away. "Well?"

"Well, you've got some nerve to interrupt my lunch with those crusty ass toes and then ask me what I've been going through. You have no idea what I've got to deal with."

"What do you mean? I don't understand?"

Traci let out her trademark sarcastic chuckle. "Just because you can't. It's tough out here."

"And you're the only one out there?"

"I'm not saying that," Traci stated. She paused. "Okay, I have been a little pushy."

"Pushy?"

"Okay, bitchy," she conceded. "I didn't tell you about the other day, did I?"

"No. You haven't said much of anything to anybody lately."

"What's that supposed to mean?"

"It's supposed to mean," she paused, and then began again, "just what I said. You haven't said much of anything to-"

"I heard you the first time," Traci said.

"Like I was saying, T, you haven't really found time for any of us the past some odd months." Before Traci could interrupt,

Sharlana continued, "We haven't hung out in a while. As a matter of fact, we haven't been out of town since you and Jordan got serious."

Traci's voice became very defensive and irate. "What do you mean, since me and Jordan hooked up? What's the problem? A woman can't get a man and spend some time with him?"

"I never said that. I'm just saying that you're doing exactly what Pam and Tiffany did. Do you remember when they met their boyfriends? You were saying the same thing I'm saying about you."

"I did not. Don't get me confused with them."

"Yes, you did. As a matter of fact, that point is moot because the fact is that you don't really hang out unless something is happening and you want someone to talk to."

"It's not even like that. I'll go anywhere when you guys set something up."

"That's the point I'm making exactly. You used to be the one that set up stuff to do."

"That's also because I was the single one with the most time on my hands."

"You can't let him consume you. You still gotta be your own person throughout your relationship."

Anger slid up Traci's back and heated her neck. "So, you're saying I'm not the same person I was before?"

"Ask the girls for yourself."

"I ain't asking them anything!"

Traci thought about how Jordan was with his friends. He never stopped hanging with them. They did the same things that they did before he met her. Traci made a mental note to ask Jordan about it.

"Forget I ever mentioned this," Sharlana said. She changed the subject. "So, what were you saying about the other day?"

Traci was boiling, but she realized Sharlana had made a valid point, not to mention she had forgotten what she was about to say. She grabbed her Pepsi and took a sip. "I went to meet Solomon the other night."

Sharlana's brown skin turned raspberry.

Traci tossed a piece of crust to an overweight albino pigeon that waddled near. She began slowly. "We met at this little restaurant and he basically begged me to give him another chance."

"I know you didn't give him the time of day, did you?" Sharlana never forgave Solomon for not being there during Traci's pregnancy.

Traci suddenly wished she had never brought up the subject.

"Well?" Sharlana persisted.

"I told him he should've been there for me. I told him that I found a man who loved me as much as I loved him." Traci could feel herself becoming angry at the fact that she even went to meet him.

"How did you end the night?" Sharlana prodded.

"I left the restaurant and went home."

"Oh."

Traci hated feeling like she was being interrogated about her own life. In between these thoughts, her cell phone rang.

"Mr. Styles is on his way to see you," her secretary informed her.

Traci smiled. "You told him where I was?"

"Yes. He left about five minutes ago."

Sharlana slid her shoes back on and jumped up. "I guess that's Prince Charming?"

Traci wasn't going to let Sharlana put her in a bad mood. "Whatever. I'll see you later."

Just as Sharlana stood, Jordan appeared through the front gate. Sharlana gathered her soda and sandwich and headed for the gate.

Sharlana waved to Traci and said a quick hello to Jordan.

Jordan was wearing a black V-neck sweater, blue jeans and a beaded black and cream necklace. He smiled at Sharlana and gave her a one-armed hug.

"What's up, Ms. Sharlana?"

"Nothing." She nodded her hello and blended in with the rest of the lunchtime crowd that walked eastward up L Street.

Traci popped an Altoid, quickly wrapped up her food, and stood to greet him properly. "Hey, baby."

"How have you been?" He kissed her gently on her top lip before moving to the bottom and then returning to the top. Traci fell back on her feet.

She didn't know whether it was a look of love or if he was trying to look through her. Regardless, she didn't feel too comfortable with his steady gaze. She offered her half-eaten sandwich. "Hungry?"

"No, I'm good. I was just stopping by because I was in the neighborhood."

"And you're not hungry. You stopped by just to see me?" Traci inched closer.

"I guess you can say that. Actually, I came over to invite you to dinner."

"Where?"

"My house. I'm cooking tonight."

"I wouldn't miss it for the world."

Jordan walked Traci back to the office. They held hands on the way, enjoying the silence and each other. They reached the side of her office, hugged for a minute, and kissed for two. As she entered her office, the phone rang.

"I know you didn't tell him you went out with Solomon, did you?" Sharlana asked.

Traci laughed.

Sharlana wouldn't leave well enough alone. "Aren't you scared Solomon will say something if he ever meets Jordan?"

"Even if Solomon was next to Jordan, he wouldn't know it."

"Don't be so sure. This world ain't that big."

"Well, the world might not be, but in the Maryland, D.C. area, there is more than enough open air to get lost in."

"Don't put anything past anybody. Great minds think alike."

"Meaning?"

"Meaning you picked two men who are similar."

"They are not alike."

"Sure they are. Both are black, tall, athletic, love basketball, good looking, good cooks, and ladies' men. You better quit trying to replace your father. Be honest, T."

Traci couldn't argue with that, but she didn't want to admit it.

"If Jordan found out about the pregnancy, do you think that he would've dated me back then? Hell, no!"

"You can't say that," Sharlana debated.

"You can't say he would've either," Traci challenged.

"Anyway, you're making a mountain out of a mole hill with the whole pregnancy thing. What's important is that you have him right now, and you better take the necessary steps to keep him."

"I'm going to tell him tonight that I went out with Solomon."

Sharlana laughed. "What would you like on your tombstone?"

Traci joked, "I don't eat pizza."

****

Traci reached Jordan's house, rang the bell and waited for what seemed like hours. Suddenly thoughts of Deanna and Jordan had her immediately reaching for her cell phone. A few seconds later he unlocked the door.

Jordan blessed the open air with his sweet aroma. "What's up, sweetheart?"

Her foot tapped. She waited. "Nothing. What took you so long?"

Jordan's smile evaporated some of the pain.

"I was throwing another woman out the back door," he joked.

"The one with the stump and the bad case of acne? she cracked back, downplaying his remark.

He threw his head back and laughed a hearty laugh.

The sun was setting and Traci could feel the warm air change to a cool breeze as they embraced.

"I'm glad you invited me over."

"I know you are," he said confidently.

"Don't be so sure about that."

"Look, before we begin, let me apologize." He peeled her away. "The thing with Deanna wasn't handled right. I know you may have taken things the wrong way, and I am sorry."

Traci brought him back into her arms and held him tight.

"I know how to make a sista feel good," he whispered.

She stepped back. "How?"

He gave her an envelope with her name on it. "With this."

Traci shook the envelope. "Is there a ring in here?"

"Maybe. Maybe not." Jordan kissed her again and left her standing alone as he walked out the door.

The note read, "Go upstairs, sit on the couch, relax, and have a drink!"

Traci went upstairs, hung up her coat, and sat on the couch. The living room was immaculate and Coltrane blasted from the stereo. She slithered out of her blazer, unbuttoned the first few buttons of her blouse, threw her head back and exhaled. Behind her, faint streams of smoke floated up from sticks of vanilla incense.

A pause in the music brought her back to reality. She grabbed the glass of white Chardonnay and noticed a napkin with handwriting on it underneath.

"When you finish drinking the glass of wine, go to the kitchen and look in the refrigerator."

The note didn't give any further instructions. What did Jordan have planned? Whatever it was, it excited her.

Traci thought about where their relationship was headed. Then she thought about the whole dinner thing with Solomon. Looking around the room made her realize that dinner was indeed a mistake. She should be concentrating on Jordan, while putting her past behind her. She wasn't going to allow him or anyone else to disturb the groove she had going with Jordan. She finished most of her drink before quickly strolling to the refrigerator. Did he want her to look inside the refrigerator or on top? She neared the kitchen. Her eyes were immediately drawn to the handle. There was another note on the handle of the refrigerator, written on a small rose-colored invitation.

"I invite you to chill with me tonight!"

It was neatly written and signed. There was a little arrow at the end of the note. She turned the note around and read the rest.

"For all the times you've bathed my soul with your love...your bath now awaits."

She repeated it to herself before putting two and two together. "My bath now awaits," she said aloud. The wine began to warm her. This wasn't the first time Jordan had revealed his romantic side. Usually he took her out to eat or to a play. She reminisced about the time he said he planned on taking her to a basketball game and ended up taking her to an opera at the Metropolitan. They each took turns reading the words on a little screen in front of them. Just the thought brought a smile to her face. She turned out the lights and walked toward the bathroom while Coltrane still blew his saxophone in the background. She yearned to be in a hot tub and just sit for hours.

She pushed the door open. "Wow!"

Beautiful. There were candles all over.

Jordan's bathroom was just the right size for her to feel like she was on an island all to herself. There were vanilla candles all around the sink and bathtub. One peach rose stood inside a little glass vase positioned in front of the bathtub like an officer guarding the Queen of England. On top of the toilet seat sat a beautifully wrapped gift box. The gold wrapping had abstract paintings of black women dancing. She shook the box gently before carefully removing the wrapping like it was packed with dynamite. She peeled the wrapping off layer by layer, but after a minute of folding up each piece of paper that fell from the box, she decided it was Christmas and ripped through the rest.

She opened the box and noticed another invitation on top of clothing. It was the same as the rose-colored one that she had received earlier.

"This is what I want my woman to greet me in when I come home!"

She put the note to the side and picked up the clothing that was neatly folded.

It was simple, yet beautiful: a navy thong with a see-through navy blouse. As she held the top piece to her chest, she noticed another piece of paper on the bottom of the box.

"The rose is peach,

and your sexy thong and blouse are navy blue.

You've got twenty minutes to soak

in this bath I ran for you."

Jordan had a habit of making every inch of her applaud him. No man existed that would ever know her and her body the way Jordan did. As she recalled some of the things that he had done, she stared at the tub. It looked beautiful. On the edge of it sat tiny Hershey's Kisses and in each corner of the bathtub sat the head of a peach rose. She began to slowly undress while pondering the reason for all of this. She didn't know why Jordan had gone through all the trouble. It wasn't that she didn't like the special things he did, she was just always cautious when guys did things for no reason.

She slowly dipped her feet inside the tub, careful not to feel all the warmth at once. Her body felt like it was being rubbed by a thousand palms. She slid into the tub so that the only thing left outside the water was her head. While leaning back, she noticed the little Hershey's Kisses had something handwritten on the tag.

One read, "Exotica," while the other four had "Almond" written on them. She opened the one that had "Exotica" written on it. Her forehead wrinkled as she put the tiny crystals to her nose. It smelled like...suddenly it hit her that these were the bath salts she saw at a convention she and Jordan went to in Atlanta. There were tons of different fragrances by this company called 4ladieseyesonly. She remembered telling Jordan that she loved the Almond scented bath salts. But how did he manage to get these without her knowing? And to top it all off, he had the nerve to save them for this long. She sprinkled the salts inside the warm bubbly water. It gave off a beautiful scent. Coltrane continued to play in the background while inside the tub, Traci exhaled.

Chapter 12

JORDAN

I could still hear saxophones filling the living room as I eased my key into the door. *I bet she's nice and relaxed.* After quietly entering the house, I tiptoed to the bedroom and waited while she followed the remaining instructions.

I cracked the door and could hear her getting out of the tub. What the hell was she singing in the background? Luckily, I wasn't with her because of her singing.

If my timing was correct, she would be reaching to get her towel and reading the note that said for her to go into the freezer. Within minutes she was in her see-through blouse and thong. I watched her intently as she went straight to the freezer. From the back I could see that the thong had done its job, which was to cover up nothing. She had a beautiful heart shaped butt that commanded my attention. As she reached into the freezer, her butt gave a little wiggle that sent Sambuca into an uproar.

"What the-"

I closed the door so she couldn't hear my laughter. In this note, I instructed her to put five ice cubes into a bowl. Along with a cherry freeze pop, she retrieved the other ingredients: peanut butter, chocolate syrup, a bag of candy that I left on the counter, and last but not least was the butter knife. I hid in the closet, and seconds later she came into the bedroom. My bedroom was modestly furnished in cherry wood. The bed reached halfway to the ceiling with a matching chest of drawers and two nightstands on either side. A picture of my son Kendal at age three sat atop the dresser with a few bottles of cologne and a few old coins. The walls were painted eggshell with a burgundy border. A lone candle burned by the bed.

There was one remaining note on the bed. Traci sat on the bed and put the note by the light to read.

"Press play on the CD player near the bed, look underneath the pillow, and get the black silk scarf, blindfold yourself, then lie down and await your knight in shining armor."

"Jordan, you are crazy," she whispered to herself. She spread out across the bed.

I waited for my cue. One minute later, the music came. The Isley Brothers were doing it.

The electric guitar played a slow soulful intro to the song, "Tears." "Thank you baby, for the years you've given me," Ron Isley sang to Traci. "For each beat of my heart, for every breath I breathe. Thank you sweetie for the best times in my life. Through the good, through the bad, you're always by my side. I never thought I'd meet someone who would love unselfishly. I appreciate the way you love and sacrifice unselfishly," was all I heard before I slowly crept out of the closet.

In my best voice, I sang quietly with the chorus, "I can't hold back these tears, let me cry. Although a man ain't supposed to cry. If I hold back my tears, I'd just die.

I don't know if I scared her or not, but she jumped slightly and scrambled for my hand, "Jordan?"

"I hope I wasn't one of the Isley's because you sure didn't move fast enough," I joked. "Just lay back and enjoy the ride."

"Why did you want me to get all--"

"Didn't I just tell you to relax, woman?" I barked softly.

She answered by gently placing her hands to the side.

As my eyes adjusted to the darkness, I could see her lying on the bed wearing the see-through top that exposed her hardening nipples. I grabbed the vanilla massage oil and stood up to leave.

"Where are you going?"

I started to come back, but continued to the kitchen to heat the oil. *Don't make it too hot, Styles! You don't want to burn her before you taste her.* I had waited all day for this. I wanted to make things right for her. She was going through a lot with the fire and all. This would be the perfect ending to a hard day's work.

I returned and climbed over her. "Did you miss me?"

She was still blindfolded, only this time she was lying on her stomach. I placed the oil near so I could reach and pour. Strategically I dropped a line of hot oil down the middle of her back, onto each butt cheek and down her thighs. She flinched, relaxed, flinched, let out a long eager moan before resting her head on her folded arms.

"What are you doing to me?"

I ran my hands gently down her back until I reached her firm chocolate buns. Slowly parting her legs, I reached in between and my fingers dove into something warm. Her legs clamped together not allowing me to pull my hand free.

"I'm trying to put out this fire."

The Isley Brothers were fading and Debarge's "Love Me In A Special Way" blended in. I undressed and straddled her, positioning Sambuca in between her cheeks.

"I should be asking you, did you miss me?" she groaned. Sambuca's heat warmed her frigid cheeks.

"Shhh!" I commanded. "Let me handle this."

She obliged.

"Stretch out your arms," I directed. I guided her arms to the opposite edges of the bed. I started at her shoulders and slowly rubbed each until I reached her fingertips. The oil heated her body and my touch warmed her sexuality. Every spot the oil saturated was followed by deep sensual kisses.

"Turn over."

I assisted by placing my hand underneath her and lifting her. I eased off her blouse and thong. While she lay on her back, her hands instinctively covered her breasts. No matter how long and how much time we spent together, she was still uncomfortable about being totally naked. Maybe it was something about her past. Whatever it was, I was willing to work through it.

Damn! I enjoyed watching her when she didn't notice I was looking. "Do you ever just look at me?" she would always ask. If she had a clue, she would never ask. I had told her about various times when she was either coming out of the shower, or just walking away, and I would stare. One thing that I was going to have to work on was girlfriend appreciation all times of the week!

I moved her hands from her breasts, kissed her lips, and massaged the nipples that stared back at me. Her body tensed for a few seconds before she let her guard down and relaxed. "You okay?" I asked.

"Why wouldn't I be?"

I pulled her against my body and held her tight. "Just asking." I paused before whispering into her ear, "Traci, I hope you know that I love you more than anything."

She took a deep breath. "I know."

What started out as a simple peck on the lips, turned into five minutes of slow tongue dancing. I removed her blindfold and we sat on the bed enjoying each other's sexuality while our fingers traveled to familiar places. She moaned as I found different ways to stimulate her. My hands remembered that she loved her breasts to be cupped. My mouth remembered how much she loved to be kissed on the nape of her neck. And my fingers recalled times they slid across her clit, causing glands to swell and juice to drip.

Her hands found my chest and eased to my piece of chocolate that hung like a bell on a grandfather clock. She caressed the sides until he saluted. She quickly placed her other hand on my testicles. Tiny drops of pre-joy erupted, letting her know that we applauded her efforts.

After turning her around and backing her up against the door, I took her from behind. Sambuca's head entered her moist lips and we both sighed. It felt so good to be inside of her walls that clung to me like I was their savior. I took all of her. I entered with the gentle force of a loving man possessed.

I loved her like Donny Hathaway's hit, "A Song for You!" I gave her the old time loving that rocked her until her face pressed against the cold wall. Sweat dripped off my forehead and dropped to her cheeks. She screamed for me to slow down and give her a second, but she respected my gangsta. She respected the way we fucked like we didn't know one another. She respected the way I slapped her ass and gave directions for her to open up and let me in. She respected the way I made love to her pleasure palace and fucked her pussy until it ached.

We paused, and a minute later, Sambuca pressed the issue. She responded by arching her back. Her ass automatically reached for the sky. I responded by inching all nine into her with a forceful ease. Now, my sweaty chest clamped down on her sweaty back and I slowly moved from left to right, stirring up juices I had helped to create. It felt so good to make love for five minutes and fuck for the next five. My rhythm went from smooth long strokes to jagged pumps that infiltrated her soul and stopped her breath. She wanted me to stop, but continue. I obliged. I rested inside of her and could feel her muscles clamp down on my rock hard piece. Her inner fire hugged the shit out of me. I reached around and massaged her clitoris with short strums of my forefinger. She began a slow motioned rocking of her hips.

I wanted to cum, but not like this. I wanted to suck her tongue and taste the salty sweat that traveled around her nipples. She gave in and lay on the ground in position: on her back, knees against her breasts. She whispered for me to come down, but I wasn't ready. I wanted to see brown skin and pink palaces. Seconds later I walked over her and dropped to my knees. Our lips met again.

I pinned her hands above her head as our fingers made a perfect fist. She gripped me tight and brought me closer. I could feel her heat and smell her scent. It turned me on. Made me want to eat all of her. That would have to wait because I had to be inside of her. Wanted to make her pussy melt. Make her cum. Bring an orgasm she wouldn't forget.

I teased her lower lips with my swollen head. I moved Sambuca up and down until she shuddered slightly. He wanted to swap spit. Her hips swiveled as she tried to suck me in. I accommodated her. For five minutes she could feel every inch slowly enter, and every inch slowly exit. We kissed. Our sexuality joined hands. They acted like it was their first time as each tried to hold on. No one wanted the feeling to end. Sensing her buckling under pressure, I began my assault on her orgasm. I wanted hers to come out and play with my mine. They needed to meet. Needed to show each other that they cared.

She sucked my tongue as I entered with aggressiveness that brought out the beast in her. I fought. She battled back. I wanted her to cum. Wanted her to scream. Wanted her to release. I relinquished my grip on her hands and guided her legs to the spreadest of eagles. Her breathing was hard and ragged, and my strokes were strong and purposeful. With every down stroke, she met me with a thrust of her hips. I could feel the earth inside her womb shake and rotate around my ship. She gripped my back with such force that I winced and my pace matched her ferocity. We continued to fuck like wild animals. Her body jerked as I blessed her with deeper, longer strokes. Her legs locked around me. Her nails dug into my skin. Knowing she was cumming brought me to my peak. Two more strokes and I felt a gush of fluid slither down my shaft and drip down my testicles. Her eyes rolled backwards. As she screamed my name, I delivered a stream of hot cum.

I remained inside her as we rested together. We cuddled on the floor, me on top of her, her holding me. For five minutes no one spoke. We each reminisced about the past forty minutes.

Five minutes later I sat on the couch, waiting for Traci to get out of the shower. It felt good to have my baby back.

She returned, sat down next to me, and rested her head on my shoulder. She took a few deep breaths and patted my knee. "I have something to tell you."

I grabbed her hands and soothingly rubbed her palms. "What's up?"

"I went out with Solomon," she blurted.

Who the fuck is Solomon? My hands automatically drew back. "What?"

She sat in silence. I couldn't speak. The lit candles didn't have the same sensual effect they had moments ago.

Traci's face fell into her waiting hands as she scooted toward the front of the couch. "I went out with Solomon," she repeated weakly.

Tears made concern overtake my anger. I tried to move closer to comfort her, but anger caused hesitation. *Don't comfort her ass, Styles. But then again, she wasn't asking for you when she was with this Solomon dude!* I didn't know what to think. I took a step back and realized that she had picked a fine night to tell me this shit. I massaged my temples, but concentration seemed to evade me.

"Who the hell is Solomon?" I wanted to know the answer, but at the same time, I didn't.

There was no response.

"Who in the hell is Solomon?" The silence was killing me. A million things ran through my head. Was she sleeping with the guy? How long had she been going out with this guy?

Traci seemed stuck for words. Hell, I was stuck for words.

"Jordan, I-" she started.

I wasn't about to let tears wash away my feelings about the whole subject. *How do I know it's the first time she's ever pulled this shit? As a matter of fact, would she have told me had she not seen Tony waving to her at the restaurant?*

I turned the music off, blew out the candles, and turned on all the lights.

"Are you going to finish? I need some answers now!"

She sat on the edge of the couch, hands still cradling her head. "I-I-I don't know where to begin," she sobbed. "I didn't mean anything by it. It was just dinner."

Who was doing the eating? "Well, if it was just dinner, then how come you couldn't come to me and tell me?" I barked. Without waiting for an answer, I continued my tirade. "How come I had to find out from Tony?"

After wiping her face with a tissue, she turned to me and whispered, "Can you give me a second and I'll explain?"

I sat on the couch and tapped my foot to the uncomfortable sound of street life in the faint distance.

After dabbing her eyes, she put her hand on my leg to hush the tapping. "It wasn't anything, Jordan. It was just dinner."

I moved my leg away. "So, how come you couldn't just come out and tell me?"

"You wouldn't have understood."

"Why not? Did you at least try to make me understand?"

"Would you have let me Jordan? You are not the easiest man to talk to at times," she explained.

I stood up and paced the room. It made me feel good. Sweat continued to drip down my back and fall on my naked ass.

"What do you mean, I'm not the easiest man to talk to?" I screamed. I wanted to get control the situation, but my emotions were going haywire. I knew deep down inside I was validating her claims with my aggressiveness, but I couldn't help it.

"See, there you go. When we have a difference of opinions, you have to try and see things from my perspective sometimes."

"Enough of seeing things from perspectives. I want to know about this date thing." I was getting sick of beating around the bush. *Bring it to the forefront, Styles!*

"Listen. A friend of mine called me the day after we had that argument about Deanna."

Without waiting for her to finish, I interjected. "So, this is about Deanna coming over to the-"

"No, Jordan! This is not about Deanna. Hell, it's not even about the person who I went out with. I just made a mistake in not telling you."

That made me feel better, but it didn't make my feelings subside. "You're damn right you made a mistake in not telling me. But guess what, I've got a whole lot of time on my hands now. So, go ahead." I folded my arms and waited patiently.

Traci fumbled with the strings on her top. She excused herself and changed into jeans and a T-shirt. I threw on a pair of sweats.

Don't say a word, Styles! Let her sweat like a camel in the desert with corduroy humps.

She returned, sat on the couch, and whispered, "Let me just start out by saying that I'm going to be honest about everything right now. There may be some things that you might not like or understand, but I'm going to get it out."

"That's fine." By this time, I was prepared for anything.

"Well, do you remember when you asked me how many times I've been in love, and I said that it was really only once?"

I reluctantly nodded.

"Well, that's who it was."

I shook my head in disbelief, not sure which way to take the conversation. I had an idea that that's who it might have been, but now she had confirmed it.

"How did this come about? Did you call him or did he call you?"

"He called me," she admitted. "He called me at the hotel a few weeks ago, and we talked for a bit."

"So, you gave him your hotel number when your house caught on fire? You must've called him and told him about the fire, huh?" I wasn't in the mood to hear anything right now. Just hearing about this shit had my blood pressure rising.

"I didn't give him my number, Jordan," she bellowed. "My mother gave it to him."

"Your mother?"

"Yes, my mother. She thinks he's a nice guy, and I guess they talk every now and then."

This entire calling business didn't compute. I didn't want to hear any more of this, but for some reason, I had to stay and get to the bottom of it.

I continued to put the heat on. "Have you been talking to him all along?"

"The first time I spoke with him was the other week. Then he called me and asked me to meet him so we could talk about things."

Traci apparently was not feeling too comfortable with the question and answer session because she never looked in my direction, instead choosing to speak to her lap. *If she doesn't like the hot seat, she shouldn't be bringing other chefs to the kitchen where your pots are, Styles!*

"And you politely accepted his invitation?" I thought about things for a second before coming to my own conclusion. "So, that's the friend of the family, huh?"

"What do you mean?"

"That time we spoke about friends calling, you said that the person that called you was a friend of the family."

Trapped by her own words, she confessed, "Yeah. I just didn't want you to think anything."

I shot up. "What more could I possibly think? You are a sneaky-"

"Watch yourself, Jordan." Traci got on the defensive quickly. "Is it okay when your secretary comes over to talk?" She asked, quickly changing the subject and shifting blame. "Hell, what about the whole note and Monica issue we went through?"

"Do we have to go there for the umpteenth time?"

"Maybe!"

"This isn't about me, it's about you," I reminded her.

"It's about the whole trust issue. It was hard to recover from that. I mean, if you can talk to your friends, then what's the problem with me doing it?"

"Does he mean that much to you?"

She hesitated. "No."

"Then you guys shouldn't have anything to discuss, right?"

"Just like you and Deanna shouldn't be discussing anything at your house, right?"

"That's different. That was business!"

"And this wasn't?"

"I don't know what it was. All I know is that you're chillin' with a man you love."

"Used to love, Jordan."

"Used to. Still do. It's all the same thing."

"Are you going to hear me out or are we going to get nowhere and argue?"

"I won't say another word."

Traci sat for a second, pondering where to begin. "We had dinner, and I asked him some questions that were never answered."

"Okay."

"I'm just going to get it out in the open."

To get it in the open, you gotta open your damn mouth!

Traci grabbed my hand, looked into my eyes, and began, "Just be open-minded with this, Jordan." She took a deep breath. "When I met you I was pregnant," she blurted.

You were what? My breathing stopped, knees buckled, and a warm rush whipped through my body as the earth seemed to tilt to the left.

I snatched my hand away. "What?"

Her voice was barely audible. "When I met you, I was pregnant."

"From what?"

Traci looked at me with tears streaming down her cheeks. "What do you mean, from what?"

I didn't know whether to comfort her or to continue to be angry at the news. "I don't mean from what. I meant, by whom?"

"Solomon."

Shit! When did she get the abortion? I sat down and tried to recover from the massive blow I had just been hit with. I felt compassion for her losing a child, but at the same time I was confused about my feelings. I knew that if I suddenly lost my son, itwould be a mess. My ex-wife, Serene, had put me through a lot, and when she left town and moved to N.Y., it was horrible.

Kendal was fifteen at the time, and I wasn't ready for him to go, but the court said that she could move.

Traci looked at me, moved closer, and put her hands out. "Aren't you going to say something?"

I accepted her hands and held them tightly. I wanted to comfort her, but couldn't. "I gotta go."

With that, I explained I had to think about what was going on and she could stay until I got back, or she could lock the door behind her.

Chapter 13

TRACI

$\mathcal{J}t$ had been days since Traci had last spoken with Jordan, and she knew not to bother him when he got in one of his moods. Usually when they argued, someone would leave the house and go out for a while before returning. This time, neither side seemed to want to take charge. If he wanted to be stubborn, then so could she.

Traci sat at work and wondered what she should do this weekend. She and the girls had done their thing this past weekend and now should be her time with Jordan.

The phone interrupted her thoughts.

"Hello, Ms. Johnson. This is Ms. Braxton."

There was a very long pause by both.

"You there, Ms. Johnson?"

Traci cleared her throat and responded, "Yes, I'm here. I've been here for the past three and a half weeks, waiting to go back home."

"I didn't call here to argue today. I just called to inform you that your home is done and you can move back in today." She paused and waited for a thank you. Realizing the wait could go on forever, she continued, "There will be someone there until about eight o'clock tonight. If there is a problem, you can contact me on my cell phone."

Traci muttered a thank you and hung up. Her first call was to the movers. Luckily, someone had cancelled today and they could move her things back into her apartment by early afternoon. She immediately called Sharlana to invite her over for lunch and to tell her the news.

****

"I'm going to call the girls tonight," Sharlana screamed.

"I really don't feel like being bothered with a bunch of noise tonight," Traci tried to explain. She knew that there was no way to get Sharlana to forget about it.

Sharlana pulled out her cell phone and perused her contacts. "We won't stay long. I'll just call up a few of the girls. You need to be around some friends tonight, anyway."

"You're right," Traci conceded. "Speaking of friends-"

"What?"

"I gotta talk to you about that shit you pulled the other day with Celeste."

Sharlana gave her a few "yeahs," then left the office.

Traci sat at her desk and checked her messages for the fifth time. Like the four times before, the service repeated, there are no new messages.

Oh, well, she thought. *Why cry over spilled milk?* She whipped her keys out and headed for the door. Finally sleeping in her own bed was going to be perfect.

****

Butterflies danced around the pit of her stomach as she held her breath and pushed the key inside the doorknob.

She heard the familiar click of the lock, closed her eyes and took a huge gulp of air.

She stepped into the living room and opened her eyes. Her jaw followed her pocketbook to the floor. Traci looked around to make sure she was inside her own house. She slowly walked to the front door and looked for her name on the mailbox. "T. Johnson," it read. She came back in and shook her head. *Who...why...when*, was all she could think as she approached the living room.

The furniture was beautiful: a chocolate Boerner Model D sofa with matching loveseat and chaise. For as long as she could remember, this was high on her list. Once before she had saved up to get the couch, but things happened and other bills had to be paid. Beautiful, soft, Italian leather upholstery, double topstitched at the seams was a thing of beauty. Her hands sank into the chocolate leather and followed it from end to end.

After sitting for what seemed like hours on the new furniture, the doorbell rang.

"Hey, T," Sharlana yelled. She barged through the unlocked front door with three bags in tow.

Traci tried to straighten herself up before turning toward Sharlana. "What's up, girl?"

Sharlana stopped short in the living room. "Damn! This is some bad shit." She walked closer to the furniture and ran her hand alongside the ridges of the sofa. "This is some expensive shit, Tee. Where'd you get this at?"

Traci didn't know what she should tell and what she shouldn't. "I bought it the other day."

"So, you finally got it, huh? Now I won't be hearing all the complaints about the black leather crap you just got rid of." She paused and thought. "As a matter of fact, where is that furniture? I could put it in my study room."

Traci didn't know what to tell her. She didn't know where any of her furniture was. Hell, she didn't know where this had come from. "I gave it away to one of my mother's friends," she answered convincingly. "They needed a couch. You didn't need it as much as they did."

"You're right," Sharlana agreed.

Traci wanted to desperately change the subject. "What's in the bag?"

Sharlana reached down and pulled out four bottles of liquor. "A bottle of vodka, Kahlua, Hennessey, and a bottle of Chardonnay for the women who like to act like ladies."

Traci laughed and led Sharlana to the kitchen. After showing her all the work that was done in the kitchen, they went upstairs and sat on the bed. Traci had taken part of the insurance money and bought a huge oak sleigh bed, giving the movers extra to set it up. Other than two old-fashioned dressers and an old-fashioned nightstand, nothing else touched her floor. She had three large framed Ansel Adam pictures of trees and forests hanging on her walls. This was her way to get away, without actually getting away. On her nightstand was a CD player that played many sounds of nature. She had a choice of rain, babbling brooks, or other sounds of the night. The sounds comforted her when she didn't want to be alone. Next to her CD player was an old picture of her mother and father holding her at her first birthday party. It was the only picture she had of her parents together.

"Have you thought about your dilemma?" Sharlana asked.

Traci ignored her and turned her CD player to the rain track.

Sharlana repeated, "Have you thought about your dilemma?"

"What dilemma?"

"Uh, duh. Jordan."

"No. I've got other things on my mind besides Jordan."

In fact, Jordan was all Traci had on her mind lately. Usually he would've called her by now. This wasn't like him. Traci began to doubt herself for telling him anything.

"Do you think he's going to start seeing someone else?" Sharlana asked.

That thought had never entered Traci's mind. Why would he start seeing anyone? After thinking for a few seconds, Traci replied, "No. I'm not worried about that. He should be worried about whether I'm going to start seeing someone."

Sharlana laughed off Traci's comment because she knew that Traci wouldn't bring it to that level. "If you would've listened to me, you wouldn't be in this mess right now. Not everything is meant to be told. You gotta keep some things to yourself."

"And you don't think telling him I was pregnant was something I was supposed to expose?"

Sharlana finished the last of her drink and put her glass on the floor. Traci continued to glare at her until she removed the wet glass from her newly finished floor.

Sharlana wiped the tiny wet ring from the floor with her hands and held onto the glass. "Do you think he tells you everything?"

Traci shrugged her shoulders.

"Did he tell you everything about his little secretary?"

"He didn't do anything wrong," Traci defended.

As a matter of fact, why was she defending him in the first place? She was tired of hiding her feelings and wanted so desperately to open up, completely. Now was her time. She sat Indian style on the bed and leaned back against the bedpost.

"I really loved Solomon. I mean, I really would've done anything for him."

"I know."

"And if he would've asked me to marry him a year and a half ago, I would've been the happiest woman in the world."

Sharlana reached into her pocketbook and pulled out a tissue.

Traci accepted and dabbed her eyes. "I'm sorry, Lana. I'm acting like a big baby."

"Don't worry about that."

"It's just that his proposal was over a year too late. Furthermore, since he's been out of my life, I've adjusted so well and moved on. Hell, I know you don't care about Jordan, but he is good to me and I can't ask for anything more. And not telling Jordan about the pregnancy was wrecking my conscience."

"It might've wrecked your relationship," Sharlana added.

"If he can't handle something that happened before him, how do you think he would handle something that happened after him?"

"I hear you, girl." Sharlana bounced up and pulled Traci to her feet. "You just need to take your mind off the both of them. Come downstairs and I'll fix you a nice drink."

The doorbell rang as they hit the kitchen.

Twenty minutes later, Traci, Sharlana, Mona, and Precious sat in the living room, reminiscing about old times. Traci hadn't seen Mona in quite a while. When Mona went back to Jamaica to visit her family three years ago, she met Trevor Clayton. This man changed her life. Not only did she go back to visit four more times in two months, but she married him in her Stella moment. She moved back to Jamaica, only to divorce him after four months.

Precious, who fit her name to a tee, was a jewel among jewels. She worked for Traci for the past four years and was a genuinely beautiful person who was as naïve as they came.

After a half an hour of avoiding the subject, Mona decided to be the brave one. "How's Jordan?"

Traci put her drink down and rolled her eyes before giving her trademark smile. "Fine, I guess."

"What do you mean, you guess?" Mona replied.

Traci looked at her and laughed sarcastically. "You of all people should know what I mean."

"Me told you what to do to him," she chastised in her thick Jamaican accent.

"And what was that?"

"Fix 'em some red rice and have him going crazy over you."

Traci looked at her and smirked. "And who said he isn't going crazy over me now?"

"That look you got when me say him name," Mona responded.

Precious chimed in, "What's red rice? Maybe I need some."

Sharlana laughed at Mona and explained to Precious, "You don't need to know what that is. That's some bullshit remedy Mona and her people in the islands have concocted to try to get a man to not only want you, but to need to have you."

Precious wrinkled her nose. "What do you mean, like some witch's brew?"

Mona shrugged off Sharlana's wisecrack. "No, gal. It's when you fix that buoy some red beans and rice or pasta and tro some of ya period in dere."

Wine flew from Precious' mouth and onto the coffee table.

"I'm sorry, Traci," she said.

Traci grabbed a napkin and wiped up the mess. "Don't worry about it. I told Mona about telling that damn story to people that don't know her. She's gonna mess around and get put in the psych ward for peeing in people's food. As a matter of fact, I hope you didn't make anything to bring over here."

Mona quickly interjected, "See, if you feed Jordan some of dat, I bet he'll be climbing all over you."

"And who says he isn't doing that now?" Traci defended again.

Sharlana, ever the protector of Traci, stepped in and stopped the conversation. They spent the next two hours watching *Disappearing Acts*, debating on how the movie should've been filmed, and who should've played the part of William Shakespeare.

Chapter 14

JORDAN

For the past week, between Traci's former pregnancy announcement, and Deanna's adulterous behavior, I didn't know what to do with the women that surrounded me on a daily basis. Tony told me that whatever happened between Traci and Solomon, it was in the past. He added that she didn't have to tell me anything if she didn't want to. I questioned whether she would've told me had he not been there watching them talk. Not only did he lecture me on forgiving and forgetting, his number one question was, if she knew all the shit I was doing before we officially got together, would she still be here? That put things in perspective. I knew we weren't going in the right direction, but I figured the present I shipped to her house would definitely cheer her up.

During the past week, I got back into writing. Instead of jumping into bed with a woman to make me feel good about myself, I was learning to deal with my problems through my own writings. I was trying to do things the right way, not just for me, but also for Traci. I wasn't going to mess up this one with a slip of the dick. Maturity is a motherfucker.

I sifted through my mail. A postcard jumped out at me.

Soul Kitchen Production presents a night of "Black Love!"

Join us in celebrating that special person or that special moment.

Invite a friend, mate, spouse or that special someone and share

"Black Love!"

Traci sprang to the forefront of my mind. I couldn't shake her no matter how hard I had tried this past week. I didn't know what made me angrier: the fact that she didn't tell me about her pregnancy or that she didn't tell me about this Solomon guy. It's not like I was insecure. I didn't care if she maintained her male friendships. To me, that was healthy, but something about him didn't sit well.

After picking up the phone for the tenth time, I decided to invite Traci to the function. Maybe I would hit her off with a little poetry to explain it all. We had gone to the Soul Kitchen Poetry reading a few times. It was that *Love Jones* atmosphere with people getting together on some positive shit. Five rings later, the answering service picked up. I left a message for her to meet me at the event.

"Mr. Amsterdam is on line four," Deanna yelled through the intercom.

Mr. Amsterdam had been on my back about getting this new contract with Webber Construction in downtown D.C.

"This is Jordan."

"Jaw-don, how's it shaking down there?" he slurred.

I knew from his slurred speech, he was having his daily Scotch. "If this is about the-"

"It's not about the new contract I haven't received yet," he interrupted. "It's about Deanna."

"Hold on," I whispered into the phone. I went to the door and peeked out and sent Deanna on her afternoon break. "What's going on?"

"Is she acting a little strange, lately?"

I didn't know how much I wanted to expose to him, and I definitely didn't like being caught in the middle. *Don't tell him anything, Styles!*

"She's been acting a little funny," I admitted. "I wouldn't say it was anything to become alarmed about."

"Well, I was just asking because I've gotten a couple of complaints from the office, and being that she's family, I've got to protect her." He paused and continued, "But if she's messing up Jaw-don-"

"Well, I don't know who's doing the talking, and if she works for me and I'm not complaining, then I guess there's nothing to worry about."

Before he hung up, we discussed how long it would be before I aggressively went after the new account. I told him that I needed about two weeks before I had something written up and then a serious proposal would go out to the company. Appeased by my answer, he told me to keep my eye out for Deanna and if anything happened, to let him know.

After her break, Deanna appeared in my doorway. "Can I speak with you?"

I pushed my stack of papers to the side and invited her in.

She looked at her hands that lay in her lap for a minute before speaking. "I'm sorry. The other day when I-"

I shook my head and stopped her. "There's no reason to apologize. It wasn't your fault."

"It was my fault. I was going to apologize the other night, but it wasn't the right time to do that at a club."

I didn't want her to have more to worry about than she already did. "It wasn't your fault. I can't help it if Traci doesn't trust me."

In fact, that wasn't the first time she had accused me of some form of cheating. When we had met, I dated a few women while I was still trying to figure out if she was the one or not. As my luck would have it, one of the women that I was kicking it to was her friend's cousin. Ever since then, I have not been clear of the accusations.

"Well, all I know is that if I never came there, she wouldn't have had any reason to doubt you this time."

"I'm not so sure about that."

"Why?"

Instinct told me to keep my mouth shut, but I decided to ease her guilt. "It didn't matter what you did. It's really about a few misunderstandings we had a little while ago."

"Like?"

I thought about which story was safer to tell. "Well, one time she found a note from my ex and took it the wrong way. My ex had a computer problem and wrote me a letter stating she was going to call me to see if I could put my disk into her hard drive."

Deanna's hand did a bad job of hiding her grin.

"I mean, don't get me wrong, I do go over the top with conversations sometimes, but if there's no foul, there's no harm, right? I can get sexual at times, but I don't mean anything by it."

Her head nod showed that she didn't agree or just didn't understand. "What happened after that?"

"After she brought my stuff from her house, I had to do some rebuilding."

My story did nothing to comfort her. She went back to being withdrawn.

"You gotta relax, Deanna."

"I try to relax, but it's hard with all of this stuff happening to me."

Besides the fact that she was dealing with a married man and she thought she had interfered with my relationship with Traci, I didn't know what else she was going through. "You wanna talk?"

She put her head down. "Not really."

I snapped my fingers cheerfully. "You gotta snap out of this funk, Deanna."

"I know what you're saying, and believe me when I tell you, this talk is helping. It's just hard to walk away."

"It's better to walk away now then be carried away in a body bag because of someone's crazy ass spouse."

Deanna looked as if she was about to cry, so I quickly changed the subject. "What are you doing this upcoming weekend?"

She methodically massaged her temples. Seconds later, her face lit up as if she had just went through a holy transformation.

"Nothing now, thanks to our little conversation. Listen Jordan, I'm just going to tell him that it's over and deal with the consequences. And if I need to talk, I don't want you shying away from me, because I know I'm going to need it." She forced a smile.

"I won't." I thought about inviting her to the little poetry slam that I was going to be at, but Traci wouldn't be too fond of seeing her when we were having our own problems.

"How did you finally know that Traci was the right one? I mean, do you think she's your soul mate?"

I thought about it before coming to the conclusion that I really didn't know the answer. I thought Serene was my soul mate, and then things went sour.

"It depends. Can a man have more than one soul mate?"

Deanna shrugged her shoulders.

"I don't know, either. I know that right now, I'm very much in love with her."

"Would you die for her?"

My heart shuddered at the idea of dying, let alone for someone else. "Would I do what?"

"Would you die for her?" she repeated.

"Whoa, Deanna!" The question caught me off guard. I knew I loved Traci, but dying was another ball of wax. Many questions filtered through my head. Would she take care of my son if I died for her? Would she die for me? "I don't know."

Deanna put her head down and whispered, "I would die for him."

My forehead wrinkled as I shifted in my seat. "You would die for whom?"

"The guy I'm involved with," she answered meekly.

I eased back into my chair knowing this conversation could go anywhere. "So, you would die for him even though he's a married man?"

"He's only married in name," she said defensively.

I threw my hands up in the air as if I was getting robbed, and laughed. "Don't get mad at me, I'm just an innocent bystander."

"I'm sorry. What were you saying?"

"I said, even though he's married?"

As she began to open up, it was easy to see that she didn't have the total control she led people to believe. The fine young black woman that came into my office every day in tight skirts, brimming with confidence, now appeared to be a vulnerable young woman that couldn't seem to find love if it slapped her in the face.

Her head remained stuck to her chest. "I love him and he loves me." A few seconds later she dabbed the corners of her eyes and sniffled. "Haven't you ever fallen for someone who was in a bad situation?"

I did date a married woman when I was younger. She was thirty-three and I was twenty, fresh out of community college. My mother casually introduced us when she came to visit. Unbeknownst to my mother, as I helped her carry some things to her car, she slipped me her number. We had great sex for about three months and then her husband came home from jail. It was the first time I was ever consumed by sex. She taught me a whole lot of things that I never knew about sex. Up to that point, girls my age were happy just to have piece of me, but not her. I remember my first encounter with her. I came in ten minutes and rolled over. Whenever I came quickly with girlfriends my age, they might've sighed and told me that they wanted more, but not her.

She said, "I'm glad you got yours, but what about mine? I'll do whatever it takes to get it back up, but when it does, I'm getting mine!" I loved her directness and when I found out that I wouldn't be able to see her again, I went berserk. After dating a few women my age, I found that they were no substitute for an older woman that had her shit together. So, in a way, I understood what she was going through.

I admitted, "I did fall for someone once, but you gotta know where to draw the line."

"But it's easier for you to draw the line because…" Her voice trailed off.

"Because what?"

"Can I be honest?"

I cleared an imaginary path with my hand. "Go right ahead."

Deanna continued, "Because you can be in a relationship with another woman and not really fall for her, because your penis is doing all the thinking."

Damn! She's making a lot of reference to the penis lately, my brotha. I was very taken aback by her openness.

"Damn!"

"C'mon, Jordan. I might be young, but I'm not completely naïve. Men are physical and women are mental."

She had hit the nail right on the head. Women definitely were mental!

She continued with a little more assertiveness. Sticking her chest out, she stated, "When I give my body to a man, it comes with a lot more than the physical."

Damn freak! "And we don't give more than the physical?"

She gave me a weird look.

"Contrary to popular belief," I said, "not all men are in it for the booty."

A guffaw followed. "You've never been in it for the sex?" she asked.

"I never said that. I was young before."

"Four score and seven years ago," she quipped.

"Funny."

"When did you change?"

"When I matured."

She grabbed a note pad and a pen and laughed. "Hold up. I gotta write this down." She put the pen and pad back down and continued, "When men mature, they slow down?"

"Pretty much."

"Please tell me the age they start maturing so I can start dating men that age."

"A man's maturity doesn't have a number."

"How do you tell then?"

"You can't. You have to do a lot of talking and praying," I said with a chuckle. "And you were doomed before you started with him anyway."

"Why?"

"Because you can't build a house on quicksand. The foundation that you're building your relationship on is filled with deceit and lies."

"I know what you're saying, but it's a hard situation to get out of. I don't want to throw away the time we've invested."

"But, everyday you stay, it takes two more days to leave."

Deanna stood and gave generic applause. "I guess I need to sign up for your class, Introduction to Relationships."

"My stuff ain't tight enough for me to be teaching a class."

"Maybe you need more research and on the job training," she said while seductively moving closer.

My mind started to race. I quickly took off the running shoes. "You have any suggestions, Ms. Simons?"

She gave me a hug, maintaining her hold a few seconds longer than necessary.

Minutes after she left, I heard a sharp knock at the door. A funny feeling hit me in the pit of my stomach and a smile erupted. Women weren't the only ones with that intuition shit. I knew my baby received my present and was on her way to shower me with praise.

"Come in, Ms. Traci!"

The door inched open, followed by a voice. "Did you say, come in, Mr. Tasty?" Tony laughed hysterically. Seconds later, he barged through the door dressed in a royal blue sweatsuit. His cologne was overpowering, and his hair was unusually unkempt.

I ignored his comment and continued doing my paperwork. He acted as if he was looking at one of the paintings near my desk before snatching the pen out of my hand.

"Don't act like you were working, Negro! I just saw your secretary leaving with the top of her blouse opened."

We both laughed.

Tony sat down and analyzed me while he opened up a Tootsie Roll.

I pointed to the candy and laughed. "Don't mistake your fingers for one of those and bite it off."

"Your jokes continue to be as dry as that eczema caked up on the back of your neck," he snapped.

"Yeah, yeah, yeah. You're late!"

He checked his watch and didn't say a word.

I looked up and watched him watch me. He didn't say a word. He just stared and kept popping Tootsie Rolls like they were Flintstone vitamins. After I finished my last paragraph, we left for the gym. On our way down the elevator, he continued to stare and rub his chin.

"You all right?" I asked.

"The question is, are you all right?"

The elevator opened. We walked through the noisy corridor and past a group of people outside smoking cigarettes. I gave a few head nods to a couple of co-workers, adjusted my bright red jacket and threw my gym bag over my shoulder as we prepared to walk two long city blocks. L Street was always crowded with people, vendors, and smoke. I coughed as a bus paused in front of us, let a few people out and chugged down the street. To our immediate left, the smell of peanuts and smog filled the air that remained damp from the early morning shower.

"I got everything under control, why?"

"Because you're acting a little strange."

I didn't like being interrogated about my business. Tony usually meant well, but sometimes his timing stunk. "Are we going to work out or should we stop at the local coffee house so you can give me some fatherly advice?"

"Cut the shit, Styles. You're going to mess around and lose that good woman over some bullshit."

I was getting tired of hearing about what I was going to miss out on. "What about what she'll be missing out on? You always think it's my fault. I've been faithful!"

We stopped at the traffic light and Tony looked at me as if the thought had never crossed his mind that I would be doing the right thing. He shrugged his shoulders and conceded, "You're right. I never looked at it that way before. I'm just so used to you being the one fucking up."

I gave him a sarcastic laugh as we hurried across the street. "I know I'm right. You act like it's my privilege to be with her. I wasn't the one caught out there with another man at some damn restaurant."

He nodded his head again.

"Can you believe that since we've been together, I ain't been with no one else?"

"If OJ can be seen in a black church, anything is possible, I guess," Tony joked. "You guys need to get your shit back to normal."

"I'm doing that."

"How?"

"By doing what I'm supposed to be doing! I know how to make things right. I'm not new to this game," I boasted.

Tony knew that his point was well received, so he abruptly changed the subject. "Isn't Kendal coming next week?"

That reminded me that I had forgotten to clear the closet out in the spare bedroom. This new schedule of holidays and summers was killing a brotha. Kendal had been down south for about eight months now. He'd be back up to see me for the whole summer and then for Christmas break. Something was going to have to give because I knew that I couldn't raise a child like this. There were a few times when Serene called me to put him on the phone so I could yell at him. I wasn't going to be a hit man to my own child.

"He'll be here in two weeks."

"When was the last time you spoke with Serene?"

Tony had just said the dreaded 'S' word. "She left a message last week, but I didn't call her back. I'm going to see what she wants though."

Tony let out a sly grin and asked, "When she gets here to drop off Kendal, are you going to let her stay over?"

"Apparently you don't know me if you gotta ask that."

"You never know."

"I know. I'm not going there and have her breathing down my neck again. I don't care what the sex was like. An hour of pleasure isn't worth another three months of her calling, and three more months of her getting adjusted to the fact that we won't be together, ever!"

Tony playfully patted me on the back. "I'm glad you're finally learning all the things I've been trying to teach you over the years."

"Yeah, I'm learning the craft from a teacher that graduated from the school of love with a GED."

"Yeah, yeah, yeah. What are you planning on doing with Kendal over the break?"

"Nothing much. It's just spring break. Shit, I need a break just as much as he does."

"Don't he get bored just sitting in the house?"

"Just because we aren't at hoop games and going out all the time doesn't mean we aren't having fun. We talk, grab a few pizzas, and play video games."

He shook his head. "Freaking video games?"

We reached our destination, gave our ID cards, and walked toward the back. "Yeah. He gets to talk his little stuff to me without me beating his ass for talking back. I'm trying to do some things that friends do. I don't want him to see me as authority all the time." The dressing room was empty, but it smelled like someone had left stale socks lying around. We sat down at adjoining lockers and began to undress. "You need some kids."

"I'll leave that to your aggressively swimming sperm." Tony stood and stretched his arms out and began a terrible job of backstroking. "I guess mine back-float and die, but I'm not complaining. I love my free time."

"I bet you do. You wouldn't have so much if you got a job," I said, throwing my socks into the locker.

Tony got up and headed for the weight room without waiting for me.

Chapter 15

TRACI

"Traci, I'm sorry about the miscommunication and I hope you like the little present that I got for you. I know things aren't going great, but meet me tonight at the Soul Kitchen at 6:30 and it'll all be better. I've got some things I want to tell you anyway."

Traci listened to the message over and over again before hitting the save button. The message only confirmed what she already knew: he had given her the furniture and he still cared. Traci's heart felt like a weight had been lifted off of it. She knew he wasn't going to leave her, and hearing his message gave her affirmation. What had her slightly miffed was what he had to tell her. The one thing she had a problem with was surprises. She didn't know if it was a setup for a let down, or if he was being genuine. She convinced herself that it was a good thing. Maybe he wanted to make that move.

Traci had had her fair share of proposals when she wasn't ready. The one man she desired had waited too late to give her the ring she coveted, so she decided that maybe marriage wasn't for her. Only one of her friends was married and she didn't seem too enthused about it, so marriage wasn't as high on her list of priorities as it was when she was younger. Her mother had never married, but she always stressed the importance of Traci having children after she was married, which brought her back to Jordan.

Another issue she had was having children. She wanted to have at least four children, but Jordan never confirmed or denied wanting more children. The few times that she was lucky enough to engage him in a conversation about it, he always said that it would be discussed when the time was right.

The past few days gave her plenty of time to think about her past pregnancy. In her thirty-something years, the only time she got pregnant was when she and Solomon weren't together. Their relationship had turned purely sexual during their last four months together. It was amazing that when they were together for six years, her period came regularly, even though they used protection sparingly. When the emotional ties were severed, she was impregnated.

She quickly dialed Sharlana's number and told her that they were going to the Soul Kitchen, and she would pick her up at six. Sharlana insisted on knowing why they were going, but Traci kept silent about Jordan calling and told her that they needed to do something different. She mentioned something about broadening their horizons. Traci then phoned Precious and asked her to meet them down at the café by six.

****

Traci sat in front of Sharlana's house and checked her make-up. This time she had kept it simple, yet magnificent: a touch of foundation to hide the ugly little zit on the left side of her chin, and a touch of new lipstick called Shema that made her lips glisten.

Sharlana got into the car dressed in a tight fitting black cat suit with her hair pulled back into a ponytail. Traci looked herself over and thought that between her tight jeans and Sharlana's cat suit, it would be a wonder if anyone would want to listen to poetry.

Traci looked Sharlana up and down. "What's up with the hooker outfit?"

"Damn! Need you talk with your big butt jeans on?"

Traci turned up the music as they sped to the café. The ride was filled with both of them performing horrible karaoke renditions of everything from R&B to rap music. When they arrived, Traci quickly parked and informed Sharlana that tonight was her treat.

"What time is Jordan coming?"

Traci shot her a surprised glance. "What makes you think Jordan is going to be here?"

Sharlana quickly dismissed her comment. "By the grin that's splattered across your face."

Traci made a feeble attempt at hiding her smile. "What grin?"

"Whatever."

It was a cozy little bar located in a shopping center near the stadium where the local basketball team played.

They entered and adjusted to their vibrant surroundings. Bright red lights flickered above, and music traveled from wall to wall. Traci looked around to see if she spotted Jordan, but with all the people in front of her, she couldn't quite make him out. She saw a friend from college and exchanged pleasantries before spotting Precious at the bar.

They hugged and sat down. Sharlana waved to a friend a few tables away and left to greet her.

"What are you drinking?" Traci asked.

Precious giggled and nodded toward a tall brotha with his back turned. "Him?"

"Who?"

Precious nodded toward her left. "The guy right there."

"Oh!" Traci took a step back to admire his broad shoulders, but mistakenly bumped into a man standing behind her. His drink splashed the sleeve of his cream blazer.

The man turned and huffed, "What the-"

Traci turned to apologize. "Sorry."

The man wiped his blazer, continuing to hem and haw.

Precious reached in her purse, pulled out ten dollars and pushed it into the man's hand. "This should pay for the drink."

He inspected the crumbled ten-dollar bill. "This ain't gonna cover my suit jacket getting all fucked up."

A hand reached over Traci and grabbed the man by the shoulder. Traci turned around and almost spilled her drink.

"Hold up a second, Traci."

"I-I-I can handle this, Solomon," Traci stammered.

By the time she commented, Solomon was in between her and the guy, whispering something into his ear. With his arm firmly around the stranger's shoulders, he led him away. A few seconds later, Traci could see the man nod in agreement. Solomon walked back toward Traci and Precious, smiling that million-dollar smile of his.

Traci's mind was racing and her fuel was low. *What in the hell was Solomon doing here?* How could she have not seen him standing so close? Poor Precious had no clue about who he was, or what type of trouble was about to go down. Traci quickly scanned the room for Sharlana, who was nowhere to be found.

Solomon grabbed Traci by the hand. "What's up, baby? You have a habit of messing up suit jackets when I come around."

Traci cringed at the sound of the word, "baby." She gently pulled her hand away, careful not to make a scene. "Nothing is up. What are you doing here?" The familiar scent of Obsession tickled the sticky air that hung over the bar.

Solomon's eyes followed the same places Traci's eyes visited. "What's wrong, a man can't get no entertainment?"

"It's not that. I just never saw you in here before."

"I've been going to a lot of different places lately."

Traci grabbed her Cosmo from the bar. "Is that so?"

"That's so." Solomon bent over and whispered in Traci's ear, "So, who's your little friend?"

With all the commotion, Traci had almost forgotten that Precious was still there. She didn't want to introduce them, but they seemed to have already met, informally.

"Precious, this is Solomon. Solomon, this is Precious."

Solomon grabbed her hand and threw on the charm. His full black lips pressed the back of Precious' hand. "It's a pleasure to meet you."

Precious giggled and repeated exactly what he said, only hers sounded genuine. Precious left for the bathroom. Traci followed.

As Traci nervously strolled behind Precious, she carefully inspected the crowd to see if she spotted Jordan. Luckily, he was nowhere in sight. Once they got into the bathroom, Precious turned and asked who Solomon was. Traci explained that she had dated him for a little while when she was younger. As soon as Precious began to press the issue, Sharlana walked in.

"That's why your ass wanted to come to this place tonight, huh?" Sharlana grilled.

"What are you talking about, Lana?"

"Duh," she said, pointing toward the door. "That big black muthafucka out there."

Traci put her head down and laughed to herself. She knew she was going to hear an earful about Solomon being here. She should've told Sharlana that she was coming to see Jordan in the first place.

"Sorry to be the bearer of bad news, but that big black muthafucka out there didn't come to see me."

"Well, why is he here?"

"I don't know. This is a free country you know. People don't have to call me before they come out."

Sharlana eyed Traci suspiciously. "There's something fishy going on, T. If there's something you have to tell me, please let a sista know. I hate finding out shit like this."

"If there was something to tell, I would tell it."

Sharlana continued to watch Traci with a careful eye, waiting for her to break.

Precious added, "I don't know if you're speaking about the guy we just met out there, but I can tell you that Traci surprised to see him."

Sharlana cut her eyes at Precious. "Did anyone ask you?"

Precious, all of five feet, two inches, walked over to Sharlana and stood in front of her with an evil glare. "Don't let the nice persona fool you, Lana." Precious was a little thinner than Sharlana, but just as tough.

"It's Shar-lana."

Traci was getting tired of the sniping. "Listen ladies, you two can fight later. I'm the one that is about to have a serious problem on her hands."

The focus was brought back to Traci. Sharlana took a seat next to her on the adjacent sink.

"What the deal, T?"

Traci shook her head, embarrassed. She took a deep breath and decided to put all of her cards on the table. She confided, "When I decided to come here, it was because Jordan called and said that he was coming."

Sharlana's mouth became an instant safe haven for flies. "Oh, shit!"

Traci agreed, "Oh, shit is right. I don't know what I'm going to do."

"What do you mean, what you're going to do?" Without waiting for an answer, she continued, "What you need to do is go out there and tell that big black muthafucka that your man is coming and it's in his best interest to leave."

Precious butted in. "I wouldn't do that. What if after he finds out Jordan is here, he wants to stay to size him up?"

Sharlana debated, "Why would Solomon want to size up Jordan?"

Precious answered, "Because that's what men do. Don't you know that?"

"Of course I know that. I was just wondering why Solomon would stay. He has nothing to gain, but everything to lose."

Sharlana had a point. It would not benefit Solomon to make her mad and risk her not talking to him, Traci thought. And what if they met tonight? This would put an end to her fighting with Jordan about Solomon. And for Solomon, it would assure him that nothing would ever go on between them. Then Traci began to think about the clash of the personalities and how it could blow up in her face.

For as long as she had known Solomon, he had been very unpredictable. He was a very nice guy for the most part, until he was messed with. She remembered one time she went out with her girls and a guy that bought her a drink had decided to follow her around the club. Luckily for Traci, Solomon had decided to stop by and check her out. When she informed him about the guy, Solomon promptly went to him and brought him back over to her and told the guy that if he had anything to say to her, to say it then. Embarrassed, the guy decided that he didn't have anything else to say. Jordan, on the other hand, would've went to the guy, pulled him to the side and let him know the deal. She felt safe with each one, but tonight she didn't feel safe with either of them.

"I'm going out there to tell Solomon to leave," Traci said.

Sharlana stood up and adjusted her hair. "If you need me to come out there with you, just in case shit goes down, I'll go."

"I got this one. But the next one I'll let you handle."

Sharlana winked at her. "Bet."

Traci checked herself in the mirror and adjusted her bra before heading back into the lion's den. She located Solomon at the bar entertaining quite a few young ladies. He did look good tonight. She stopped short and took a deep breath.

Traci's heart pounded. She could literally count the steps. There were about twenty steps that separated her from the man she loved for years. Twenty steps away from her first child's father. She looked up to see if he had seen her coming and had the decency to get rid of the other women.

"Hey, baby. What's up?"

Traci knew the voice and spun around when she felt a slight tug. Uncharacteristically, she began to sweat. She dabbed her forehead and collected herself.

"Jordan?"

"Who were you expecting, the Michelin Man?" he replied with a boyish grin.

Traci's heart stopped. Everything around her slowed to a snail's pace as Jordan's mouth remained open and moved, but she couldn't hear anything coming out. Traci looked to her left and people were moving their heads to the beat, but there was no music playing, or so it seemed to her. Jordan continued to mouth things while Traci nodded.

She put her hand up to shield herself from Solomon's eyesight. She turned back toward the bathroom and grabbed Jordan's hand. "I don't feel so good, Jordan."

He put his arm around her and guided her to a table near the rear. "Are you okay?"

She shook her head and moved her chair so she faced the window. "I don't know what's going on."

"Is your friend here?"

Her head popped upright. "What?"

Jordan grabbed her thigh and slowly eased his hand up and down her leg. "I said, is your friend here?" He scooted his chair over and kissed her lightly on her ear. He looked between her legs and whispered, "You know, your little red headed friend. The red monster. The showstopper. The cock blocker. The puddle of red rain."

She sighed. The anticipation of getting out of the present situation had begun to stress her even more than her initial reason for coming. "Oh. I'm sorry, Jordan. I'm just kinda confused right now."

He continued to rub her leg. "Confused about what?"

All Traci knew was that she wanted out of this whole situation. She didn't want to see Jordan, and she damn sure didn't want to see Solomon tonight. She searched for Sharlana, who hopefully could divert one of them. As she panned from left to right, Jordan did the same.

She turned to face him. "I'm not confused about anything. I have to run to the bathroom. As a matter of fact, I do think my period is coming."

Jordan smiled confidently. "And you don't think I know you."

Traci bolted toward the bathroom. Perspiration continued to slide down her arm.

Sharlana closed her compact. "What are you doing back in here?"

Traci didn't feel like explaining herself anymore than she already had. She took a paper towel and wet the end of it with warm water and began dabbing her eyes. "I've got problems," she answered slowly.

"Are you okay, T? Did Solomon do something out there?" Sharlana was seething. "I knew I should've straightened his ass out myself."

Precious stood by the sink and watched as Sharlana consoled Traci. "Is there anything I can do to help?"

Sharlana looked her up and down. "Only if you're about six feet. Your little ass can't handle this situation. My girl, T, needs a big bitch to make moves."

"It's nothing like that. I didn't even get a chance to make it over to Solomon."

Confused, Sharlana asked, "What happened?"

Traci quickly turned her head and began crying.

"Oh shit, T. Jordan is out there, too?"

Traci nodded.

"You want me to talk to Jordan? I can keep Jordan company while you handle Solomon."

Sharlana continued to map out a plan, as Traci continued to map out her thoughts. She had to do something quickly. Jordan obviously asked her to come to the spot to tell her something, so she couldn't leave him. Solomon somehow came to the spot on the same night and fucked her whole evening up. She decided to go out there and stand up for her man. It was time to let the cat out the bag to everyone involved. In all the years she had known Solomon, she always let him talk his way back into her life, but this time, it wasn't going to happen. She had all but erased Solomon from her heart when he disappeared, but when he called she finally realized that she had no control over her heart. But she did have control over her body and what she did with it.

Traci wiped her eyes, shook her head, and instructed Sharlana with renewed vigor, "You keep Jordan company, and I'll handle Solomon."

Precious stood by the sink. "What can I do?"

Traci looked back at her and smiled. "You can sit near the bathroom just in case I have a nervous breakdown out there."

Precious smiled.

Traci directed Sharlana to where Jordan was sitting. "Give me about five minutes. I told him I was checking on my period."

Sharlana turned to ask what that was all about, but Traci had bolted toward the bar.

On the way to the bar she kept whispering, "You get more bees with honey."

"What took you so long, Traci?" Solomon attempted to greet her again with a smooch.

Traci pulled back. "Can we go to the other bar near the front of the place?" She shuddered. "It's cold back here,"

Solomon slapped a twenty down on the bar. "No problem."

Traci walked quickly so she would be out of sight in case Jordan decided that Sharlana wasn't good enough company. She glanced over in the direction they were in and found that Sharlana had seated herself near the window with Jordan's back toward the crowd. As they walked toward the front of the café, Traci wondered how she would get rid of Solomon.

Solomon asked her if she wanted another drink. She politely declined.

"If you don't feel like drinking or socializing, why did you come out?"

Traci pondered whether to tell him about the poetry, but decided against it just in case he was suddenly into that, too. "I came because we were having a girls night out. You know, the happy hour thing."

He looked around. "Where are your girls at now? Aren't you guys supposed to be socializing and checking out all the guys?"

"I'm just not in the mood," Traci said. Just as she finished her sentence, a man's voice was heard over the loud speaker.

"Welcome to Soul Kitchen's poetry night. If you can, please find a seat near the front and be blessed with a little knowledge, wisdom, and culture."

Solomon extended his arm. "Would you like to join me this evening, as we are blessed by a little knowledge, wisdom, and culture?"

Traci's head snapped. "What do you know about knowledge, wisdom, and culture?"

"I told you I've been doing some different things. I'm trying to work the creative side of my brain. We all know the freaky side of my brain is always working."

"You come here often?" Traci asked, aware that it sounded like a weak pick-up line.

"Nope. Tonight's the first night." Solomon bent down and whispered. "A little bird told me about this spot."

Traci was baffled on how to get rid of a man that was there on his own. She thought about just leaving, but that wouldn't have done anyone any good. She needed closure. Needed him to know that she had moved on. Wanted to lay everything to rest. Needed him to know that she didn't have the same feelings.

Her mind was telling her to say all of this, but her mouth chickened out. "Solomon, I'm about to find my girls."

Solomon peered around her and smiled. "Well, look at Ms. Sharlana coming our way. I haven't seen her in a while. And look at her. She looks like she done went and got herself a man." He nodded his head appreciatively. "Not bad."

Traci couldn't dare turn around. Her feet were stuck, but her neck had a mind of its own as it swung 180 degrees. Sure enough, Sharlana and Jordan were coming their way. Jordan walked with confidence as he bypassed a few eager women. Sharlana followed in the back, in shock. It was do or die. Traci had to make a decision within the next five seconds.

Traci left Solomon without uttering a word. She met Jordan halfway.

"Hey, sweetheart." Her shaking hands wrapped around him. She held him close and nodded for Sharlana to take care of Solomon.

In the background, she heard Solomon say, "Hey, Sharlana. Long time no see."

As they spoke, Traci relinquished her grip on Jordan's arm. "I want to grab a drink from the other bar. He made me a drink earlier that was very good."

As Jordan led her away, she breathed a sigh of relief. She wondered what she would tell him.

Jordan ordered her a drink. "So, what happened to you? I waited for you to come out of the bathroom and it seemed like the toilet spit out Sharlana. You know I like your girl, but damn!" His humor eased her tension. She wished he would tell her about seven more jokes.

"I was speaking to-"

The man over the loudspeaker came back on. "I would like to welcome you once again to Soul Kitchen's poetry night. If you can, please find a seat near the front. The show starts in two minutes."

Jordan grabbed Traci's hand. "You can tell me later. We've got to get seats," he said, leading her toward the café. "Is Sharlana sitting with us or is she going to chill with Muscle Head over there?"

"Who knows," Traci answered without turning around. Precious was walking out as Traci and Jordan entered the cozy room. Precious whispered something about not liking poetry, and getting a phone call that she would tend to since everything seemed to be okay.

Jordan found seats in the front. Traci felt so safe in his arms, but at the same time, she felt violated by Solomon's presence. She didn't know how or why Solomon was there, but she hoped Sharlana would do something so he would leave.

Traci rested her hand on Jordan's thigh as they waited for the performance to begin. They were seated next to a couple that didn't seem to care that they were in a public place. The man, a cutie of Latino descent, turned the front of his black and white Kangol up and winked at Traci as he continued to nuzzle on his girl's neck. Jordan soothingly massaged the back of Traci's hand as he scanned the room. He silently acknowledged a few people he knew while the place continued to fill up.

Rose colored candles were on the four tables in the rear and on all the ledges that surrounded the place. There were two rows of five separated by a small aisle. About fifty people occupied the cold silver chairs that surrounded them. Luckily they had arrived early and got seats in front where they were sure not to miss a thing. A four by four platform with an old-fashioned microphone was used for a stage. To the right of it was a local band called Burgundy Jazz. An older gentleman with platinum cornrows blew on the saxophone while a thin young white woman plucked the bass. Behind them, a heavyset black man with oversized shades beat on the drums. Jordan nodded his head as the saxophonist began a sultry solo that brought applause from the audience. The backdrop was unique: a huge canvas painting of an old New Orleans saloon, with a few people sitting at the bar. On canvas, a lady sat at the bar with a huge white brimmed hat, smoking a cigarette, while a man stood in front of the jukebox.

When the emcee came to the stage, the bass player and drummer brought the volume down as the emcee informed the audience that the first poet was ready.

Traci marveled at how a young poet, Kasim, rocked the crowd. The brotha came out on stage and wrecked it. A woman in the back yelled for him to do his thing. He smiled and continued to indulge everyone with his words. Even the men shook their heads in agreement with his message. After he left the stage, Traci turned around to see if Solomon and Sharlana had come into the lounge area. It was a pleasant surprise to find that they were nowhere in sight. Traci finally relaxed.

Jordan leaned over and kissed her gently on her forehead. "Want something to drink?"

Remembering the Cosmo that she had just downed minutes ago, she replied, "I've had enough."

"I'm glad you're back."

"Me, too."

Traci felt a slight tug on her shoulder. Her heart stopped.

"You scared the shit out of me," Traci whispered to Sharlana.

Sharlana's voice was just as low. "I had to let you know the situation-" she started, but stopped when Jordan turned around to acknowledge her.

Traci removed her hand from Jordan's thigh. "On second thought Jordan, could you get me a bottled water?"

"Sure." He stood and asked Sharlana, "Want something?"

Sharlana shook her head. "I'm good. Thank you."

Jordan cracked a smile. "Where's your man?"

Sharlana gave a confused look.

Traci butted in, "Never mind him."

Sharlana sat in Jordan's seat and whispered to Traci, "That brotha didn't want to leave, T."

Traci looked behind her nervously. "He's gone, right?"

"Now he is."

Traci clutched her heart and fell deep into her chair. "Whew."

"Do you know what it took to get his ass to leave?"

"What?"

"I had to promise him that when it was all over, you would fuck him."

Traci grabbed Sharlana's arm. "What?"

Sharlana laughed. "I'm joking. But damn, I had to tell him something."

Traci's eyebrow arched for battle. "What did you tell him?"

"I said that you would call him later. And I also explained that you were supposed to meet your friend here. I said something about you guys having problems and this should be your time. It was either that or he was going to stay and try to talk to you now."

Traci nodded. "You're right, Lana. Either that, or him coming in here and sitting behind me."

"Did Jordan ask you about Solomon when you guys walked by?"

"Girl, Jordan didn't even see me talking to him. He thought that Solomon was your new boyfriend."

Sharlana doubled over. "He thought what?"

"He thought that-"

"Here's your water, baby," Jordan said.

Traci grabbed the water and looked at Sharlana, trying to figure out if Jordan had heard any of their conversation. "Thanks."

Sharlana jumped from Jordan's seat and told Traci she would be in the back socializing.

Jordan sat down and pulled Traci close. This is the feeling she wanted to have. There was no substitute for security. This is the man she wanted to spend the rest of her life with. She counted her blessings that she had Sharlana in her corner. If she had never needed her anytime before, today was the day.

Traci took a sip of water and turned to Jordan. "On the phone you said that you had something to tell me."

He scratched his head for a second. "I forgot. With me being under the influence of love, I don't know what the hell is going on." He gave her a smile that went straight from her heart to her panties. Just hearing his deep voice say the word "love," made her nipples stand up. It had been a while.

"C'mon, Jordan," she playfully whined.

"Should I tell you?"

Traci's voice was soft. "Do you want me to beg?"

"That would be a start."

"You want me to get on my knees in front of all these people?"

"We could always walk to the back and when it gets dark-"

She slapped his arm.

"I'm just joking." As he finished his sentence, the emcee walked toward Jordan.

She smiled and spoke into the microphone. "Mr. Styles, we were calling your name." She continued, "You were busy laughing with the young lady." She walked back to the stage and informed the crowd, "If you guys don't know this next performer, let me introduce him the right way. This brotha was a regular with us for years, but he got away from the poetry scene for a while. To my surprise, he called the other day to let me know he was coming and he needed a little time to do his thing. So, without further ado, I bring you the poet formerly known as Wild Style, Freaky Styles but now prefers to be known as Mr. Jordan Styles."

The audience that knew him shouted out his name, while the rest of the crowd that didn't, gave him adequate applause. Jordan turned to Traci. "You wanted me to tell you, right?"

Traci scooted back in her seat, aware of all the eyes glued to her back.

Jordan walked to the center of the stage and peered across the room. He wore a tan crewneck T-shirt underneath his black jacket that showed off every ripple in his chest. He looked into the silent crowd and gave a sexy grin. "Do you ladies mind if a brotha gets comfortable? It's a little hot up here with all you fine looking black women out there." There were a few loud hums heard around the room.

Jordan peeled off his jacket and placed it on the speaker next to the band. He whispered something to Platinum Cornrows and walked back to the stage. A few feet in front, there were red, blue, and burgundy lights that hit every part of the stage. He walked toward the front and unscrewed a few of the lights until the stage was dimly lit. He slowly climbed back onto the platform, and on center stage stood a perfectly chiseled black god, with a blue light filling the space around him. As if on cue, Platinum Cornrow began blowing his sax softly in the background, with the drummer and bass player filling in.

Jordan took a deep breath, looked intently at Traci, and began:

"I love you, baby.

Freddie Jackson couldn't have said it better that..." he broke off into a cute little off key chorus. "You are my lady. You're everything I need and more." He went back to his baritone voice and moved closer to Traci.

"Remember the other day, when I tiptoed in and closed the door?

If my memory serves me correctly, your suit had less while mine had more,

I had on black and you had on your birthday suit,

But I, for some reason, thought the contrast was cute.

You looked like an angel; only we can't make love to angels because God says it ain't right,

But somehow you brought out the giant in me even though it's a feeling I tried to fight.

I mean, I love being with you so much that when I can't make love to you,

I grab my memory and my oil and take you anyway.

They say you gotta love the one you with,

Shit, I love and lust after the one I'm with."

Jordan grabbed the mic from the stand and turned his attention toward the crowd. "Now ladies, how many of you would love for a man to be the man?"

Behind Traci, a lady yelled, "Preach, brotha, preach."

He continued, "I mean, be the man

By taking command

of your soul.

Keep the heat up so high that your heart never gets cold.

Make you breakfast in bed, but his lunch is under your covers,

He'd be the corporate brotha in the day or throw on a black skullie at night and be that undercover brotha.

That ain't afraid to take you to the park,

After dark.

He'd be the one that knew just how to please you,

His shit be so real, you'd be draped across the chair with small doses of amnesia.

He knows when to lie in bed afterwards until he was no longer soft,

And knew when you had your fill of him and got a warm rag to wipe you off.

See Traci, I am that brotha that no longer wants to be undercover."

Tears streamed down Traci's cheeks. Aware of all the stares, she straightened her back and sat proudly.

Jordan continued, "Traci, I don't think you heard me, baby. I said that I no longer want to be that brotha that's under covers, without you."

Traci didn't know what Jordan was about to do or say, but she couldn't take it anymore. Before he really embarrassed her, she got up and hugged him on stage. They embraced for a few seconds before the emcee came to the mic and shouted, "Now ladies, are we feeling what this brotha has to say or what?"

In unison, the ladies snapped their fingers and yelled, "Oh, yeah."

Jordan sat down next to Traci and pulled her closer and whispered, "I'm not done telling you what I came to tell you."

Traci dabbed her eyes and whispered back, "I knew you weren't, but I wanted to save something for when we got home. And speaking of home, thank you for the gift. I love it, baby."

"It's nothing. Just a little housewarming gift."

Traci thought to herself that that wasn't just a little housewarming gift. Jordan must've spent a pretty penny, but she guessed they both would be using it soon.

The emcee got back up and looked at Jordan and warned the crowd, "I feel sorry for this next brotha that has to represent after those powerful words. He grabbed me a minute ago and said he had to go on while the ladies were still hot and bothered. And this is his first time, so please be nice to..." she paused to make sure she was reading it right before continuing, "Mr. Action Jackson."

Traci froze. For a moment, she thought that the lady had introduced someone named Action Jackson.

Sure enough, Solomon strolled to the front and took his place on the same stage. The ladies across the room reacted with a few claps and whistles as his thick bass voice flooded the room. "Pardon me for a second, I not only want you to hear me, I want you to see me." He screwed the lights back in and the stage was once again flooded with light.

He continued to play to the crowd. "Remember what the emcee said, ladies. This is my first time, but in my head I've done this all before, only you guys weren't watching," he joked. He cleared his throat and looked at Traci for a second before focusing back onto the crowd. "Ladies, my last name is Jackson, and because of some of my wild and crazy antics when I was younger, I was nicknamed Action Jackson. Don't put too much stock into the name. Remember, I was young."

An older woman in front barked, "Well, you sure look like you still have some action left in you!"

Solomon smiled and clapped his hands. "I would like to applaud the brotha that was doing his thing before me. He touched on some very important points that had me putting pen to paper in the back." Solomon turned around and motioned for the band to stop playing. "I want them to hear me. I'm not sugar coating this one."

The same lady in the front yelled, "Give it to us, baby!"

Solomon stood on the stage and waited until he had everyone's undivided attention.

Traci turned to Jordan and watched as he smiled with admiration. Traci didn't have any idea that Solomon even read books, let alone wrote poetry. Was this some of the new things that he claimed to be getting in to? If so, why did he have to wait until this night to do it?

Traci turned to Jordan and whispered nervously, "I'm ready to get going now."

Jordan put his finger to his mouth. "Shhh! I gotta see this shit. I know Sharlana is going to shit a brick with her man about to blow up her spot." He looked around. "Where is Sharlana at anyway?"

Traci looked around nervously and shrugged her shoulders. "Jordan, there's something-"

Jordan hushed her with a pat on her knee. "After this, baby. We'll leave right after this Action Jackson dude. I like his style."

Solomon took a sip from his drink, placed it onto the brown stool that stood beside him, dug into his back pocket and unfolded a piece of lined paper.

His voice was commanding. "Holla if you feel me.

I mean, this ain't no dream.

If you listen real closely, you can still hear her scream.

Because she felt all of me.

Every-last-single-inch.

She loved my big bottle of Sprite because that's what we used to quench

her thirst.

See, he came later, while I came and still remain first."

Solomon's paper hung from his outstretched hands as he looked directly at Traci and continued.

"Back in the day, I wasn't man enough to take you like I knew I could,

But I'm man enough to come back and get you and deep down inside you always knew I would.

I bent down and cried when I found out you carried my seed

But back then, I was only thinking it was another mouth to feed.

Now I'm feeding fuel to this fire

He may be able to take you to the mountain top-" Solomon raised his hand above his head and continued, "but I see shit that's a little bit higher.

See, baby, I'm older

And like that poem about footsteps in your bathroom, I'm willing to carry you on these broad shoulders."

Jordan turned around and realized that he was talking to Traci. Jordan looked at Solomon and then at Traci. "No, the fuck he didn't," Jordan half-whispered, scooting to the edge of his seat, ready to pounce on Solomon. Traci, aware of the drama that was about to transpire, grabbed Jordan's leg and held him back.

Traci looked around and pleaded, "Sit back, Jordan. Please don't cause a scene."

Jordan whispered back, "The only scene is you being able to see me beat his ass!"

"Not here, Jordan. Please," she begged.

Sweat dripped from Jordan's furrowed brow. He looked around and everyone seemed to be enjoying what "Action Jackson" had to say. He eased back and began rapidly tapping his feet.

Up front, Solomon watched the anger in Jordan's face linger, so he continued talking directly to Jordan, "See, undercover brotha, I be the one that chilled with her in the restaurant.

And you be the one that bought her that whack ass La-Z-Boy recliner

With that tired ass little brown foot stool

I gave that to charity and got her the shit she's always wanted. I'm a grown ass man from the old school,

That knows how to give a woman what she wants, not only for what she asks,

I be the one sipping on the good stuff, while you're in the bathroom drinking from your flask."

Solomon got into a defensive stance and shouted to Jordan, "So bring it, Nigga, please.

You be the one that bought her that canvas shit, I got her the good wood from Belanise."

The emcee, now aware of the situation, ran to the stage to intervene. She locked her arm around Solomon's and clapped. "Let's give a hand to Action Jackson ladies." A sweaty Solomon stood next to the emcee and hesitantly relinquished his grip on the mic. He figured that this wasn't the time. Jordan, on the other hand, slowly counted to ten as Traci began to nervously draw little circles in his thigh.

"I'm going to crack this dude as soon as he walks over here," Jordan threatened with venom.

"And what's that going to do, get you arrested?"

He shook his head in disgust. "I really don't give a fuck."

"What are you going to do when Kendal gets here and you're sitting in jail?"

Even though Jordan didn't want to be rational, when it came to his son, he took himself out of the situation and dealt with it accordingly. "You're right, but trust that I'm not going to let this shit rest."

The emcee kept talking to Solomon on stage as she waited for Jordan to exit the place. Traci, recognizing the stalling technique, began to lead Jordan out of the café.

Chapter 16

JORDAN

Get a grip, Styles! This dude had my blood pressure boiling. So many questions ran through my head, but I had to come to some sort of solution. First thing I was asking myself is when did he become Sharlana's boyfriend? Why didn't Traci tell me about him when I joked about him? What in the hell was he doing there? Is this why Traci was acting so crazy all night? And just to think I was about to try to make some serious moves.

"Jordan, let me explain," Traci started as I put my car in fifth gear and did ninety-five on I-95. She grabbed the dashboard and pleaded, "Can you slow down, please?"

I looked at her in a state of shock and shouted, "Can I slow down? Can I slow down?"

"Yes."

I was getting tired of the bitching, so I made my Volvo's right eye blink as we sauntered toward the shoulder.

Traci turned to her left and watched as traffic flew by. The Volvo kept its steady drive-by creep until he rested on the shoulder.

"Are you going to stop right here?"

How about you stopping here and I keep going? "Where would you suggest?"

Noticing that we were about two feet away from on-coming traffic, she flopped back into her seat. "This is fine, I guess."

I cut the Volvo's lifeline, turned his voice off, and made his hug recline. For two minutes, there was no response from Traci. I thought about whether to speak up or drop her ass off home. I should've let Sharlana take her home when she offered.

After five more minutes of cars speeding by, I grew tired of the silence.

"Speak!"

Traci's face fell into her hands and she started crying. "I'm sorry, Jordan."

I didn't wait for almost ten minutes to hear, I'm sorry! "This, 'I'm sorry shit' isn't going to work!"

She looked up at me and pleaded, "What do you want me to say?"

"I want you to tell me why you didn't tell me who he was?"

"When?"

Dumb plus stupidity didn't equal progress. "When I saw Sharlana talking to him!"

"You thought that it was Sharlana's boyfriend, and I didn't have time to tell you that it wasn't."

"You didn't have the five minutes before the show started to lean over and say, 'Jordan, the guy I used to sex was right in front of you?'"

"Yeah, that would've been the perfect time to do things."

"It would've been a little better than letting me look stupid! Here I am, up on stage talking about undercover and then he comes and uses my shit against me!"

"Is this about him getting the best of you?"

My head snapped in her direction. "Hold up, no one said anything about him getting the best of me!"

"I wasn't saying that. I was just saying that-" she started, shook her head and stopped. "Never mind."

"Let's not do the never mind thing. Let's talk about this." I imitated his voice and repeated what he had said earlier. "Nigga, please. I got this wood from Belanise. Is Belanise even a fucking word?"

Traci remained silent.

I continued, "Nigga, please. I got this wood from Belanise. I should've put my wooden foot in his Belanisian ass. And what was he talking about some La-Z-Boy recliner. You told him about the chair I bought for you?"

"No. That's the part I didn't understand."

"Why did he say he gave it to charity?"

"I would never give anything you gave me to charity. I really love the chair and the other pieces."

Huh? "What other pieces?"

"The matching sofa and loveseat that came with it."

"The matching what?"

Traci sat back, unsure of whether to continue.

I repeated, "The matching what?"

Traci spoke weakly, "Sofa and loveseat."

"What color were they?"

"A mahogany brown."

"I didn't buy you any mahogany brown sofa and loveseat!"

Traci seemed confused for a second as she rubbed her head to gather her thoughts. "Hold up, you didn't buy the mahogany sofa, love seat and matching chair set?"

"Hell, no!" As soon as I said that, I realized that it didn't come out right. "I don't mean that I wouldn't. It's just that I knew that I didn't have the money like that right now."

"What did you buy me?"

Tell her! I didn't want to say a word, but I had to defend myself. "A brown La-Z-Boy recliner."

Traci felt embarrassed for me. She didn't utter a word.

"Where did the furniture come from?"

Traci shook her head again and whispered, "I honestly don't know."

****

Tony laughed hysterically. "Belanise?"

I wasn't about to take this shit from him, too. "Yeah, Belanise," I half-heartedly admitted.

Tony forced himself to stop laughing for a second before continuing, "Is Belanise even a-"

"It's not even a fucking word," I interrupted.

Tony shook his head in disbelief. "I can't believe that dude had the balls to come on stage and use some of your own shit against you. I know you wanted to beat his ass, huh?"

"His ass and her ass. All those people knew what was going on, too. If I could've disappeared, I would've."

Tony asked the waitress for another soda as he checked out the ladies at the table next to us. "Don't sweat it, bro. I bet no one even knew he was talking about you."

"You're right."

"Sike. Everyone knows your ass got played," he teased.

You deserve it, Styles! You would be giving him the same shit.
"Real funny. I can handle the shit though. I'm a bigger man than
he is."

"How big was the guy?"

Here go the jokes. "Six-seven."

Tony burst out laughing. "Just say that you were the smarter
one."

"Yeah. Yeah," I said, brushing off his comments. He was
having a ball kicking me when I was down. I didn't really mind
because if I didn't see the humor in it, I would be trying to find
out where Solomon lived.

Tony quit laughing and got serious. "What was dude like?"

"What do you mean, what was he like?" I didn't believe he
was asking me to give him a rundown on the brotha.

The waitress returned with a pitcher of soda and a plate of
wings. Mad Wingz was the bar we frequented on Saturday
evenings because of the twenty-five cent wings that were
followed by the homegrown dollar pints. The place was usually
packed after four in the afternoon with college students trying to
get a cheap meal and people who didn't want to wait in line for
three hours to get into one of the restaurants downtown.

Tony wolfed down a wing and licked his fingers clean. "I
mean, what was the guy like? Was he in your league or was he a
step down?"

What was he like? "I don't know. I wasn't looking at him like
that. Were you looking for me to hook you up or something?"

"Nah. I was just wondering whether you got a little jealous
because you saw where she came from and where she is now." He
continued to spew joke after joke.

He was definitely trying to push buttons that I didn't want pushed. "I'm not getting jealous over somebody she used to mess with. That would be like you getting jealous over that guy that's dating Cynthia now, right? I mean, so what if he's a big time banker that can take her anywhere?" I knew how to push his buttons, too. Cynthia was Tony's last girlfriend who left him when she felt the relationship was going nowhere. No matter how hard Tony pleaded, she would not come back. Two months after they split up, she began dating her banker.

Rather than respond, Tony silently dipped carrot after carrot into the blue cheese and popped them into his mouth like they were Chicklets.

"Why so silent now?" He had no response. "And stop eating all the carrots. You look like a big ass burnt Easter Bunny."

I broke him down. He couldn't contain his laughter. "I understand, but what about the furniture?"

"That's the part that I'm still confused about. I don't know how he found out about my gift."

"How do you know he did anything with your stuff?"

"She told me that she had a new couch, chair and love seat."

"Didn't you buy her the chair?"

"Yeah. That's when his little comment about the La-Z-Boy Recliner hit me in the stomach."

"Did she say where the stuff came from?"

"She told me that she didn't know."

"Do you believe her?"

I looked at Tony and raised my eyebrow. "Honestly?"

He waited patiently for my answer.

"I do."

"What are you going to do?"

"Find the motherfucker and deal with him."

"Be careful. You don't know anything about him. No sense in getting shot over something like this."

I stood up and looked Tony directly into the eye. "I got this!"

TRACI

"I'll hold," Traci muttered into the phone. She wanted some clarification, so she called Ms. Braxton. The only people with access to her home were the construction people.

"She seems to have stepped out of the office for a second," the lady responded.

Traci asked impatiently, "Can you tell me who worked on my house while I was gone?"

"I'm sorry. I'm not authorized to release any confidential information."

Traci's patience was wearing thin. "You mean to tell me that you can't give me any of my own information?"

The lady corrected, "No. What I'm saying is that I'm not authorized to release any information. I'm only the secretary."

"Can you tell Ms. Braxton to call me ASAP?"

"I will do that, Miss-"

"Johnson. Traci Johnson," she spat before slamming the phone down. She walked toward the furniture and ran her hand up and down the deep mahogany wood. It was finely crafted and looked beautiful in her living room. Traci sat down and replayed the evening over and over in her head. She should've left when she saw Solomon there.

A sharp knock at the door startled her.

"Who?"

"Me," Sharlana said.

Traci opened the door, retrieved her newspaper and led Sharlana upstairs. On their way, Sharlana paused to look at the furniture again. "It is some good furniture!"

Traci changed into a long T-shirt and shorts, then propped herself against a pillow. They began dissecting the previous evening.

"Have you spoken to Solomon yet?" Sharlana asked as she stretched out on Traci's bed.

"Nope."

"Are you going to?"

"I think I should. "

"You think you should?"

Traci thought about what she was saying and corrected herself. "I meant to say that I am going to speak to him."

"What are you going to say?"

"I haven't thought about it yet. I still can't-"

The phone rang in the middle of Traci's response.

"Hello."

"This is Ms. Braxton."

Traci put the receiver on her leg and said to Sharlana, "This is the bitch that had my house done."

Sharlana urged her to pick up the phone and speak calmly.

Traci put the phone to her ear and immediately switched tones. "Ms. Braxton, I need to know who was working on my house."

"Is there anything wrong? Did someone take something from your house?"

"Not really, well, it's hard to explain."

"If someone stole something from you, we'll do everything in our power to get your stuff back."

"It's nothing like that." Traci said, making sure she didn't say anything to alarm her. All she wanted was the company's number so she could find out how Solomon got into her house. "I just need the number so I can send them a thank-you note. They did a wonderful job."

Ms. Braxton's voice sounded compassionate for the first time. "That is so nice. Would you mind putting it in writing so I can have something to show my boss?"

It didn't surprise Traci that she was pleasant only because she wanted something. "Sure. I can do that. It wouldn't be a problem."

"Good. I'll send you an e-mail and let you know where to mail your letter."

"Before you get off, do you think you can give me the number of the construction people?"

"Sure. The name of the company is Better Builders Construction Company." She gave Traci the phone number and street address before reminding her to send the letter to her boss.

Traci wrote down the information and immediately dialed the number for the Better Builders Construction Company. Sharlana looked on intently.

"Hello, my name is Traci Johnson and I need to speak with a manager."

The voice on the other line was stern. "Pertaining to?"

Traci didn't know what it was pertaining to. "Um, someone worked on my house and I want to ask them a few questions."

She could hear papers being shuffled in the background. The man returned and let her know that the boss would be on the phone momentarily.

"I'm about to get in the boss's ass," she told Sharlana.

The phone was muffled, but she heard him say," It's line one, Boss."

Traci heard the line click and then a voice shout, "Hello."

****

"Are you okay, Traci?"

Traci shook her head and attempted to sit up, but was too weak and fell back onto the bed. She felt something cold being placed on her forehead. "What are you doing, Lana?" she said groggily.

"Trying to help your ass out."

"What happened?"

Sharlana took the cold rag off her forehead and placed it next to the bed. "Do you want the funny version or the serious one?"

"At this point, I just want to know what happened."

Sharlana felt Traci's forehead. She removed her hand and said with a snicker, "When you heard that man's voice, you passed out."

Traci's reaction showed confusion. "Huh?"

Sharlana blurted, "Solomon is the boss!"

Chapter 18

JORDAN

I arrived at the gate twenty minutes early. I perused the newspaper for a few minutes before getting up to walk away the nerves. I sat back down, nerves shot to shit, left leg tap dancing on the dirty linoleum as the right leg watched. A bead of sweat slithered down my back before soaking into my skin.

Ten more minutes passed and I got up to pace again before nerves made me find a seat in front of the large filthy window that separated the buses from everyone else. A long stream of cool air left my mouth as I tried to rub the denim off my jeans.

Five minutes later a bus pulled into the station. Two older, heavyset black women with frosted Afros strolled off. An older white man with a paper brown, raggedy, double-breasted suit followed. About twenty people got off the bus and there was no sight of Kendal. A few minutes elapsed and no one else got off the bus. Confused, I walked to the bus driver, who was entering the building, and asked if this was the last bus coming in. He explained that there would be another one in a few hours. I expressed concern about my son. He described a boy of Kendal's size and his oversized Afro that boarded the bus.

"That's him."

"He was on this bus," the driver said.

I double-checked the passengers that remained in the terminal and still couldn't locate him.

The driver pointed to the bus and told me to check to see if he was asleep in the back.

I walked to the bus and attempted to look through the window. Fog impeded my view, furthering my adrenaline rush. I could hear muffled noises in the background as I ran up the five stairs that led to the inside.

Shit! "Kendal!"

Kendal jumped up, knocking a young lady to the floor. "I-I-I was just talking, Dad," he stammered. He went to reach for the young lady, but she ignored his extended hand and stood by herself. The girl, who looked about sixteen, was dressed in tight fitting jeans and a shirt that clung to her over-aged breasts.

"What's going on?" I knew what it looked like, but I wanted him to tell me.

"Um, nothing. We were just-"

"We were just getting to know one another," the girl interrupted.

Kendal shot her an annoyed look. His reaction led me to believe that he didn't want her speaking up for him.

"We were just talking," Kendal said.

"Let's go, Kendal," I instructed firmly. I gave Kendal and the girl a once over before turning to walk away. I knew Kendal's next move was to kiss her goodbye, and without turning around, I yelled, "Now!"

We walked to the car in silence. He kept his eyes straight ahead, never making eye contact. We were definitely going to have our sex talk, real soon. I got mines at sixteen, and so was he.

He had grown a few inches since I had last seen him. He now towered over me by at least three inches. As usual, his pants were neatly pressed and hanging off his butt. He had on a navy blue New York Giants football jersey with a gold chain dangling from his neck. I wish we could've started the day off another way, but what was done was done.

I took three deep breaths and changed my mood. I put my arms around his shoulder. "You hungry?"

He rubbed his stomach and grinned. "Starving."

He threw his bag in the trunk and we whisked down I-95. On our way, he told me about his new friends, new neighborhood, and his new basketball team.

He eased a tape out of his pocket and popped it into the car stereo. We both bobbed our heads to the beat until someone in the song rapped, "Bitch betta have my money."

Wide-eyed and without missing a beat, Kendal ejected the tape, turned the radio on, and adjusted his head nod to a different beat. For the rest of the ride, we chitchatted about my new job, where I lived now, and how I had been practicing for the past few weeks so I could beat his butt in basketball. He laughed, jumped out of the car, and ran into McDonald's.

"You got a girlfriend yet?" I asked in between fries.

Two quick slurps of chocolate shake and his attention went to a fly that walked on the outside window like he had stock invested in McDonald's. "Nope."

I moved closer, pointed to his chin and let out a chuckle. "You getting a little fuzz underneath your chin. The girls liking that?"

More fly watching followed by more slurps. His cunning grin, which had kept him out of a lot of trouble, erupted. "I never said that."

"So, what's going on with the girls? I see you had one on the bus just that quick," I prodded.

His twisted lips went in the opposite direction of his eyes. He paused, leaned over, and tilted his head toward me. "You didn't say anything about my hair." It was neatly twisted in cornrows.

"It's nice."

He smiled and nodded in agreement.

"What about the girls?"

His eyes went back to the fly as he munched on a few fries. He mumbled, "Some of them look good."

"Yeah?"

"Yeah." His answers were short and sweet, and if I wanted details about what was going on, I would have to step up my questioning game.

"You having sex?"

He froze. My breathing stopped, my heart dropped below my stomach, and everything seemed to move in slow motion. I didn't want to hear the answer, but I had to.

Another quick "no" escaped Kendal's mouth.

Quick answers from him always meant there was something else going on. I didn't want to bring up the subject as soon as he got here, but after the whole bus ordeal, it had to be done immediately.

I took a quiet gulp of air and let it out even quieter. "We need to talk about sex, Kendal."

He took a few creases from my forehead and put them on his. "While we're eating?"

"As opposed to when? When you're sleeping?" He wasn't making this any easier. I reminisced about my sex talk with my mother when I was a little younger than Kendal. She brought out a thick book that had pictures of cartoon people having sex. My older brother gawked, and my younger sister gagged. It looked like Fred and Daphne from Scooby Doo were having sex. From then on, cartoons were never the same. I promised myself I would handle it differently.

"What do you know about sex?"

Kendal found a piece of hair on the side of his head and twisted it until it could wind no more. "Not much."

"Do you know what you call a woman's-" *Just come out with it, Styles!* I didn't know what terminology to use. Vagina! No. I should say private parts. Puddy! Too cartoonish. Twat! Canal! Tunnel! Lovebox! I repeated, "Do you know what you call a woman's thing?"

Visibly uncomfortable, Kendal dropped his head. "Vagina. Was that the word you were looking for?"

I slowly nodded my head and smiled the same tense smile he did. "I guess that's the word. Tell me what you know about … vaginas."

During his hesitation he seemed to wrestle with whether to tell me everything he knew, or part of it. The corner of his mouth curved into a slick grin and he said, "I do take health class, Dad."

"What do they teach you in health class?"

The cunning grin returned. "They teach us about the reproductive system."

"And?"

"I know where's babies come from, and how they get here."

This was the answer I had been waiting for. "How?"

He stood up and dug into his pocket. "First you give a woman this," he said handing me a dollar.

"What the-"

He grabbed my shoulder and laughed. "Just joking, Dad." He sat back down getting a good chuckle out of my near heart attack. "I know about how men and women make babies. I know that you're supposed to wait until you're in love."

"Married. Until you're married," I corrected.

"That's what I meant," he said.

We continued our talk about love, and then switched to basketball, grades, and the new school he was attending.

****

Deanna walked into the office, eyes bloodshot, feet dragging. "Mind if I sit?"

I looked up and offered her the seat across from my desk.

She slid uncomfortably into the seat. Her eyes expressed hurt, and her tapping feet indicated nervousness.

"Coffee?"

She declined.

I didn't know whether to comfort her or back off. I couldn't tell what she needed. I popped my pen on the desk and waited patiently.

She adjusted her confidence. "I need to speak to you about something important."

I placed my pen on the desk. "What's up?"

The chair creaked as she inched closer. "I don't know how to begin."

My heart warmed. I knew what she wanted. Feelings crept in.

She inched even closer.

Feelings continued to creep.

Well-manicured hands seemed to reach out.

Sharp banging interrupted my warm fuzzies. The door swung open slowly and a size ten Buster Brown shoe entered. Mr. Amsterdam's chiseled chin shuddered as he cleared his throat, commanding attention. The black pupils consumed most of Deanna's eyes as she slid deeper into her seat. Her will remained strong, but her posture relented. The grown woman with the killer body appeared to be an overgrown teen applying for a job at McDonald's.

Mr. Amsterdam adjusted his thin burgundy suit jacket and walked toward Deanna. He placed his stubby fingers on her shoulders as they appeared to buckle, and he asked, "Can you excuse us, please?"

Without verbal acknowledgement, she answered with a slow ascent as if the bailiff had yelled, "All rise!"

The door slammed and I watched as Mr. Amsterdam dug into the inside of his suit jacket and pulled out a Havana cigar. He unwrapped it, put the butt into his mouth, and slowly spun it around until it was saturated.

He took two quick puffs, threw his head back, and a flurry of halos emitted from his lips before disintegrating in the air. The stale office air was now blessed with the familiar aroma of cherry wood. It always lingered long after he left.

"Jaw-don, let me get right to it. I'm concerned about Deanna."

Two more halos were born. "Her attendance has been going downhill and her tardiness is on the rise, not to mention Jaw-don, I think you've been covering for her."

Covering? What? My body braced and my brain locked. "Covering up? How so?"

His penguin-like body shook from left to right as he prepared to sit up. Three grunts later he was at my desk, cigar in one hand while the stubby index finger of his other pounded on my blotter. "I mean covering. How many times has she been late during the past month?"

I opened my mouth to explain, but he interrupted before I could continue.

"You don't know, do you? Well, I'll tell you. She was late ten days during the past month."

Suddenly I didn't feel so good. How could a man that hired his own flesh and blood be so cruel? I knew he was a businessman first, but it did nothing for my job security. All I knew was he had never interrogated me like this before, and it wasn't a good feeling.

My eyes now had the same glare his did moments ago as I shot up to face him man to man. "Look, you said that you hired me because I had the same fire, initiative, and that certain something right?"

He stared.

"Well, if I know someone's behavior is detrimental to the company, then I should be the one to call it. I interact with her on a daily basis." We both stood, guns drawn, waiting for the count!

He twirled his gun around his finger. "Something's got to give, Jaw-don." He reached the door, opened it, and slammed his gun into the holster. "Now!"

Chapter 19

TRACI

Traci adjusted her red spring jacket and braced herself as her eyes scanned the numbers again. 2-3-0-2 L Street. The numbers on the little white piece of paper matched the large bronze numbers on the ancient brown building in front of her. Bright yellow flowers sat in the windowsills of each large window to the left of the door. She looked up the cold stairs, then looked at her watch and realized it was noon and he might be out to lunch. She was thinking of any reason not to go inside. While she pondered her next move, an unexpected breeze brushed her face, cooling her down. She fumbled with her gold bracelet before placing her hand on the black rail.

"Looking for someone?"

Traci spun around and did a double take.

The man in the blue Nike jogging suit extended his hand. "Hello, again."

Traci accepted his hand and looked at him, trying to remember his name. "Aren't you-"

"Larry," he said with a huge smile. "I'm surprised you remembered me."

"I almost didn't. You look different without your coveralls."

Larry tugged at his jacket, admiring himself. "I do, don't I?"

She smiled.

"What are you doing in this neighborhood?"

She debated for a second whether or not to tell him her real reason. Hell, she didn't know if she was ready or not, but once she thought about Jordan and the problems they were having, she knew what she had to do. "I have to speak with your boss."

With his cool demeanor rattled, he asked nervously, "Is everything okay?"

"Oh, yes. The place turned out great," she assured him.

He wiped fake sweat from his brow and chuckled. "Phew. It was the first job I was in charge of."

"Well, you did a great job, Larry." She hesitated. "Is the boss in?"

He looked around and searched the street before turning back. "He should be. I see his car a few houses down. Follow me."

He walked her into the office and excused himself. She sat in a small room that had a desk, phone, coffee maker, and a picture of the D.C. skyline on the wall near the window. She smelled a hint of stale vanilla coffee that teased her nose and did nothing for her nerves. She thought about getting up and walking out, but Larry came back less than a minute later and escorted her to another room.

"The boss will see you now."

An uneasy smile escaped her. Her heart raced for the front door, but her feet stayed as still as the motionless skyline near the window. She followed him to the door and took a deep breath before entering.

Solomon remained seated as he jotted things onto a piece of paper, never once looking up. After allowing her to stand for a minute, he offered her the little brown seat across from him. Traci glared into Solomon's eyes, her growling stomach unsettled, and palms leaking. He sat across from her in his cushioned brown leather chair, rubbed his chin nervously and peered through her soul. Their eyes played an intense game of chess. No one seemed to want to make the first move. It was a battle of wills. A battle of power. A battle of first love verses true love.

He placed his hand on a pawn, looked directly at her and moved. "Does he understand you?"

Her eyes shifted. "You have some gall, Solomon."

Solomon loosened his tie, seized another pawn, and moved again. "Does he understand you?"

She remained motionless, stunned, and aggravated. "I didn't come to be interrogated, Solomon. You know exactly what I want."

His face softened as he put the chess pieces away, walked around his desk, and sat on the edge. His legs were spread. The uncomfortable closeness caused Traci to shift nervously. She didn't know whether the warmth came from the heater that never hummed or from Solomon's enormous presence.

"I understand what you want. But don't you know what I want, Traci?"

Her palms wept, heart shuddered, foot tapped, and eyes darted away from him. He inched closer and she could smell the sweet aroma that always enticed her.

"I know you feel it, too," he said confidently.

Traci felt a trickle of perspiration run down her back. She felt his soft brown eyes scanning her body. She felt his breath slither down her face and across her lips. Her voice was shaky. "You know I feel what?"

"Us. I know you feel us."

Traci was angered by his confidence, but marveled at his perception. She continued to tell herself that it was too late for him to crawl back into her life. It was too late for him to be the man that she wanted him to be. Shit, it was too late for him to fill a void that was already being well filled. She regained her composure.

"I'm not feeling anything right now, Solomon. What I am feeling is that it's time to do the right thing."

Solomon cocked his head to the side and squinted as a sly grin crept across his face. "I'm more than willing to give you back his furniture, but can we at least make a deal?"

Traci knew Jordan wasn't going to go for any kind of deal, but she didn't want to risk losing him. At this point she was willing to give a little to get a lot, just as long as sex wasn't involved.

He repeated, "Can we at least make a deal?"

"What kind of deal?"

Solomon grinned.

Chapter 20

JORDAN

"Dad?"

Shit! My puffy red eyes widened as I searched in vain for Halle. Only seconds ago, her beautiful bronze tits bounced in my face as I gripped her firm behind. I closed my eyes, grabbed her waist, and moved her back and forth until a warm wave of fluid flooded Sambuca. Now it was my turn to bless her with a warm rush of my fluids.

"Dad?"

I closed my eyes and her face flickered in the dark as I waited for her to appear again. Two more screams from Kendal, and Halle was gone for good.

"What?"

"It's ten o'clock."

"And?"

"And you promised to go to the park with me today."

I growled, swung my feet to the edge, and eased them into my awaiting brown grandfather slippers. As I began to walk toward the door, I heard him take off for the kitchen.

By the time I got dressed and walked into the kitchen, he was already rustling through the cereal boxes.

"You're up early. What's for breakfast?"

"Nothing over easy with a side of nada." He snickered. "Just joking, Dad. Your bowl is on the table."

His sense of humor warmed me. It surprised me at how much he was beginning to turn out like his old man instead of his mother. Serene didn't have a sense of humor and never encouraged his crazy antics, so he suppressed them when he was with her, and became rigid like her. But with each passing hour with me, he seemed to be coming into his own. His natural bubbling personality was starting to take over the withdrawn young man I had picked up from the bus station.

I shook my bowl of dry flakes. "What happened to the Frosted Flakes?"

He smiled. "We ran out, so I fixed you some Corn Flakes."

I leaned over and looked into his bowl. "What are you eating?"

"The rest of the Frosted Flakes."

I couldn't be mad at him for doing something that I would've done. I dipped my spoon into my dry bowl of Corn Flakes. I scooted a few flakes out of the way, searching for moisture.

"What happened to the milk?

He laughed again. "There was only a little bit left and you had so many Corn Flakes that I didn't want to spoil your breakfast with it." He pointed toward the counter near the sink. "I opened a can of Carnation Milk so you can enjoy a full bowl of cereal, Dad." He finished his cereal and pushed his bowl to me. "Or you can always use the rest of my milk. I didn't backwash."

****

Another drive with Kendal meant more tape popping, more music switching, and more hearing loss. Sundays weren't my day to play ball, but Kendal was eager to play and I was just as eager to show him who was still king. I called Tony and invited him to join us. He said he would stop by after twelve. He had an early appointment with some lady that worked for the president. I didn't bother to ask.

We stopped at the store and picked up a few bottles of Gatorade before heading to the park. When we arrived, the park had two full court basketball games going on. The young kids played on the far side, and the men played closer to the entrance.

"Which court do you want to play on?" I asked.

Kendal looked at both sides for a second before letting out a distraught sigh. "It doesn't matter. I really wanted to play you in some one-on-one."

"We don't have to stay here."

"Where's the closest park?"

"It's downtown. It'll take us about forty minutes to get to, but if we go now, we can play for about an hour or so before everybody gets there."

"We're here now. We might as well stay. And isn't Uncle Tony coming?"

I had totally forgotten. "Oh, yeah."

Kendal grabbed the ball and yelled, "I'm going over where the real players are. You can stay and play with the old guys. If you need to score any hoops, call me over and I'll save you."

I walked to the court where guys were huffing and puffing. While I stretched, I watched a few minutes of the game. When they finished, I sauntered toward a few of the players that were getting ready to play.

An older black man with tiny red shorts and thick green goggles said, "We need one. Wanna play?"

When he pointed to the rest of his teammates, I knew we were doomed. The other three had to be over fifty and looked as if they had been playing all day. I nodded and introduced myself to the rest of the guys. "You been playing for a while?" I asked.

The eldest of the tribe coughed and grabbed his chest. "This is our first game. We'll be leaning on you to carry us to the Promised Land."

It was going to be like playing against the Los Angeles Lakers with Moses, Methuselah, Jonah, and Job on my team. I knew that it was going to be a workout that was welcomed, but not expected.

The team we were playing looked at us and smiled confidently. One guy I played against last summer looked at me and shouted, "Watch out for his jumper. We can let the other guys shoot."

They checked the ball in and informed us that we were going to eleven by ones.

After about ten minutes of running and sweating, we were losing seven to two. We had no chance. I looked over at the sideline and noticed about ten guys waiting to play next and if we lost, we would have to wait another hour to play again.

The big guy on their team missed a shot and I grabbed the rebound. I dribbled the ball up court and scooted past a defender while another flailed at the ball wildly. I dribbled between my legs and past another before spotting Moses under the hoop. I threw the ball behind my back and Moses caught it and threw a wild hook shot toward the hoop. Their big man jumped in the air to block it, but Moses had lofted the ball high in the air and seconds later it came swooshing through the hoop. The hecklers on the sideline whooped and hollered as we ran back down court. Score was now seven to three. Three more bad shots by the other team, one jump shot by me, two lucky shots by Jonah, and we were in the game. Score was now seven to six. They scored the next two points and my old Bible members were running out of steam. I purposely threw the ball out of bounds to get them some well-needed rest.

"You can get em', Dad."

I turned around and saw Kendal on the sideline cheering us on. While someone retrieved the ball, Kendal threw me my Gatorade. The cold drink cooled my temperature and replenished what little energy I had left.

We scored the next two points and the score was now nine to eight. The sun continued to beat down and sap our energy. We had possession of the ball and needed the next point to tie the game. I got the ball at the foul line, faked like I was taking a shot and got their chubby player in the air before driving to the hoop for an uncontested lay-up. Nine to nine.

"We ain't letting these old men beat us," the feisty young one with the large Afro piped.

I let out a sarcastic chuckle and prodded the elders on. We traded baskets during the next three minutes, making the score tied at ten apiece. The heat took even more precious energy from our aged bodies. The crew of guys on the sideline maintained their heckling as our younger opponents felt us wearing down. The chubby one faked Methuselah and had a clear lane to drive in for the lay-up, but decided to take a fifteen-foot jump shot.

The ball circled the rim before spinning out. Job grabbed the rebound and was fouled hard by Feisty Afro.

Feisty Afro stood over Job and yelled, "Get up, old man. I didn't hit you that hard."

Job clutched his ankle and spun over before letting out a loud groan. Jonah sprinted toward Job and tied his sneakers tightly to avoid further damage to his ankle. Feisty Afro looked at me and slid me a slick grin. "You gotta pick one from the side."

Before I could select the tallest man in the park, Kendal stepped forward and said, "I got a basket for you, Dad."

I patted him on the butt as he ran onto the court. A year ago, he wouldn't have wanted to play, but now his confidence was high. It was a beautiful sight.

I dribbled the ball at the foul line and looked Feisty Afro directly in his eyes. "I'm about to take you to school."

"Nigga, please!"

I dribbled and threw the ball over his head. He spun around to intercept my pass only to find that I never let it go. He turned around with a look of bewilderment as I threw it off of his head and caught it. Before he realized what I did, I was on my way to the basket. As their big man rushed toward me, I gave Kendal a head nod and lofted the basketball toward the hoop. He leapt high in the air, catching the ball. He kept rising with the ball and slammed it through the hoop with authority. The sidelines went crazy as Feisty Afro ripped his shirt off and stormed off the court.

"Your son sure did save your ass," Tony yelled.

I turned around and saw Tony hugging and congratulating Kendal.

I pointed at the elders and corrected him, "I saved their ass is what you meant to say." On the sideline, Job continued to nurse his swollen ankle as the others crowded him, reveling in what appeared to be their only moment of glory at this court. By the round of applause they received from the hecklers, winning really didn't come easy for them.

Kendal ran toward me, grinning from ear to ear. Enthusiastically he asked, "How'd you like my dunk?"

I admitted I was very impressed, but we had more work to do on the court. I hoped at least one of my prehistoric teammates would quit. My teammates didn't seem like much, but they put up a hell of a fight. We prepared ourselves for the next battle.

Tony said he would watch some of the game before he left to take care of some business. "You got your hands full this game," Tony said.

I quickly sized up the four guys that walked on the court. The leader of the pack was a new guy that stood all of five feet, five inches. He had on long red shorts and a white T-shirt with white tube socks that reached his kneecaps.

My team assembled at the free throw line and matched against the people opposite of them. They were one short.

I told Tube Socks he had to get another guy.

"He's coming in a second," he grunted.

Aware that it was only getting hotter, Jonah complained that it was time to get the game started. He told them to pick someone off the sidelines until their savior came to help them out. I shot Jonah a cold stare. It was always the ones that had no game that initiated all the shit.

Tube Socks looked in the direction of the parking lot and shouted, "Here comes our fifth man."

Methuselah adjusted his weathered basketball jersey, tapped me on the shoulder, and displayed a worried look. He pointed toward the parking lot and uttered, "We got our work cut out for us. I used to play against that guy in a league down in D.C."

I turned around to find out who I was going to have to shut down. For a second, everything was deathly still. I did a double take. I looked over at Tony as he casually conversed with a few hecklers while Kendal stretched for the next game.

Tube Socks greeted their savior as if he was the next Jesus. "What's up, Solomon?"

Solomon threw his jacket to the side and greeted the rest of his teammates. "What's up, fellas?"

Tube Socks informed him, "What's up is that we almost had to pick up a guy from the sideline. You know we're trying to win all day. I hope you still got game."

Solomon jumped up and touched the rim with ease. "I can still jump through the roof."

"Enough of the chitchat," Moses yelled. He pointed at me and continued to scream, "We don't care who you got because my man right here is going to give you more than you bargained for."

Solomon quickly looked in my direction and did a similar double take. He stepped back and sized me up before checking out his surroundings. He was preparing for something.

All of his teammates jumped in front of the four players on my team, which left Solomon standing in front of me. He attempted to impose his size and will with an intense glare. No one knew or understood the magnitude of the match-up that was about to take place. He stood at six feet, seven while I was five inches shorter. He was muscular, but thin, while I had a more natural weight and thickness going for me. I never thought he played ball. Hell, I never thought I would have thoughts about one of Traci's ex-boyfriends. I knew I had an advantage, which was Traci. He wanted what I had. With his confidence brimming,

I started to wonder whether I had what he didn't want. Either way, I was about to force my presence on him.

He checked the ball and threw me an underhanded smirk. "Didn't know you played ball, Poet!"

I looked at him with a haughty stare that chopped him down a few inches. "Didn't know you sold furniture."

Instinct told me to run up on him and bash his head in right there, but Kendal was next to me and I definitely didn't want any trouble while he was there. I put the beef on the back burner and decided to make the best of the bad situation.

For the next ten minutes we went back and forth. Solomon was better than I thought, but nothing I couldn't handle. When he scored, the hecklers let me have it. With Tony watching the onslaught, I decided to step my game up another level. My teammates were not doing so well against the stronger players. Even Kendal was having trouble guarding the speedy Tube Sock.

I checked the ball in. "What's the score?"

Solomon wiped his bald-head clean and rubbed his sweat on the ball before hurling it directly toward my chest. "Seven to three, Poet!"

I caught the ball before it knocked the wind out of me. "Been lifting, huh?" I heaved the ball back at his chest with the same force.

He caught it and his mouth curled into another sly grin. "Don't have to lift for you guys." He bounced the ball three times and tucked it under his arm. "Put your money where your mouth is, Poet?"

He was putting me in a position where I had to defend my manhood, my integrity, and myself. I looked at Moses, who was doubled over and grabbing on his shorts, then at Methuselah, who was leaning against the gate, and I realized I couldn't do it with them. While I assessed the situation, Solomon assembled his teammates together to talk.

Tony walked over. "Damn, Styles. I told you that you were going to have your hands full. What's the hold up?"

I nodded toward Solomon. "Homeboy wants to play for some money. I know we can take these guys."

Tony peeked around me, looked at my teammates, and shook his head. "Not with them dead ass dinosaurs. And not to mention, homeboy is eating your ass alive out there."

Throw salt on the wounds, why don't you! "He ain't eating me alive. He's only got two baskets and I've made all three of ours."

"What you gonna do, Poet? We playing or what?" Solomon yelled.

The hecklers became restless. I needed more time to make this decision and the prehistoric dinosaurs needed more time to heal.

Fuck it, Styles! Get in his pockets! "Let's do it for twenty-five!"

Solomon chuckled as though I meant twenty-five cents. "Twenty-five? I wouldn't play hard for twenty-five. What about a buck?"

Don't do it! I knew one hundred dollars was a lot and it probably wasn't a good idea, but I had pride knocking on my door. "Let's do it!"

Solomon dribbled the ball a few more times before letting his players know it was on.

"One more thing," I said. "We start from scratch and I get to pick my own players."

Chapter 21

TRACI

Inside the living room, Kendal fidgeted opposite Traci.

Traci was unsure where to take the conversation, so she continued to search in vain for something to say. Kendal, aware of the thick cloud of boredom that lingered above their heads, grabbed the remote and turned the channel.

"You watch Springer?"

She wrinkled her nose and shook her head.

Just as he reached to change the channel, she interjected, "I don't mind though."

Jerry Springer looked into camera and smiled, "Today's show is about women that can't and won't let go." Kendal quickly found the remote again and for the next five minutes, they watched Emeril cook up a Curried Shrimp dish.

During a commercial, Kendal blurted, "I make my own decisions."

Traci's brow was furrowed as she turned in his direction.

Kendal noticed her look and repeated, "I make my own decisions."

"Oh. Okay." Traci had no clue why he had just said that.

Kendal stood and walked toward the kitchen. "Want something to drink? We have soda, cranberry juice, orange juice, and water."

Traci smiled. "I'll have cranberry juice."

Kendal disappeared into the hallway. A minute later he emerged with a tall glass of juice and sat across from her, tapping his foot nervously.

"What were you just talking about, if you don't mind me asking?"

His mouth twisted wryly as he searched for the right words. "My mother said a lot of things about you and my father," he confessed, "but I'm old enough to make my own decisions."

Traci's soul warmed and her heart fluttered. She stood up, smiling with satisfaction as she accepted the drink and gave him a hug. "Thank you, Kendal."

The door handle trembled as Traci took her seat across from Kendal. A combination of the heat and uncertainty caused a bead of sweat to glide down her damp forehead. Instead of her whole life, the past year flashed before her eyes. The trembling of the door conjured up feelings and so many emotions that lay dormant. While her passion raced to greet, her feet remained idle. Her emotions: angry, confused, and petrified. While she always maintained total control of her life, her heart did its own thing.

The lock clicked and the door swung slowly open. Traci heard the rustling of plastic bags and then watched Jordan slip into the kitchen without noticing her.

Kendal leapt from his seat and disappeared into the back, leaving Traci to sit nervously and watch the paint dry on the walls.

In the kitchen Jordan rustled bags and slammed cabinets. He yelled, "Kendal, you hungry?"

"No!" A few seconds passed. "Dad, Traci's in the living room."

The cabinets no longer banged, the bags rested comfortably against the linoleum and everything in the house remained hushed. Traci thought about going into the kitchen, but decided against it. She didn't want to wear out her welcome before she even got a chance to speak.

Jordan took a few deep breaths and cleared his throat. Traci pushed herself to a standing position and took slow calculated steps toward the kitchen.

She called softly, "Jordan?"

Silence answered.

"Jordan?" she repeated even quieter.

He responded weakly, "I'm in the kitchen."

Traci proceeded to the kitchen cautiously, not knowing what to expect. She inhaled long winds of dry air before turning the corner.

She forced her lips into a grin and walked into the kitchen. "I was just stopping by to see-" Her voice trailed off and her brows drew together in an agonized expression. A muscle in her jaw quivered as her expression grew serious. Her steps slowed as she approached. "What happened?"

An unspoken pain was alive and glowing in his swollen blue-black left eye. "Nothing," he replied nonchalantly, leaning on the opened refrigerator door.

"Are you sure? Did you go to the doctor?"

One corner of his mouth pulled into an uneasy grin. "Just a little war injury."

Her uneasy grin matched his. "What happened?"

After putting the remaining items into the refrigerator, he leaned against the counter and drew three deep breaths. "I was playing basketball earlier and got elbowed."

She moved closer and her fingers lightly traced the swell of his eye. "Did the guy at least apologize?"

Jordan snatched his face away. "I'd rather not talk about it."

Traci gave a curt nod and followed him to the living room. Jordan put on a jazz CD, threw his head back against the black leather couch, and blew exasperation into the air.

Traci didn't know what to do. She didn't know whether to explain to him about the sofa and chair or to just forget about it until another day. She chose the latter, and her head fell into his arms. She wrapped her arms around his waist and listened to the unsteady rhythm of his breathing.

Smooth jazz love songs blended in and out as she comforted him with a steady massage of his hands. He wasn't his usual receptive self, but he didn't seem to shy away either, so she continued to draw circles inside his palms with her fingers. Seconds later, Jordan began humming along with the song and put his arm firmly around her waist. His strong hands took command of the pain that found a home near her lower spine. He continued to massage through the next song and Traci's legs began to shift from side to side. She couldn't remember the last time they were intimate. She couldn't remember the last time they just held each other and kissed. She was going to make sure nothing interfered with their evening tonight.

Jordan lifted himself up and took a few sips of red wine before returning to his reclined position to continue his assault on Traci's sweet spot. His hand slid underneath her shirt and rubbed with the passion of teenage love. He started at the base of her back and rubbed until he reached her shoulder blades. Traci moaned and fell deeper into his arms. With a slight nudge, he lifted her face so their lips could meet. She tasted warm wine on his lips as their tongues collaborated on a smooth jazz melody of their own.

Her hands trailed down Jordan's chest and rested on his stomach as she continued to suck on his tongue and kiss every part of his face. Jordan lay back and allowed Traci to probe his face and neck with short kisses while her tongue continued its journey down his tense brown skin.

Traci squirmed as his hands inched closer to her spot.

"Dad?"

They shot up and adjusted their clothing as though they were just caught by their parents for making out. Jordan cleared his throat and turned to face Kendal.

Kendal stood by the kitchen, tossing the basketball in the air. "Mind if I go to the park for a bit?"

Jordan looked at Traci and smiled before answering. "Go ahead. What time are you coming back?"

Traci could see the wheels turning inside his head.

Kendal hurried to the door. "In about an hour."

Jordan checked his watch and laughed. "Take your time."

"Do you need anything before I come back?"

Jordan playfully patted Traci's thigh. "Nope. I've got everything I need."

As soon as the door slammed behind him, Jordan asked, "Traci, can you make sure the door is locked?"

Traci walked to the door and clicked the lock.

Before she could turn around, the lights went out and Jordan was behind her.

He pressed his body against hers. "Don't move."

Unaware of his next move, she froze. Her mind wanted her to turn around and speak about the issues they were having so they could have closure, but her body was on a different page. Her body instructed her to stay still and receive the lovin' that she so desperately wanted and needed.

As Jordan pinned her hands above her head, she could feel the heat and moistness of his breath as he laid his two hundred and thirty pound frame against her body. In the background saxophones slowly pumped sensual melodies into her mind and she closed her eyes and brought everything back to the Poconos. Last summer, she took Jordan to the Poconos and told him that he was on a sexual retreat and he could have anything and everything.

Jordan continued to bark instructions. "Taste this."

Traci's eyes remained closed while her mouth opened slightly. She smelled wine on his breath as he lightly kissed her ear lobes and whispered how much he missed her. His hands glided alongside her hips and met around her taut waist. She flinched as his forefinger probed the inside of her belly button. More caressing was followed by more whispers, which were followed by more tingling sensations. It had been such a long time since she had felt like she was wanted. Her neck craved his lips. Her lips craved his. Her insides yearned for his thickness, while an orgasm screamed it wanted to come out and play.

She tried to turn around, but Jordan's body was still firmly pressed against hers. Her breasts pressed against the door and she could hear faint traces of street life.

"Taste this," he repeated.

Her mouth opened wider, anticipating the sweetness of fruit or candy, but like before, there was nothing. His hands continued to creep toward her inner thighs. He casually unbuttoned her jeans and slipped his fingers inside her panties. She let out a moan as she anticipated the movement of his hand further down into her pot of gold. He paused and made love to each muscle in her shoulders with passionate kisses. Song after song blended and faded like the memory of all the arguments that proceeded. His tongue traveled from her shoulder blade to the nape of her neck and found a home on the inside of her right ear. He firmly gripped each of her buns and gently slid her jeans down around her thighs. She closed her eyes and took another whiff of the wine, Jordan's scent, and sweat that mixed in the air.

"Let-me-get-these-for-you," she drawled as she shifted from side to side and eased her pants off.

Once naked, he whispered, "Don't move." She hummed with the music as she waited for her knight to touch her with his mighty armor. She wanted to turn around, but decided it was more exciting to follow his directions.

Traci wanted to take him right there, but Jordan had other plans. Sambuca stretched from the cusp of her cheeks to the small of her back. She could feel every inch of his pulsating tool as it throbbed against her. "Jordan, can I-"

He interrupted her by spinning her around, introducing his tongue to hers. With every sip of his tongue, she reached a new high. As he kissed and sucked her neck, his forefingers and thumbs pinched her nipples. She moaned. Traci, not to be outdone, massaged his chest and followed his hairline leading directly to Sambuca. He let out a groan as she wrapped her hands around the shaft and slowly pumped up and down as he continued to pinch her nipples. They found a rhythm. Jordan's hand continued to play with the hairs that guarded her gold while her hand continued to stroke the master of ceremonies. He lifted his forefinger to his mouth and put a dab of saliva on his hand before returning to her inner thighs. She leaned against the door, arching her back so her gold could meet the wet forefinger that was sent to probe. He slid his finger gingerly up and down her moist slit. His wet finger lightly touched her lips.

"Taste this."

Her face instinctively turned away, but seconds later she relented to the pressure, closed her eyes, and opened her mouth slightly. She didn't particularly care to taste her own juices, but she knew it turned him on immensely. His wet finger circled her lips before finding her tongue. Traci wrapped her tongue around his finger and bobbed her head slowly in an up and down motion. Against her stomach, Sambuca hardened even more as she continued a deliberate massage of each testicle.

The music went off and they were left with only the sounds of the world to entertain them. No one seemed to miss a beat. Traci closed her eyes and heard a sensual murmur from Jordan with every shake of his shaft. And he heard deep moans every time his finger entered her smelted gold.

She knew what he wanted. She knew what he loved. Today she wanted to give him whatever he wanted, and then some. Her hands no longer massaged his thick tool, but instead wrapped around his neck and drew him in to enjoy the sweet taste she had. He reached around and gripped each cheek with renewed vigor and reintroduced his lips, swapping her juice.

In the Poconos, Jordan made sure he took her anywhere and everywhere. They made love by the indoor pool. They had sex in the bathroom. They fucked by the large window in the evening. Since that day, she hadn't really gotten that wild, but she knew she would have to do that every now and then to keep him satisfied. His sexual appetite was unique. He didn't want it all the time, but when he did, he wanted it all!

With her body temperature rising with each kiss and each rub, she decided to take over. She wanted to make him feel like she felt so many other times.

With Sambuca in hand, he pressed it against her leg and whispered, "Taste this."

She obliged and slid down his chocolate frame until she rested on her knees. She kissed his athletic thighs while massaging his growing tool. Sweat dripped down his stomach and onto her hand. She loved the musty smell of his love. The only sounds now came from him. Moans were followed by slow urges to indulge. She hated to be asked, but loved to hear him beg. She took long licks of his thighs as she inched her way to his tool that had always provided her with great pleasure. Cars beeped outside and kids screamed nearby. Inside, business was being tended to. She was going to do whatever it took to keep her man happy. She knew what he liked and how he liked it. And if she did it right, it wouldn't take long.

Her tongue found his sweet spot in between his thighs and testicles. She took deep whiffs of his scent and long licks of his soul. He shuddered as she stopped suddenly and sucked lightly on his thigh while her hand maintained its steady pace on his tool.

Jordan's hands left her shoulders and gripped the sides of the door as she continued her oral journey to pleasure. Before he could give out another order, Traci, already comfortable between his legs, lightly flicked her tongue across the head of his rock hard penis. His body shook as the warmth of her mouth enveloped the head. Appeased by his reaction, she continued to inch pieces of his thick chocolate flesh into her mouth while holding on to his testicles as if her life depended on it. He stood above her, legs spread wide and hands remaining at the opposite corners of the door.

Jordan began rotating his hips with steady pumps as inch after inch entered her awaiting mouth.

Her hands followed a trail up to his chest. She pinched each of his nipples as she remained still and let him enter and exit her mouth at will.

Minutes after his easy glide subsided, she eased him out of her mouth, letting her tongue trail to his testicles. She licked each one appreciatively. Jordan responded with a few "damns." She knew what would bring him over the top, and she was pulling out all the stops. Her two hands clasped around Sambuca and moved slowly in an up and down motion while she noisily slurped on the head. Jordan loved when he could not only feel, but also hear her handling her business.

Jordan grabbed her shoulders and brought her to him. She knew that he was closer to his orgasm and she wanted him to cum, just not in her mouth.

"Taste it," he begged.

She engulfed the tip. She slid her tongue down one side and up the other. She made noise. She gagged. She touched her breasts and pinched her nipples. She toyed with his orgasm and teased hers. She gave him sloppy head. He fell into her rhythm. She made her own beat. She could feel his vein. She knew he wanted her to let him cum in her mouth. She was not yet comfortable with it, but today was different. She wanted to please him, by any means necessary.

She hesitantly conceded, "Just this once."

His grip around her shoulders tightened. His strokes became shorter. She continued to shake his shaft and noisily slurp on his head. His knees started to tremor and his hands shook against her shoulders.

She braced herself as his hands found the back of her head. His grip tightened and she felt a stream of hot fluid hit the back of her throat. She gagged. She drank his seawater. His back slammed forward against the wall. "Fuck!"

Traci leaned to the side and spit into her hand the few swallows that didn't quite go down, and then she slid them down his leg. She could still taste the salty semen in her mouth as she wiped her mouth with her hand.

Jordan's face still lay against the wall, drenched.

Her hands traveled to the scene of the crime to feel his semi-hard dick. It pulsated a few times before going limp. A few drops of semen remained. She climbed up his body and stopped at his lips. She smiled and whispered, "Taste this!"

Chapter 22

JORDAN

I sat at my desk befuddled. The anticipation caused beads of sweat to form on my creased brow as I realized the day of reckoning couldn't be postponed forever. Deanna had slipped out of work last Friday without my knowledge. After my meeting with Mr. Amsterdam, I came out to find that Deanna had left a note on her desk about being sick, so business had to wait.

My finger shook as I hesitated a few seconds. I had rehearsed my speech over and over again this past weekend, but I knew as soon as I saw her face I would lose my composure.

My forefinger came crashing down on the cold black button and my tone was short. "Can you please come into my office, Ms. Simons?"

Her voice rattled as if she knew the news that was coming. "I-I-I'll be right there, Mr. Styles."

Seconds later, Deanna entered and sat opposite me. *Relax and get this shit over with, Styles!* I took a few deep breaths and began with a voice shakier than I would have liked. "You know why you're here, right?"

Her head dropped and she shrugged her shoulders in mock resignation.

"Hello? Are you with me?"

She turned away from me. "I'm with you."

She was going to try to make this harder than it should be. I didn't know whether to just explain that it was time for her to move on, or whether to tell her that it came straight from the top. I decided to be up front about everything.

I began with cool authority. "It's time to make some changes around here." I took a sip of coffee and cleared my throat before finishing my thought. "I think we both know that the reason we're here is because of your attendance, tardiness, and work ethic of late. I don't know who has been talking to people about your being late and absent, but word has gotten to the top."

Her eyes were filled with concern. They pierced my being and searched for answers. I didn't want to bring up her uncle, but it was something that was going to be brought up whether I liked it or not.

"We have to let you go."

Her dark eyes suddenly grew wild. I saw a different person.

I repeated, "We have to let you go."

She shifted in her seat and spoke in a weak and tremulous whisper. "I'm not leaving until he gets here." Her eyes clung to mine, analyzing my reaction.

You're not leaving? My heart pumped thick red blood. I studied her carefully, trying to choose the right words to respond to her absurd comment. "You're not leaving?"

Her body language showed defiance. Leaning forward in her chair, in a controlled voice she repeated, "I'm not leaving until he gets here."

"Until who gets here?"

"Mr. Amsterdam!"

Never once in my ten years of supervising other staff have I had to deal with this type of behavior. I was supposed to fire her, but how would it look for me to have security escort the boss's niece out of the building? I decided against any action of that nature.

I fiddled with the phone. "Give me a second."

She excused herself from the room and I quickly left a message for Mr. Amsterdam to head down to the office immediately.

I called Deanna through the intercom and let her know that I would call her in when I heard from Mr. Amsterdam.

I dialed Tony and spoke to him about the situation.

He couldn't help laughing aloud. "Thank God you don't work in a postal office."

His laugh was not contagious. "I would have to post my foot in her damn ass."

"You wanted to be the Head Negro in Charge, right?"

I co-signed his sentiments. "You're right. It's difficult because I really can't say what I want to say to her."

Another laugh erupted. "I know what you really want to say to her."

"Apparently you don't. I ain't going there."

"All right. I'll take your word."

I was happy he didn't press the issue. He knew I was doing the right thing, and I never mixed business with pleasure.

He continued, "How's that eye of yours doing?"

Instinctively, my fingers grazed the tender lump that had shrunk sizably since Saturday. "It went down a lot. A good steak will do wonders for the eye."

"You put steak on your eye?"

"I said, it does a wonder for the I. I ate a large T-bone steak and totally forgot the damn eye and let nature take its course."

We both laughed. I needed a good laugh. I knew I could count on Tony to take my mind off the drama.

"Did you talk to Kendal about what happened the other day?"

"Why would I talk to Kendal about that?"

"Because you always tell him to defend himself if he gets into an altercation, right?"

"Yeah, but this was no ordinary altercation. He started getting rough, and then I started getting rough. He caught me good with an elbow," I reluctantly admitted. "What was I going to do? It was part of the game! Elbows get thrown in the heat of the game."

"You should've told me earlier he was the guy Traci used to date. I would've made sure nothing jumped off."

"Thanks, Mandela."

Tony ignored my comment and continued, "I would've sent Kendal to the car and me and homeboy would've had some words. But you did the right thing under those circumstances. As long as you got the money, right?"

"Damn right, I got the money. I'm glad your big ass hit a couple of shots."

"What did Traci say about your eye?"

"Nothing."

"She didn't see it?"

"She saw it when she came over, but we didn't talk about it."

"What the hell did you do when you..." he paused. "Never mind."

I remained silent.

"As a matter of fact," he added, "what did you do?"

"What do you mean what did I do?"

"Did you act like everything between you guys was cool? Did you tell her about the incident in the park? Did you-"

"I get it, Dr. Abby." I paused to gather my thoughts. "I just wanted to relax and not mention anything about it. No sense in her worrying."

He gave a sarcastic chuckle. "Not you, Mr. Go Tell It On the Mountain."

"I'm on some new shit now. I'm not about to have a heart attack over that. If she wants him, she can have him."

"Don't tell me that. You should've told her."

"I was frustrated," I admitted. "I just wanted her to ride me and we could just deal with the issues later."

"What happened after the riding?"

"Kendal came back and we sat and watched a movie before she went home."

"You plan on talking to her about what's-his-name?"

"Solomon?"

"Yeah, Solomon."

"I'm going to ask her what's going on."

"What if she says that there's nothing going on?"

"Then we'll speak about removing him from the situation before he causes more drama."

Playing devil's advocate, he asked, "What if she says that she's confused?"

I chuckled to cover my annoyance. "Then she's gotta go!"

"You wouldn't fight for her?"

I was irked by his cool, aloof manner of questioning something that was so new and fresh. "Fight? Would you fight if you were in my shoes?"

"Listen, Styles. You need to understand that you don't know everything that's going on. Put yourself in her..."

"Hold up, Tone. You hear that?"

He paused. "Hear what?"

"The damn violins in the background! I'm tired of your Hallmark answers. Was I giving you these answers when Cynthia was bringing you through all that mess?"

Tony remained silent.

I continued, "Give it to me without the bullshit, Tone!"

His husky voice held a challenge. "You want me to keep it real. You want me to keep it real?"

"Please."

"First of all, she ain't fucking him so what's the big deal? You used to chill with Monica and ain't nothing happened. Your problem is, you knew your intentions when you went out with Monica and you think she has the same intentions."

"I wasn't fucking her, though."

"But you thought about it, right?"

"Maybe," I confessed. "But I didn't do anything."

"Maybe she thought about it, but she didn't do anything."

"Hopefully she didn't."

Knowing my temperature was flaring, Tony quickly switched the conversation to the project he was working on.

The intercom interrupted. Deanna's voice, though soft, was crisp and clear. She seemed to have renewed energy. "Mr. Styles, Mr. Amsterdam is on line one."

I got off the phone with Tony and quickly hit line one.

"What's going on, Jaw-don?"

I didn't know what to say about the situation, but quickly decided to get to the point. "She's not leaving until you get here," I blurted.

In the background I could hear Mr. Amsterdam unwrapping a cigar. For the next minute, I listened as he lit his cigar and blew smoke into the receiver. Instead of being angry, he spoke in an odd, yet gentle tone. "Get her into the office, Jaw-don."

Get me a damn drink! I didn't know what was about to go on, but I hoped it was over with soon. I beckoned Deanna into my office. One minute later, with Mr. Amsterdam on the speakerphone, we all sat in silence.

Deanna's eyes shifted from the speakerphone to me. She smiled an unconfident smile as she waited for someone to say something.

After crossing and uncrossing my legs for the fifth time, I decided to break the silence. "Everyone is here, Mr. Amsterdam. Would you like for me to start?"

He hacked a few coughs and let out a long, audible breath. "I tried to let you handle it Jaw-don, but you couldn't seem to get that right, so I'll do it myself."

I looked at Deanna and she returned a look of disbelief at Mr. Amsterdam's audacity. He had never spoken to me in such a tone before. My guard went up as I prepared for everything.

"Deanna," he barked, "you are terminated as of today. We will give you a month's severance pay before you leave, but today will be your last day."

She tilted her head, staring at the speakerphone in disbelief. She let out a loud, hard hum before she spat out the words contemptuously, "That's bullshit!"

What? My head swung from the speakerphone to Deanna. This had all the makings of a soap opera that I didn't want to watch.

More coughs erupted from Mr. Amsterdam's clogged lungs. "Excuse me! I am the boss!"

She chuckled nastily, "I never said you weren't, but you can't fire me!"

His anger became a scalding fury. "I said, you are fired, Deanna!"

A sudden thin chill hung on the edge of his words. I had never heard Mr. Amsterdam so angry. I knew when he got angry that he could be cold, but this was borderline satanic. Had he no compassion for his own flesh and blood?

Another nasty chuckle erupted from Deanna's section. "I'm not leaving until you and Aunt Carol get here to discuss what I'm going to do about my financial situation."

Mr. Amsterdam said nothing. I could hear more inhaling and hacking on the other line while Deanna sat patiently across from me with her hands folded and legs crossed. I didn't know if I should've stopped them while they were ahead, but I knew it was best to stay out of their business.

Deanna inched closer to the speakerphone and uttered casually, "Do you want me to call Aunt Carol or are you going to tell her what you're doing to her favorite niece?"

His tone was irascibly patient. "I'll make some calls, Deanna. I've already spoken to your aunt about the situation, and she wants no part of it. Let's not make this bigger than it is. Accept the severance pay and go about your business. I can't offer anything more than that. I think thus far I've been more than fair with you, right?"

I could feel Deanna watching me as I watched the speakerphone. My eyes shifted from the speakerphone to Deanna. Her eyes were bulging with fire. I knew now that her wide-eyed innocence was merely a smoke screen. She spoke to Mr. Amsterdam with such ferocity that it seemed to catch him off guard as well. Mentally, I excused myself from the rest of the conversation. It was a battle I was not supposed to be a part of.

Deanna broke the silence. "What's it going to be, Uncle Willy?" she mocked.

"If that's the way you want to play bitch, that's the way we'll play!" Mr. Amsterdam's line went dead before she could respond.

Deanna's eyes watered, and she remained absolutely motionless for a moment. She took a deep breath, adjusted her smile, and walked toward the door. She grabbed the door handle and spun to face me. "This bitch will be in her seat waiting for the boss!"

.

Chapter 23

TRACI

Traci sat at her desk, planning her next move. "What would you do if you were in my shoes?"

Sharlana slid to the edge of her seat and shook her head disapprovingly as she continued to eat her turkey club. "I would jump the hell out," she joked in between bites.

"Seriously, Lana. I'm in a tough situation."

"What's so tough about you telling Solomon to mind his own damn business?"

Traci's spoon searched her pint of butter pecan for pecans. "It's not that simple."

"What's not simple about it? Do you love the man?"

Traci's right brow was high and rounded as she slid a spoonful of pecans into her mouth. "Who?"

"Solomon?"

Traci's spoon remained stuck in her mouth as she pondered the question to which she already knew the answer. She hesitated before letting the words slowly escape her mouth. "Yes, I still love him." Before Sharlana could interrupt, she continued, "But I'm not in love with him. There's a difference."

"Just like there's a difference between a hole in your head and a hole in your brain. You gotta get that brotha out of your system. What's it going to take?"

That was the million-dollar question Traci asked herself on countless occasions. Until he called recently, she thought she was completely over him. He had a stranglehold over her emotions.

"I don't know what it's going to take," Traci admitted. "He just called and left me a message. I'm debating on whether to call him or not."

"What was the message?"

Traci didn't want to tell Sharlana everything because she knew how stupid she looked with each passing tidbit of information. Her spoon glided alongside the almost empty pint of butter pecan ice cream, carefully picking up every last morsel. She thought about whether or not she should just sit Jordan down and tell him everything. She needed Dr. Phil!

Traci huffed, "He wants me to meet him next Friday."

Sharlana's voice jumped an octave. "Meet him where?"

"At Friday's, near Greenbelt, for drinks and then he wants me to attend a function he's speaking at."

Sharlana's expression grew grim and resentful. "Speaking about what? Fucking women over and leaving them paranoid for the next man that comes into their lives?"

"C'mon, Sharlana. He seems to have changed somewhat."

Sharlana was caught off guard by Traci's protection of the man that once wreaked havoc through her life and even put their friendship to the test. "Why are you defending him?"

"I'm not defending him. I want this over as much as you do. Believe me, I love Solomon for being my first love, my heart, but

I'm in love with Jordan. I have to go, Lana. He promised if I met him, he would give me back my furniture and be out of my life for good."

For Solomon, she held back tears of disappointment. Tears of anger. Tears for her unborn child. For Jordan, she held back tears of guilt. Tears for fear of losing him. Tears for stupidity.

Sharlana's warm hand found Traci's neck. Traci propped her folded arms on the desk and her head sank deeper into them with each rub.

"Let's do something tomorrow night," Sharlana said.

Traci sat up, yawned, and reached for each side of the room, stretching every limb. "What?"

"I'll figure it out."

A smile warmed Traci's forlorn appearance. "As long as there's some drinks, okay?"

Sharlana got up and headed for the door. "No doubt. We'll pick you up around seven."

Chapter 24

JORDAN

I repeated to myself, "This bitch will be in her seat waiting for the boss!" I didn't know where that had come from. Hell, I debated on whether I should report Mr. Amsterdam to the Better Business Bureau. The one thing I did know was that I needed to leave the office before he got here.

I heard two sharp knocks at my office door.

"Come in."

Mario peeked inside the office and smiled. "What's up, J?"

Not now, Mario! I didn't need for him to be in my business. "Hey, Mario."

He took a seat in the chair across from me and continued to smile broadly. "Did you hear about the party a few of my actor friends are throwing? There's supposed to be quite a few small time producers coming."

I nodded and slumped further into my leather chair.

He continued, "You coming through or what?"

"I don't know Mario. I got a lot of stuff going on right now."

He forced a demure smile.

I added, "But I'll make sure I at least try to stop by, even if it's just for a few minutes to check you out. What time?"

"About seven. Can you do some talking to the little lady out there?"

"I can't promise you. Why don't you invite her on your way out?"

He shrugged his shoulders and walked out the door.

As if on cue, Mr. Amsterdam appeared in the doorway two minutes after Mario left.

With short, purposeful strides, he marched to my desk with an expression of pained tolerance. The heavy bags under his eyes paralleled Chinese teacups, and his large blank eyes resembled lumps of black sugar waiting to dissolve into them. He cleared his throat, moved into my personal space, and spoke with a slight twinge of wonder in his voice.

"What's going on with you and Deanna?"

"What do you mean, what's going on with me and Deanna?"

His forefinger landed with a thud against my desk. He yelled, "Are you having relations with my niece?"

A snide chuckle burst through my unsuspecting lips. "Relations?"

"Yes, relations! She's never acted like this before. Her behavior has been very aggressive toward me and I think you have something to do with that," he barked loudly, pointing at me as if I was already convicted.

Veins surfaced like large chocolate noodles alongside my neck. "I think you better sit down, Mr. Amsterdam," I said with calm anger.

His hand fell to his side and his eyes shifted nervously. We had never had a confrontation of this magnitude, and he seemed to realize that after sizing me up, this job was not worth getting his ass kicked. His tone reflected his softened stance. "I'm sorry about the tension here, Jaw-don, but I'm just upset, confused, and bothered."

I remained standing, not allowing him to look down on me or feel any false sense of power. "Grab a seat, Mr. Amsterdam," I said firmly.

He relented. We stared into space looking for answers.

"Should I call her into the office?" I asked.

He shifted anxiously in his seat.

In a friendlier tone, I repeated, "Should I call her into the office?"

He nodded and searched his pockets for a cigar. Realizing that he didn't have any with him, he clasped his stubby hands together and rocked slightly. I pressed the intercom button and called Deanna into the office.

The minute it took for her to arrive was long enough to reflect on the situation in front of me. We were about to have a meeting to fire his niece whom he thought I was having relations with.

Deanna pushed the door open ferociously, strutting vibrantly with her head held high. She took a quick hard breath and walked closer. We exchanged glances. Between her and Mr. Amsterdam, the unwelcome tension stretched even tighter as he didn't bother to look her way or acknowledge her presence.

She spoke to all, but gazed only in my direction. "I'm here for the meeting."

Mr. Amsterdam's voice was courteous, yet patronizing, as he finally looked her way. "I'm so glad you could make it to the meeting, Deanna. Sit!"

She sat opposite him, smiled smoothly, betraying nothing of her annoyance. "Not a problem. As a matter of fact, can we get going? I have work to do."

A hint of perfume teased the humid room.

Mr. Amsterdam searched again for the cigar that was not in his pocket, swung his seat toward her and stated with firmness, "You have no more work to do here, Deanna. Your job is finished at Marigold Industries."

My head dropped and I pinched the bridge of my nose with my thumb and forefinger. It felt good to disappear. I wanted to be far away from the bullshit of this firing. The bullshit of Mr. Amsterdam's new attitude and the bullshit of corporate America.

Deanna stood and demanded in a shrill voice, "Why? Why? Why?" Without waiting for him to answer, she continued her barrage of questioning. "Why am I getting fired?"

His face became flushed.

"Because I won't sleep with you any longer?" she bellowed.

Sleep? Any longer? Words caused my head to spin. My dark eyelids opened and shed light on the situation that needed to stay concealed. A heavy trickle of sweat glissaded from underneath my armpit. I didn't know what was going on or what she was talking about, but this was a conversation I know I didn't want to have.

His eyes flashed with outrage as he tried unsuccessfully to clear his throat while stumbling to stand. Once he gathered himself, he pointed at her and spat venomously, "You better watch your mouth, Deanna!"

She walked closer and challenged, "Or what?"

They stood face to face, neither willing to give in. Her soft brown eyes dueled with his rock hard hazel ones. It was a match made in hell.

You gotta do something, Styles! I wanted to stay out of this, but it was clearly up to me to keep the peace between...shit, I didn't know what to call their relationship.

I immediately rose to regain control of the situation, but stopped short when my phone rang. I debated on whether to pick it up or not, but after hearing it ring for a minute, I realized maybe this would stop the madness.

"Hello."

I nodded a few times and gave a few um-hums before dropping the phone back onto the receiver. This is going to be some shit. Mrs. Amsterdam never comes to the office. In the short time I was employed here, she's never come to the office. I informed Mr. Amsterdam that his wife was on her way to the office.

His eyes quickly left Deanna and glanced in my direction. He began rubbing his hands together with his head spinning back toward the door. He adjusted his glasses as though he had x-ray vision. "Did she say where she was?"

I shook my head. "She did say that she was on her way."

Mr. Amsterdam looked at Deanna and then at me. He began biting the insides of his mouth as he paced the room. I didn't know what was going on, but I'm sure Deanna knew more than her unaffected posture led us to believe.

Mr. Amsterdam hurried to the partially fogged window to search for his wife's car. Deanna looked at me, shook her head, and mouthed an apology. One minute she was screaming at Mr. Amsterdam about not sleeping with him any longer, and the next she was apologizing. Her emotions seemed out of control and Mr. Amsterdam seemed bewildered. For the next minute, Mr. Amsterdam paced, not saying a word to either of us.

With his back still turned, Deanna walked forward, stopping a foot short of him. "I made the call and told her to come."

He spun around. Horror terrorized his eyes. "You did what?"

"I told her to come," she repeated.

A thick vein appeared on the side of his temple. He gritted his teeth and his eyes dug slowly into Deanna's flesh. If looks could kill, she would've died instantly.

For the first time in a while, I saw them in the same camera lens. The contrast was unbelievable, given the content of their relationship. They were about the same height, only Mr. Amsterdam was quite a bit bigger than her. He looked like he could've been her father, but his actions showed that the only relationship that was feasible was one of a Sugar Daddy.

Mr. Amsterdam continued to glare at Deanna as they challenged each other to make the first move or say the first dumb thing. The ringing phone broke the silence.

I answered the phone and spoke slowly. "He's in my office, Mrs. Amsterdam."

As the receiver hit the base, Mr. Amsterdam rushed to my desk and interrogated, "Where is she? Did she say she was coming up?"

That's right asshole, Elvis is in the building! "She's in the lobby downstairs and she didn't want to come all the way up here if you were somewhere else in the building."

Sweat dripped down his cheeks and all of his energy left. All the fight he had left seemed to evaporate as time continued to tick away. He shot a glance at the door and then at Deanna. She seemed to be the only calm one in the office.

She looked at me, then back at Mr. Amsterdam. "Why is everyone looking at me?"

Her words were playful but the meaning was not. Her eyes glowed with a savage inner fire that was not going to be put out with a little cup of water. Mr. Amsterdam stood still, almost stone-faced.

I looked at my watch and knew that it would only take Mrs. Amsterdam four minutes at most to get here, and one minute had already elapsed.

"What's it going to be?" Deanna asked Mr. Amsterdam as she folded her arms and shifted indignantly from side to side. Her patience was being tested.

He looked at the door and then at his watch. More perspiration left his nervous ducts. "What do you mean, what's it going to be?"

"Meaning, I could just sit here and wait for about two or three more minutes and exercise my right to explain my firing to the boss's wife, who in fact owns half of this business, or I can keep my job and walk out the side door."

Mr. Amsterdam wrestled with the thought before shaking his head in disagreement. "I can't do it."

Deanna applied more pressure as she walked toward the front door and placed her hand gently on the knob. "Is it worth all of this because I don't need sex in my life anymore?"

Embarrassed, Mr. Amsterdam looked at me and realized I knew what was going on, so he could speak freely. "We had a deal."

Deanna spun around and walked forward with renewed aggression. "We didn't have a deal! You wanted to have your cake and eat it too, but I'm tired of this arrangement. Plus-" her voice faded.

Mr. Amsterdam walked closer to her. "Plus, what?"

Her head dropped. "I met someone."

Mr. Amsterdam wiped his damp forehead with the back of his hand. "You can have him, too. I don't care about that."

Her head snapped in his direction. "What?"

Mr. Amsterdam grabbed her shoulders and pleaded, "I just need you to be with me on this one and get the hell out of here."

"Do I keep my job?"

Mr. Amsterdam knew his time was running out, but his stubbornness wouldn't allow him to make a deal with the devil. He shook his head violently. "No!"

Deanna returned to the door and yanked it open. It hit the back wall with a thud. "That's okay! I'll handle this!"

Mr. Amsterdam ran to the door and closed it quietly. "Okay, okay!" He grabbed Deanna's hand and led her across the room to the side door.

She turned to him as they walked, speaking as if nothing had just happened. Tears streamed down her cheek. "All I want is to keep my job."

He stood by the side door, hoping she would come to her senses. "I didn't say you were keeping your job. What I am saying is that I'll give you six months severance pay instead of one month if you'll just leave." His eyes softened, hoping her stance would follow.

She wiped her tear away with a quick swipe and eyed him with a calculating expression while she did quick math. "One year!"

He did some calculating of his own. "Eight months?"

A sharp knock brought his attention back to the door. He glanced at the door and then back at Deanna.

"Okay. One year," he said before opening the door and shoving her through.

I now understood how your whole life could be changed in a matter of seconds. Seconds were like pennies: in the big scheme of things, they didn't seem very valuable.

I got up, adjusted my tie, and yelled for Mrs. Amsterdam to come in.

Mrs. Amsterdam walked toward me with the grace of an Egyptian queen, but possessed the look of the queen of England. She stood five feet even with strong features: a broad nose, square chin, and eyebrows that were penciled into a high arch. She always wore an expensive business suit. Her business attire was usually complemented with a nice string of pearls, or a gold and diamond studded necklace and pendant. Today she sported a cream suit, pearls, and a matching church hat with a brim that flopped as she walked.

I extended my hand. "It's so nice to see you again, Mrs. Amsterdam."

She accepted my hand and spoke softly, "It's nice to see you, Jordan. How have you been doing?"

Her fragrance overpowered what was left of Deanna's scent. She breezed by and headed straight toward her husband.

"You know how it is, Mrs. Amsterdam," I replied.

She smiled in agreement.

Her motherly instincts took over as she rushed to his side, wiping sweat from his brow and sliding her arm around his waist. "What's going on?"

Mr. Amsterdam glanced back at the door that remained shut and took in a few deep breaths before turning to his wife. "What do you mean, what's going on?"

She moved away from him and looked him up and down disapprovingly. "Look at you!"

He glanced at the areas of his body that she had just inspected. "What's wrong with me?"

"Never mind that." Without waiting for a response, she continued, "Your secretary called the house and said that I should come down."

More beads of sweat crept from underneath his hairline. He muttered a few words then fell silent. He looked at his wife, put his hand to his mouth and a barrage of fake coughs escaped his hand. She patted him softly on his back.

"Are you okay, Bill?"

Out of the corner of his eye, he peered at me, silently asking for help.

Let his ass sweat! I wasn't going to be caught up in this mess, but better judgment made me change my mind. I interrupted, "Mrs. Amsterdam, maybe you should take him out of here. He doesn't seem to be feeling too well."

Her right hand quickly found a home on his forehead. Sweat dripped from his badly receding hairline as she checked his temperature. Her hand moved from his forehead to his neck and throat as though she had an extensive background in medicine. Mr. Amsterdam, knowing she was taking the bait, continued his hacking cough until she escorted him toward the front door.

With Mr. Amsterdam hunched over, Mrs. Amsterdam turned and asked, "Can you tell the secretary thank you for asking for me to come and check on him? She said he looked extremely sick and with him being the strong black man he is...well, you know," she said as her words trailed out the door behind her.

Come in and check on him? This shit is getting messed up by the hour. I raced to the side door to see if Deanna had left. When I opened the door, she almost fell through.

At this point, I didn't know which Deanna to expect.

Returning to my desk, I decided to cut to the chase. "What in the hell is going on?"

She took refuge in the seat opposite me and shifted from side to side. "Let me explain," she said softly.

Explain to me why you're fucking your uncle! Explain to me why you're sleeping with the boss? Explain to me why you called it off? I shook my head at the turn of events and begged, "Please tell me what's going on?"

She inched closer and continued, "It's been rough on me lately, Jordan."

My body language showed I felt no pity for her as I maintained an intense glare. I was tired of the fidgeting and the beating around the bush.

My voice was direct and unfamiliar. "Are you fucking your uncle or what?"

Her chestnut eyes narrowed suspiciously as if I had some nerve asking her about her business.

"Yes." She hesitated, and then corrected herself. "I am fucking him, but he's not my uncle."

What? Even though I knew the answer to my question, it still shocked me when the words flowed from her mouth. I didn't know which question I should follow up with. She reached inside her pocketbook and fumbled with a tube of lipstick. The thought of Mr. Amsterdam and Deanna had my head whirling. I didn't know whether to feel sorry for her for dealing with a situation like this, or to feel sorry for him for indirectly paying for sex.

"You got what you wanted, right?" I asked.

"Which is?"

"A year's salary."

Her back straightened and tears crept to her pupils. "You think all I wanted was the money?"

My eyebrow arched inquisitively and I remained silent.

She continued, "Well, it's not. I wasn't the one that approached him. He was the one that came to my school to do a business presentation! He was the one that approached my group about an internship! He was the one that decided to help me out with school and then moved me to the city so I could be closer to him! He is the one who's married, not me!"

I interrupted, "But you're the one who knew he was married. You're the one who was fucking him all this time, and you're the one who wasn't living up to your responsibilities on the job."

Her head fell and her chin slammed against her chest.

I added up everything up and realized that Mr. Amsterdam was the mystery meat that Deanna was always talking about. My stomach churned at the thought.

"He's the married man, right?"

Her eyes remained glued to the ground. She nodded.

"And his wife was the one that called your house, right?"

She nodded again.

"And when you started messing up at the job, he had no choice but to fire you."

Deanna's flailing hand blindly searched for the tissue box located on the table next to her. She wiped and blew her nose loud enough for the people in the next building to hear.

"Can I explain?" She knew her secret was out and it wasn't a pretty one. My mind still searched for the reason behind her escapade with Mr. Amsterdam. I wanted to know more, but at the same time, I didn't.

My response was unemotional. "I'm listening."

"Have you ever been in love with someone, not because of the physical, but because of their knowledge?"

What? I had no clue where she was going with this one, but I shrugged my shoulders as if it could happen, although it hadn't happened to me.

She continued, "Well, when he came to my school, I was amazed at the knowledge that he had. He spoke to a group of two hundred business majors and rattled off figure after figure."

The figure of every woman in the place! 36-24-36. 34-22-32...

"He was explaining to us different business practices, how much capital people needed, and how much they grossed in their first year. I mean, I was impressed at how much he knew and I wanted to learn from him. Then, when he said he needed a few interns that summer, I immediately jumped on it. I went up to him after the seminar and introduced myself. I told him how much I was interested and how glad I was that I had decided to attend his seminar. He said I had the same fire in my eyes that he had in his own eyes quite a few years ago. I ended up interning for his company that summer. The good thing was that I never had to leave the campus because all of the work was on the computer, and the next thing I knew, he offered me a full-time job."

"But when did he tell you that the job entailed other duties?"

"It wasn't like that at first," she uttered defensively.

"How did you get from working with him to sleeping with him?"

She seemed more perturbed as the questioning became more personal. She fiddled with the lipstick before slowly easing it back into her pocketbook. She looked up at me and mumbled something incoherent.

I moved closer. "I couldn't hear you."

She began slower, "I said that I never looked at him like that. He came to the campus a few times to check on our progress. We had small talk and that was pretty much it. By the end of the summer, I had to e-mail him the progress of the three other interns and he returned my e-mails instantly. It was always a nice note thanking me for the great work. He would also comment about the wonderful talks we had. It felt nice to be appreciated. The guys at my school were only interested in one thing, but he was different. I could have male contact without worrying about someone getting in my pants."

I started to comment, but decided the timing wasn't right.

She continued, "And then he offered me a job full-time at twenty-five thousand to start. It wasn't great money, but coming out of college, it had potential. I told him I wouldn't mind leaving North Carolina, but at that time I wasn't financially stable to be on my own. That didn't bother him because in his next breath, he offered to help me out."

"And you didn't think anything was odd about a boss offering to help an intern move?"

"A little bit," she admitted. "But he told me I would be a great asset to the company."

You were definitely a great ass, with a set of titties! If she didn't see the smooth talking from that far, she would never see it. "So you just moved out here, not knowing anyone?"

"I was hungry and trying to get my foot in the door."

"But fucking him to get ahead?" I was amazed at how smart, yet dumb, she was.

"I never dealt with him physically to get ahead. It kinda just happened."

Rain kinda happens! Someone growing on you kinda happens! Fucking doesn't kinda happen! There was no way she was going to convince me that they just kinda ended up in bed together. My pencil tap-danced on the desk as I awaited the next chapter in her book.

Not sure where to take it, she gave me a smug grin and shrugged her shoulders as if to say that was all she was going to tell me.

"That's it?" I asked.

Her shoulders bounced up and down again.

She expressed her grief in getting me wrapped up in everything, but also explained that some things couldn't be avoided. I told her I was sorry to see her leave, but everything happens for a reason. She gave me a hug, wrote down her number, and told me whenever I need to talk she would listen. I told her if she ever needed a recommendation, I would be more than happy to help her out.

"I hope we can continue our conversation another time," she said before exiting.

Chapter 25

TRACI

$\mathcal{T}$oday was a day of cleansing. Traci needed to clean out her closet and empty things and people who were not healthy for her. She had a list of people to call and places to go.

First on her list was Celeste. She didn't realize how much their whole ordeal affected her, so she was definitely a high priority. She didn't need any other things weighing her down.

Sharlana gave her Celeste's number and, surprisingly, didn't ask any questions about it. On the fifth ring, Celeste's answering service came on.

"Celeste, this is Traci. When you get a chance, please give me a call. It's time to lay some things to rest. You extended your hand the last time we met and I..." her voice trailed off. She cleared her throat and continued, "Anyways, we are hanging out tomorrow and I would love for you to come. It's just me and a few of my girls. Call Sharlana and get the location. Bye."

A rush came over her as she hung up the phone.

Next on her list was Solomon. She dialed his number and left a message for him to call her immediately. After her talk with

Sharlana, she realized she had to confront her feelings about Solomon head on. Her heart could no longer lie about what it truly felt. Deep down inside she knew she was in love with Jordan, but Solomon coming back into her life made her question her true feelings. During the past month, she wondered whether it was possible to be in love with one person, while still loving someone else. Jordan controlled her wants and needs, but Solomon controlled her desires. It was time to get her feelings in order.

Minutes later, she phoned Jordan to finally come clean about things, but was surprised to hear about the day that he was having. He went into a brief description of the events that unfolded at the office, but said he'd give her the rest of the details later.

After hearing all of this, Traci decided that now was not the time to be telling him about what she was thinking about. She wanted to explain her sudden mood swings, her unwillingness to bend as of late, and her anger. She decided to go another route.

"Me and the girls are going out to dinner tomorrow. Want to come?"

Jordan politely declined, stating he and his friends were attending a function themselves.

Knowing she had some making up to do, she figured she would be a little more aggressive. "Mind if we tag along?"

"We, who?" he asked suspiciously.

"Me, Sharlana, Precious, and maybe Celeste."

"The one from the-"

"Yes. That's the one."

"I won't ask."

"Thanks." She hesitated for a few seconds, giving him time to think. She didn't want to be too pushy, but she still wanted him to know that she was into him and what he liked. "C'mon. It'll be fun. We haven't all hung out in a bit. First we can go to the function and then we can all head to dinner."

Jordan agreed a minute later and they set a time to meet. Traci hung up with Jordan, called Sharlana, and informed her of the new plans.

****

"I don't have a good feeling about this evening," Sharlana warned as Traci eased into the passenger's side of her car. She continued, "You remember the last time I said this."

A full moon hung in the night sky. Maybe that was making Sharlana act so funny.

"Let it go," Traci said.

Sharlana looked at Traci, smirked, and shot her an inquisitive look. "Let what go?"

Sharlana sped down the street with the music blasting.

"Girl, I ain't hardly thinking about Jordan and that drunk chick with the burgundy shirt and scuffed up shoes that we caught him with last year around April 15th."

They both laughed. A young girl with yellow spandex and a bright red blazer passed as they sped off. They reminisced about some of the odd outfits they wore over the past ten years as they continued toward the club.

Sharlana got out the car and did a full spin to show off her outfit. "Do I look alright?"

Traci checked her makeup in the mirror, laughed, and without acknowledging her spin, responded, "You look fine for a woman that don't give a damn about a man."

"Whatever! I know my big ass is simply divine," she said in a horrible British accent.

Traci slammed her door and walked around to check out Sharlana's outfit. Sharlana sported tight blue bell-bottom jeans with a multi-colored halter-top that fit snug to her little breasts. Traci, on the other hand, chose black jeans that hugged every inch of her hips, paired with a sandy brown T-shirt that made her breasts seem much larger.

"What time is Precious coming?" Sharlana asked.

"She said she would meet us here. Did Celeste call?"

"She said she had plans today, but said that if she could stop by, she would. She also said she was very happy you called and is excited about us hanging out again." She paused and grabbed Traci's arm. "Thanks for calling."

Traci playfully snatched her arm away. "I wasn't calling for you. I'm just trying to let bygones be bygones."

"I knew you weren't that hardcore."

They turned the corner and spotted Precious near the front of the line. They eased in front of Precious, who was dressed in her retro gear: two nappy Afro puffs, a matching faded denim jean outfit with an earth-toned V-neck shirt that showed enough cleavage to have babies from all over calling her momma."

A few people had snide remarks for Traci and Sharlana as they bypassed them and jumped in front of Precious. They chatted while checking out some of the fine brothers that stood in line behind them.

"What about him right there?" Precious asked.

Sharlana looked the man in the blue suit over and shook her head. "I'm not feeling him," she said. She pointed to a Puerto Rican man about six feet, three inches and solid. "I'm feeling that one right there, though."

Sharlana and Precious continued to debate and took it to the leading men in the movies. Precious loved thick chocolate men, while Sharlana preferred the light-skinned slim ones. Traci continued to search for a familiar face. They were fifteenth in line and it was going to be at least another twenty-minute wait. A hint of marijuana smoke traveled through the thick air, causing a few gentle coughs. A police car slowed down, checked the crowd, and pulled off even slower. Two men in back argued about lighting up while the police were near.

"Over here," a voice shouted from the side of the building.

Traci turned, saw Tony waving from a side door, and led Precious and Sharlana toward him. He greeted them with hugs, took them through the side, and escorted them to a table near the front.

Traci slid into her seat. "Tony, where's Jordan?"

Tony looked at his watch and shook his head. "I told him to be here by seven, and if I know that brotha, he'll be here when it's time to leave."

Jordan would be late, but Traci wasn't surprised. Jordan made it a habit of being fifteen minutes late to everything. It was his way of showing people that he moved to the beat of his own drum.

In the background, Bobby Brown's "Roni" blared from the speakers. Sharlana and Precious recalled what they were doing when the song came out. Traci continued to keep an eye open for Jordan.

The Strawberry Letter had only recently opened in the heart of D.C., but it was the new hot spot. Inside, it was dark, cozy, and packed with women of all flavors. The bar filled the left side of the wall with about fifteen stools stretched alongside. Women were occupying all the seats, with men positioned perfectly between them. A long, narrow walkway led to the back of the club where a stage sat off to the right. To the left of the stage were tables that seated four. Every table had a red tablecloth with strawberry candles in the middle. Track lights lit the middle of each table with a warm red beam. The walls were painted a pale red with large strawberry colored L's across the borders. As the club began to fill up, Traci noticed a few familiar faces.

Mario wandered over, spoke to all, and found a seat next to Traci. Sharlana and Precious continued their search for the perfect man while Traci took time to learn more about Mario.

"How long have you been acting, Mario?"

"Not long."

"What got you interested in the business?"

"When I was back home I used to watch American movies over and over again. Do you know what my favorite movie was?"

"What?"

"*Posse.*"

Traci snickered. "*Posse?*"

"Yeah. I like westerns and that was the only updated one they had."

"That's cool. I don't know if Jordan told you, but I used to do a little acting."

His face brightened. "Yeah?"

"Yep. Was kind of good at it, too," she modestly bragged.

"When was this?"

Traci playfully patted his leg and laughed. "Many, many moons ago. I gave it up because I didn't like the pressures of showbiz after a while." Mario's facial expression grew sullen. She didn't want to deter him from the business, especially today. She continued, "But it's not really that bad. You seem to have the drive for it. I say, go for it!"

Mario smiled. Traci excused herself and left for the bathroom.

Mario stood up and slid off his burgundy sweat jacket, revealing muscular biceps that caught the attention of Sharlana and Precious. Watching them admire his biceps, he flexed and positioned them directly under the light so they could get a better view.

Sharlana reached over and lightly ran her fingers against the Chinese writing neatly carved into his skin. "What's it mean?"

Mario glanced at the letters as though he was reading them for the first time. "That's Chinese for Asian Invasion," he replied with a sly grin.

"What are you invading?"

He smiled and inched closer. "Anything I can get my hands on that's worth some value."

Sharlana tried unsuccessfully to hide her grin. "Worth some value, huh?"

"You got it. I'm invading anything I can. I want to invade the movie industry, the talk show circuit, and a pot of that brown sugar," he said with a devilish smile.

Sharlana swirled the tiny red straw around in her apple martini, took a sip, and continued her questioning. She was impressed by his confidence.

"You don't date Asian women?"

He moved closer and opened his mouth. He pointed to a silver crown located in the back of his perfectly straight teeth and whispered, "See that crown?"

Sharlana nodded.

He added, "That's for the sweet tooth I got from eating all that chocolate."

Mario wasn't her type, but he continued to amuse her with his quick wit.

Tony interrupted, "Mario, the producers are networking with other actors over in the corner."

Mario excused himself.

Traci returned and smirked.

Sharlana shot her a similar smirk. "What?"

Traci leaned over. "You feeling him?"

Sharlana ignored Traci's ridiculous statement and finished her drink. She reached for a chicken tender and waved it in front of Traci. "Why do you think I was feeling him?"

Precious added, "Because of the way you were draped all over him."

Sharlana turned and looked at Precious with a look of disdain. "Draped?"

Precious laughed. "Yeah, draped. It's okay to enjoy the man's company. He's kind of nice."

Sharlana admitted, "He is nice, but you know what they say about Chinese men." She displayed the size of a two-inch penis with her hands.

Traci slapped her hands down. "Would you prefer a big dick and a bad attitude?"

Sharlana shook her head slowly. "I just can't do it."

"No one is asking you to marry the man. We're just saying that he's a nice guy," Traci said.

"A nice Chinese guy!" Sharlana threw her hands at the both of them in disgust. "I'm not messing with you guys tonight."

Sharlana and Precious headed toward the bar to find the men they met earlier. Traci stayed back, awaiting the arrival of Jordan.

"Is this seat taken?"

Startled, Traci turned around to see Jordan standing above her with a huge grin and a red rose wrapped in baby's breath. He kissed her cheek, gave her the rose, and took a seat behind her. Traci leaned back against Jordan's chest and exhaled.

"How's the evening been going?" he asked.

"It's been pretty interesting." Traci explained how Mario pushed up on Sharlana. They shared a much-needed laugh. She ordered him a beer and turned her attention to his injured eye. "Your eye is looking better."

He grabbed her hand, directed it to his injured eye, and guided it softly across it. "It's because of that TLC you gave me the other day."

Traci reminisced about the other evening and how well she did in helping him orgasm without penetration. She didn't mind. "I did do a great job, didn't I?"

Jordan's broad smile echoed his sentiments. For the remainder of the evening, they sat as if they were Siamese twins connected at the hip. She sipped on another apple martini and Jordan finished off a shot of Hennessey and another cold beer.

Chapter 26

JORDAN

"You drunk?"

Traci cuddled closer, wrapping her arms around my waist. "No, but I'm feeling nice," she slurred.

"How many drinks did you have?"

Traci rose and began slowly counting on her fingers. "Two before you got here and then another one during dinner." She looked up, gave me a wet kiss on the lips, and sank back into my arms. "Why, are you trying to take advantage of me?"

My hand slid down her arm and underneath her shirt as I massaged the small of her back. In between rubs, I leaned over and kissed her lips, letting my tongue trail to her neck. She tasted sweet. Her scent was even better. Our scents always blended beautifully. It was the mixture of our love. The swapping of our sweat. The marriage of our sexual beings.

As my hand probed deeper into her domain, she wriggled in her seat attempting to elude the relentless pressure I put on her sexuality. "And what if I did try to take advantage of you, would you mind?"

Her hand eased up my shirt. "Depends."

I looked around the lounge area and only a few stragglers remained. The empty stage looked cold and uninviting under the pillar of darkness. There were no more crowds cheering its occupants. The red beams of light were replaced with three distant track lights that hit the ceiling and illuminated what it could. The waitress walked near, but I waved her off. I didn't want to be disturbed. Luckily, the rest of the group had taken the party to another club nearby.

I finished the last of my beer and slid my cold hand underneath Traci's shirt to feel the warmth of her taut stomach. "Depends on what?" I lifted up my shirt and allowed her eager hands to feel my warm chest. The deeper my hand sank into her jeans, the faster her forefinger and thumbs flickered against my nipples.

"How about we just drive." She stood and offered her hand.

I accepted and lifted myself up. "Okay, Ms. Daisy!"

In the car I hit random play and Freddie Jackson began belting, "Rock Me Tonight." For the next five minutes we drove in silence as Freddie took me back to my first love. By the faraway look in Traci's eyes, he took her back, too.

Raindrops trickled on the window as we cruised downtown D.C. in search of the perfect spot. From the left, the Washington Monument called my name. It stood so powerful and alone. The pitch-black backdrop allowed the world to see its pencil shape reach high for the sky. Luther Vandross began the next song with the words, "A chair is still a chair." I pulled Traci close and blended in my off key notes with Luther's perfect rendition of the old Carpenters' song. I didn't know the rest of the words after the first verse, so I hummed in adequate harmony to the remaining chords. The magnetic pull of this powerful building drew me near. As I eased to a halt, I was close enough to see the gray and white marble that made this structure one that was recognized across the country.

Quite a few yards away, I noticed a park bench that stood underneath a huge elm tree. I parked and escorted Traci through the minor shower to our final resting stop.

I sat on the back of the bench and brought Traci close. I could feel her breath against my skin. "You okay?"

She smiled, kissed me lightly on the neck, and hugged me tightly. "Yes." Her fingers found mine and interlocked into a perfect fist. She drew in a deep breath, held her head back and exhaled slowly. "I had a wonderful evening, Jordan."

"You couldn't have said it any better, sweetheart." I turned her around so her back rested against my chest. We both watched from underneath the huge elm tree how the rain dripped on every piece of grass. I wrapped my arms around her tightly, securing her from any harm. I could feel love oozing out of every pore on her body. I wanted to do nothing but make happy this woman that felt so right in my arms.

As we continued to watch the raindrops fall, my lips descended to the nape of her neck. My finger slowly entered the inside of her belly button, only to exit just as gently. Overhead, the tree continued to shield us from the rain that fell heavier and thicker with every passing minute. With not a soul in sight, we became shadows amongst the elements.

The scent of wet grass brushed the air. A squirrel inched near the bench, sat up, and watched.

I cupped her silky bra and felt her nipples harden against my fingers. I drew circles around her areolas without touching her nipples. She reached behind and popped the bra strap. Her breasts dropped an inch before bouncing back into my hands. As the rain continued to drip, her nipples continued to call. They wanted me to make friends and shield them from the cold, but I wouldn't give in. As I continued to caress her firm brown breast, she pressed her butt firmly against Sambuca, attempting to breathe life into someone that already had arisen. With him positioned between her cheeks, she moved with gentle force from side to side.

In back, I was losing control. I reached around, unsnapped her jeans and quickly found the hairs that guarded Sambuca's teammate, his partner in crime...his soul mate.

A single raindrop hit the top of my head, soaked into my scalp and traveled down my forehead. My fingers never left the confines of her panties as she spread wider to allow easier access. The raindrops continued to trickle around us while her luscious lips below spewed viscid drops that coated my forefinger. She let out a few more moans, adjusted her rhythm, and drove her body to meet my fingers. My lips found a wet spot on her neck and clamped down on it with force as my fingers continued to probe the source of her inner wetness.

Cars splashed in the background as they sped by, unaware of the thunder and lightning that struck underneath our tree. My finger glided up her wet slit, pausing at her clitoris that grew with each touch. My thumb and middle finger held her lips hostage as I tantalized her clit up and down in a slow motion with my forefinger. It felt so good to see her writhe, hear her moan, and watch her attempt an escape I knew she didn't want.

Two quick strums of my forefinger brought more whimpering.

"Make love to me," she pleaded.

"Somebody might come."

"Exactly," she moaned.

Our little tree started to give way as God sent down buckets of rain. The leaves buckled under the pressure and allowed more drops to hit my back. Neither one of us was bothered by the sudden shower. It enhanced my sexuality. It piqued my interest in how Traci would respond to the rain.

I positioned her so she could grab the back of the bench. "You want me, huh?" I asked. I spread her legs apart, lifted up the back of her shirt, and began kissing her.

I planted a deep soul kiss on the middle of her back. "Like this?"

Her moan answered the million-dollar question. I continued my assault on her soft brown skin. My tongue trailed to the small of her back, painting long licks of love on her canvas spine. The rain on her back had an odd taste, but didn't deter my mood. After easing her pants down, my tongue purposely swerved to her wet cheeks. They were perfectly separated with rain dancing off each one. My hands greeted each one with a hard, but affectionate slap. Another moan erupted from her lips as I introduced, with a nibble, the dark line that split each chunk of chocolate.

"Damn! That feels so…"

I could feel the heat and smell the Strawberry Breeze as I buried my tongue deeper into her depths. I toyed with her as my tongue started at the top of her split and inched its way closer to her love nest before starting its journey over again. She wanted me to taste her and attempted to take matters into her own hand by arching her back in the air toward my tongue. I moved back, not wanting her to rush me. She tasted so sweet, but I wanted to lick, suck, and taste on my own terms. I lavished the inside of her cheeks with little licks before spreading each cheek wide and letting my tongue travel deeper.

She gasped, "What are you-"

My warm tongue answered by gently entering her anus.

"Oh, God!"

****

The inside of my car was soaked, but I didn't mind after the lovemaking session that had just taken place underneath the shady tree near the Monument. Raindrops in the background blended in smoothly with an oldies mix that blasted from the rear speakers. Up front we sat in silence, not wanting to spoil the moment.

Her cold hands found mine, just as her head hit my shoulder. I kissed her affectionately on the forehead and stroked her hair with my free hand. As my hand slid down her face, I felt a stream of water flowing to her chin.

Tears? I tilted her head toward me. "What's wrong?"

Words formed but seemed scared to leave her mouth. Recently, she'd often cry after our lovemaking sessions. I was under the impression that sex was her getaway from whatever ailed her, but as soon as it was over her sadness returned. I turned the music down and continued to stroke her hair, hoping she would open up.

Summoning courage from within, she sat up and wiped her cheek with her hand. Her voice shook like trees in a gusty wind. "Jordan, you know I love you, right?"

Oh, oh! I had heard these same words many times on the late night talk shows. Those words were always followed by something the other party didn't want to hear.

Our hands remained locked as I answered with a nod.

She continued, "I want to be completely honest, okay?"

I looked out the window and suddenly wished I were walking in the rain without a care in the world. All the macho stuff I fed to my boys was long gone.

She took a deep breath and uttered, "Solomon wants…"

Blood gushed to my temple as my heart pounded through my drenched shirt. My fingernails dug deep into my palm as my balled fist instinctively swung with the might of one hundred men.

Traci let out a piercing scream. For a minute the rain seemed to stop and take notice. The Monument shook.

That fucking Solomon! She brought this shit on herself, Styles! I was amazed at how his name was always popping up. My eyes remained closed as her loud cries turned to a soft whimper.

"I'm sorry, Jordan," she whispered.

My hand grazed the side of my face and I felt something wet trickling down my cheek. I rubbed some of the fluid between my fingers and tasted it. *Phew! Water.* My sense of reality started to come back as I shook off the cobwebs. Music filtered in with the raindrops lightly hitting the windshield as the soft cries of the night crept around us.

"Oh, my God," she screamed.

Fear interrupted cool thoughts of my next move. My eyelids opened and I began to check out my surroundings. I pulled my throbbing right hand toward my face to inspect the dull pain that shot from my wrist into my fingers. What in the hell just happened? Fear quickly turned to panic as I quickly turned to my right.

Her eyes met mine with horrid terror. I scanned her face and saw swollen eyes from crying, but no blood. I immediately drew my hand to my face again.

"Are you okay?" she asked weakly.

I attempted to close my hand, but halfway through, a pain shot all the way through my forearm. The middle knuckle uncharacteristically slumped to the left.

Traci bent over and grabbed something off the ground. I tried to make a fist again, but the pain stopped my motion halfway through. I looked at my bloodied knuckle and searched for the origin of the blood.

Traci dropped something into my lap.

Instantaneously my eyes fell to my lap. The rearview mirror was cracked, sitting in my lap. She reached into her pocketbook and began wiping off my knuckles.

"Are you okay, Jordan?"

Embarrassed that I just injured my knuckle on the rearview mirror, I looked at her out the corner of my eye. Barely audible, I responded, "I'm fine."

Solomon! Every time I turned around, his name was being said. If his name was spoken in my presence again, I would try to kill the messenger.

Blood still trickled from the cut as I started the car, gripped the wheel firmly, and eased between a few raindrops. The Monument remained still, watching us leave the park.

I pulled to the last traffic light inside the park and asked, "What about Solomon?"

Traci's fingers began strumming a beat on her knee while she searched for answers outside the car.

The light remained red. "What about Solomon?" I repeated firmly.

Her hands slammed together and she began cracking every knuckle she owned. In a tone that was soft and almost apologetic, she started, "I know you're tired of hearing about him. I am tired of it too, Jordan, but…"

"But?"

Her hand found my bouncing knee and tried unsuccessfully to stop it with a light massage.

The light finally changed. I peeled off.

"You love him?" The Volvo sped down a dark side street before exiting to where street lamps occupied every block.

She took a deep breath and let it out with ease. "Let me explain."

My words exited deliberately with conviction. "Do you love him?"

She hesitated. "Yes."

The Volvo screeched to a standstill after running through a stop sign. Luckily, there were no cars in sight. My hands tightened around the steering wheel causing more blood to ooze from my knuckles.

Her hands weakly gripped my arm as she drew close to me and tried to divert my attention from the road. "Let me explain," she pleaded softly.

Using my hand as a stop sign, I commanded instant compliance.

I continued to look straight ahead. Fog crept and lingered in front. I felt evil. "Get the fuck out of my car!"

Traci's innocent look turned to a look of defiance. "Are you out of your mind?"

Am I out of my mind? "Get the fuck out of my car," I repeated.

"And how am I supposed to get home?" she asked.

"Oh, I don't know. Maybe you can-" I paused and looked her directly in the eye, "call Solomon!"

She folded her arms and sank deeper into her chair. "I'm not getting out and walking in the rain. You picked me up, so you can bring me home!"

I nodded my head slowly. "Okay. You want me to put your ass out, huh?"

She smacked her lips and continued to stare straight ahead.

Oh! She isn't moving, huh? Today was going to hopefully be the first and last day I would have to put a female out of my car. I drove a few feet to the nearest parking spot. Underneath a few trees, we sat alone.

"Are you getting out?" I asked.

Her annoyed look remained the same as she sat motionless.

Cold rain hit my half-dried shirt as I leapt out the car. The enormous drops sent a wave of goose bumps down my arm, making me angrier. I sprinted around the front and shouted, "Get out."

I looked around to make sure we were still alone before grabbing the passenger side door handle. A quick jerk on the handle left me outside. With every unsuccessful tug at the door, the rain came down heavier.

I looked through the fogged window and saw her mouth crease to a sly grin. Not wanting to further injure my hand, my wet fist tapped lightly on the window. With music blaring from the inside, I mouthed so she could read my lips, "Open the fucking door!"

Another grin erupted as she inched over to the driver's seat. Seconds later the Volvo purred.

She's starting my car? It was like being in a horror movie that I didn't want to star in. Watching her intently watch me, made me realize I wasn't getting anywhere with my present strategy. After inhaling deeply a few times, I decided it was time to be a little more rational.

When she noticed I had calmed down, she opened the driver's side window enough for me to hear her, but not enough to stick my hand through.

"I'll open the door if you promise to listen to what I have to say and drive me home."

Take her home, Styles! I didn't want to ride with Traci and the ghost of Solomon. I didn't want to stay in the rain any longer, either. I walked back around to the driver's side and agreed.

She grabbed the door handle. "Promise?"

"Whatever!"

"I'm not going to open the door unless you promise to listen and take me home."

She had some nerve to be giving orders when she was in the wrong and she was without a car. I wanted to get back into my car as quickly as possible and bring her ass home just as quickly.

After I gave her my word, she unlocked the door and jumped back into her seat. I quickly opened the door and hopped back in. I turned the heat on and began driving immediately toward her house.

No one spoke for five minutes as I weaved in and out of traffic that was cluttered due to an accident.

She blurted, "I love him, but I'm in love with you."

My eyes rolled to the back of my head.

"Did you understand what I just said?" she asked.

"I promised I would listen to you and take you home. There was no agreement for me to say anything."

She nodded. "Fair. Just hear me out." She paused, turned down the music and began again. "I love you so much, Jordan. Solomon is not someone I want in my life. I don't even know why his name keeps coming up because he means nothing to me. Can't you understand that you are my world? You are who I think about every day. It hurts that I can't show you how much I really love you. It hurts that you don't believe me. It hurts that…"

"You love another man," I added.

Traci remained mute. She didn't defend nor oppose the statement. It hurt that she didn't put up a fight. My heart sank deep into my stomach. Bile crept to my tongue. I wanted desperately to cry my last cry, but my pride wouldn't let her know that she had hurt me. Pride wouldn't allow me to let these feelings surface, but somehow I had to get out the anger and bitterness.

"You want me to talk, right?" I asked. My tone was no longer filled with concern. It was time to go on the offense. I wanted to put her on the stand so I knew where to go. "I need some answers from you."

Her hung head, sunken shoulders and poor posture showed defeat.

"You love him?"

"Yes." Her answer was short and she added no further insight into it.

"But, you're in love with me, right?"

She nodded.

"I'm not trying to misinterpret between a nod and a shake. You're in love with me, right?" I repeated.

"Yes."

"And you love him, too, right?"

Her voice was strained. "Yes."

"Do you love him because he's your first love?"

"Yes."

"Do you love him because he's your soul mate?"

"No."

"Have you thought about getting back with him?"

"That wouldn't work."

"That's not what I asked. I said, have you thought about getting back with him?"

"No."

"You wish you would've had his baby?"

She stopped breathing momentarily and a single tear trickled down her cheek. She didn't answer. My soul cringed. My speed increased to ninety miles an hour in a fifty-five mile an hour zone. I wanted to get her home as soon as possible. I didn't want to hurt anymore. Didn't want to feel the pain in my heart that went from a dull throb to a horrid stabbing.

"Do you wish you would've had his baby?" I repeated.

Silence from her lips allowed me to make my own assumption.

"Hear me out, Jordan!" she wailed. "I'm getting everything situated. He won't be a problem any longer."

I continued to drive in silence.

"He said he would put your things back in as soon as I ..." Her voice trailed off.

"As soon as you what?"

"As soon as I ..."

"See him again?"

"It's not like that."

"If you see the man again, don't bother calling me. As a matter of fact, Traci, I've got nothing else to say. Go get that sorry ass nigga!"

Traci folded her hands together and cried softly. My arms wanted to reach out and console her, but pride wouldn't let me slip up. It was now that I realized I was chasing a woman that had never gotten over her ex-boyfriend.

****

"It's karma," Deanna said.

I adjusted my headset and cruised Northbound I-95. Anger caused my temples to throb uncontrollably as I switched my ten and two handgrip on the steering wheel to a pimped out, one finger, Mack Daddy grip. I threw on some hardcore rap, adjusting my attitude and my head nod. *Fuck that tired ass nigga!* Two encounters with this brotha and nothing was going right. During the first encounter, the timing wasn't right. The second, Kendal watched two grown men fighting for a loose ball, unaware of the disturbed nature of their relationship. Either way, I was not about to be made a fool of again. While my ego wanted me to find him and beat his ass, my common sense reminded me that I was the other guy on a few occasions. Was Solomon to blame or was he just being a man? *He's just in the wrong place at the wrong time!*

"You there?" Deanna asked.

"I'm here. What were you saying?"

"Karma."

"What about karma?" I asked.

"Me calling you at a time when you needed to speak to someone. Something told me to call you and it worked out because I think you needed to hear from me. Needed me to calm you down a little. Not to mention, that stuff that happened with Monica is karma, too."

"Yeah?"

"It's coming back."

"That's just that 'what comes around goes around shit!' Why are you telling me this anyway?"

"Don't know. Just making conversation." She paused. "Where you going?"

"Nowhere...fast!"

"Why don't you-"

"Oh, shit!" My heart thumped, I popped back up and resumed my ten and two grips.

"What happened?"

I eased my foot off the pedal, slowing down considerably. "Cops."

"Where?"

"In back." When it rained, it poured buckets. I pulled over to the shoulder and awaited my death sentence.

"Why did they stop you?"

"Dunno."

"Were you speeding?"

"Don't have a radar detector. Maybe."

"Remain calm," she instructed.

"Thanks for the advice," I said sarcastically. As I spoke, my eyes were transfixed on the carnival lights in my rearview mirror. "You get stopped often?"

"Once or twice. Showed some cleavage and got out of it."

The police officer got out and walked toward me. I couldn't make out a face because of the blinding white light.

"License and registration!"

"I'll call you back," I whispered as I slid the headset off. I reached for my license and registration and offered it to the officer with my left hand, not looking up, but looking directly ahead of me. "Why was I stopped, officer?"

Her voice was husky and firm. "Seventy-seven in a fifty-five, sir." She snatched the papers from my hand.

The officer was a black woman, mid-thirties with unusually large lips. No perfume filtered through the air and her tie leaned to the left. I attempted to impose my mojo as she scanned my license and registration. I cleared my throat and tried a different approach.

"Can I ask how many miles over the speed limit do you let people go?"

She adjusted her thick horned rimmed glasses on her square face and chuckled under her breath. "Usually nine to thirteen miles over, why?"

I gave her the smile. Showed all the teeth and dimples, searching hard to make eye contact. "If I was doing sixty-nine would you have stopped me?"

She didn't reciprocate my warmth. "Depends."

"On what?"

"On if you were a woman or not," she said before whirling away and walking back to her car. A minute later she returned, yellow slip dangling from her hand. Just when I thought I had her on the ropes, it all came crashing down.

She handed me my fate and gave a sarcastic chuckle. I begrudgingly accepted it before easing between the raindrops. I snapped my headset back in and phoned Deanna.

"Karma, huh?"

Deanna laughed. "Yeah, why?"

"I was just telling someone the other day that I never get stopped. Then I said that if the officer was a woman, I would be able to do my thing and get out of it."

She laughed again. "The officer was a she?"

"Yeah."

"And you didn't work it?"

"Tried to. She wasn't feeling it."

"She blind?"

"Worse."

"How?"

"Strictly clitly and all about the breasts."

She guffawed. "Damn!"

Awkward silence erupted.

She continued, "I'm strictly dickly and all about the balls."

Strictly dickly? "Did you say-"

"Strictly dickly? Yes!"

I had no comeback. *Don't go for the bait, Styles.*

"And don't forget about the balls," she added with a twinge of humor.

Her humor tickled me, her openness intrigued me, and her directness excited me.

"Where you at?" I asked.

"My skin. If I jumped out, would you jump in?"

"Depends on-" My signal faded. I didn't know if that was more karma creeping, but I wanted to finish the conversation. Wanted to hear more about this karma. Wanted to hear more about strictly dickly. Definitely wanted to hear more about the balls. Wanted some female companionship without all the bullshit. Wanted to be the Mandingo that she spoke to her friends about behind closed doors. Wanted to pump away my frustration with long, deep, purposeful strokes. Wanted to tease, tickle, and connect. Wanted to fuck like a wild man in the rain. Wanted to hear my name being called like the king of the jungle. Wanted to roar when I came, and spoon when I was done.

I hit redial. "Signal faded. You there?"

She hummed a suspicious hum. "Thought you were scared."

My forehead wrinkled as I slid to another lane. My grip returned to the gansta lean. "Of what?"

"The conversation."

"Never that."

"You coming over?"

"For what?"

"Whatever you want."

My mind chased, but a cooler head prevailed. "Can we talk?"

The excitement left her voice. "We can talk."

"Need anything before I come?"

"To cum before you do."

We laughed. She gave me the address. I told her I was about twenty minutes away. I did a U-turn on the highway figuring who gets stopped twice in one day? The twenty-minute drive had me thinking about situations that I wanted to avoid. Loud music didn't take my mind off the matters at hand, so I turned the music off and concentrated. Wanted to meet my demons head on. I wasn't afraid of the Big Bad Wolf.

I phoned Tony.

After telling me he was doing nothing, I went on a ten minute rant about life. I explained that I was sick of hearing of Solomon, sick of sexing Traci and hearing about Solomon, sick of the bullshit Traci was giving me, and sick of my job. Tony tried unsuccessfully to explain that Traci was going through some things, she needed to vent, and at least she was honest enough to bring up the subject. That did little for my anger. I expressed that I didn't want to hear about Solomon, and if she went to see him, it was over.

"You gave her an ultimatum?"

"Yup," I said without remorse.

"That'll only push her away."

"Or make her ass smarter. I'm not going to sit back and wait for her to figure out if she wants this man. You think I'm stupid?"

"Never said that."

"What you saying?"

"You don't need to give her an ultimatum."

"Now that I really think about it, it really wasn't."

"What was it?"

"It was a motherfuckin' either-or!"

We both laughed.

"Either-or? You better just let it go," Tony advised. "Maybe this is her last temptation before she'll finally settle down with your ass."

"Last temptation?"

"Yeah. Kinda like that red-boned stripper at your bachelor party."

"We fucked!" I reminded him.

"She was supposed to be your last temptation before marriage."

"And you see how that went."

"Doubt if Traci is like that."

"I ain't putting anything past her."

"What you gonna do?"

"Right now, I'm going to meet Deanna."

"When?"

"Now."

"To do what?"

"Didn't know I needed your permission, Dad!"

"Glad you finally realized who was laying pipe to your mom all these years."

"She does have a thing for overweight chocolate brothas with chronic halitosis."

"Whatever. Where are you meeting her?"

"Her house."

"Shit!"

"You tellin' me. The last statement she made was about being strictly dickly."

"Strictly dickly?"

"And all about the balls."

"What? You bringing a condom, right?"

"I ain't fucking with her like that."

"Why are you going then?"

"I just needed to talk to a woman."

Silence.

"And she's untouchable. I used to work with her," I added.

Silence.

"Hell, I won't do anything I don't want to do."

More silence.

"Look, Tone, I'm here now. I gotta run."

I hung up the phone and pulled into the parking lot of her building. The rain had slowed to a slight drizzle and the fog seemed to follow me. It was already ten-thirty and I knew I didn't want to stay long. Eleven-thirty to midnight was my limit. I silenced the Volvo, inspected my swollen knuckle, and hurried to her door.

Deanna answered as I reached for the doorbell. "Hey, Jordan." She hugged me tight and kissed my cheek.

Get those nipples off of me! "Hello, Deanna." My tone was dry, but my heart pumped fierce energy into my veins. I followed her into the house, watching the back of her sweats switch from side to side.

"It's a studio," she explained as I entered the house.

The room was huge. The walls were salmon colored with no pictures hanging. A large burgundy sectional and loveseat sat in the far right corner. Near the door was a small black kitchen table with two chairs sitting across from each other. A black candle sat in the middle of the table and gave off the peculiar scent of cedar. Opposite the sectional was a nineteen-inch color television that blasted the news. Next to the television was a petite sturdy black computer stand that housed a sleek, black computer.

She pointed toward the sectional. "Have a seat."

I walked over, took a seat on the couch, and grabbed the remote lying next to me. As she walked to the kitchen, I surfed channels.

I yelled, "You got something to-"

"Right here." She handed me a cold Molson Ice.

That's what I'm talking about! "Thanks."

She sat next to me and sipped from her own. A wave of fresh sweet fragrance breezed by my nostrils. I inhaled, cleared my bad thoughts, and stopped at a basketball game on television. We drank beers and watched the game for a few minutes.

Enthusiastically, she shouted, "Shaquille is killing the Bulls."

"Huh?"

She pointed at the television. "Look, he's hitting them with all the low post moves."

"What you know about low post moves?"

She smiled, continuing to watch the game. "Used to play."

I turned around and sized her up. She was a little thick and didn't seem like the athletic type. "Used to play where?"

"High school and two years of college."

"What happened to the other two years of college?"

She stood, lifted her sweats to her knee, and pointed to a nasty scar below her kneecap. "It's an injury I got in college."

Her bronze calf looked like she still hit the gym. Her leg was lean and powerful.

"You don't play for fun?"

"Nope. Sometimes I shoot around."

"One day we gotta shoot around," I suggested.

"No problem."

I leaned back and let out a loud sigh. She inched closer.

I wanted to ask her more questions about her and Mr. Amsterdam, but decided against it. I was enjoying our conversation, the beer, and the game.

Deanna stood up, walked around, and began massaging my shoulders. Her hands dug deep into my pain. I tensed at first, but gave in to the good feeling.

"You're tight."

I moaned as the massaging only got better. I leaned forward so she could rub my shoulders and lower back.

"I know I'm tight. Been under a lot of stress lately."

She continued to massage.

"Haven't had one of these in a while," I said.

Her hands dug deeper.

"I really needed this."

"What's going on, Jordan?"

"Sure you want to hear about it?"

Her hand slid down the left side of my neck, down my arm until it reached the tips of my fingers. It was feeling so good that I didn't want to say anything to make her stop.

"Why don't I rub and you tell me anything you want," she said.

Her thumbs drew deep circles into my neck. My back arched and goose bumps traveled across my body.

"I'm having female issues." Instead of responding, she dug deeper into my shoulder blades. My chin hit my chest and I continued, "Traci is hanging with her ex-boyfriend and I'm on the back burner."

I needed someone to tell me Traci was an idiot. Needed someone to comfort me and tell me that she would take me if she were in Traci's shoes. Needed to make love without hearing anyone's name but my own.

She lifted my shirt up to reach my lower back. It felt so good. *She doesn't work for you anymore, Styles.* I wasn't doing anything wrong.

"What's going on with her ex-boyfriend?" Deanna asked.

"You want details?"

"No. Just wanna know why you're so mad." Her thumbs and forefinger formed a W as she moved them seductively from my lower back to my shoulder blades. She repeated this motion over and over until I slumped further.

"He's invading my space. Making me fight for someone that's already mine. Making me hear his name more than I should. He's pissing me the fuck off!"

"And why does she continue to speaking with him if she knows it pisses you off?"

"If I knew that I wouldn't be here."

The easy glide of her fingers ceased. My breathing stopped as I searched for ways to get out of my last statement. I didn't want to make her out to be a substitute, but I didn't want her thinking there was a chance, either. She removed her hands and left my shirt up, allowing cold air to hit my warm back.

I pulled my shirt down and stood to face her. "I didn't mean it like that."

Her eyes glossed. "That's cool. I understand."

"I meant I wouldn't be here talking about it."

She twisted her lips.

I extended my hand. "Accept my apology?"

"I don't shake hands with friends," she said with a courtesy smile.

I opened my arms wide and invited her to embrace me.

She reluctantly moved closer and positioned herself between my arms. Her hands clasped around my waist as she laid her head on my chest. We stood silent, both caught in the moment, enjoying the mood. Her hands slid underneath my shirt and caressed my back again. No music played, yet we moved to the uneasy sound of our heartbeats. Her hands moved up my body. I could smell her perfume, feel her breasts press firmly against me, and sense the slight weather change. She sang softly, pressed even closer.

I whispered, "I guess this was better than a generic hug, huh?" I pulled away and noticed her nipples saluting me. Sambuca jumped.

She grabbed my hands and swung them slightly. "I guess it was," she admitted. "One more hug?"

Don't get too close, Styles! Sambuca can't take too much of this.

She wrapped her hands around my neck, the room began to spin, and I attempted to move away.

She persisted.

I took a deep breath and relented under pressure.

She brought me close and whispered, "She doesn't know what she's giving up. I hope that other man is worth it."

Solomon's presence clouded my judgment.

Her hips swiveled to meet mine.

Sambuca grew to full strength.

She stood on her toes, kissed me on the cheek, and then found my lips.

Her lips were soft and moist. It felt good, but wrong. I drew back only to find out her lips followed.

I groaned. "We can't do-"

Her hand slid down my stomach and wrapped around Sambuca firmly.

"We can't do what?" she asked.

"This," I responded weakly as I slid myself backwards.

Chapter 27

TRACI

$\mathcal{S}$harlana laughed hysterically. "He tried to kick you out the car?"

"That ain't the half of it," Traci explained. "After I let him back in, he started asking me do I love Solomon." She paused, twirled a mound of spaghetti onto her fork, and slid it into her mouth. "Then he asked if I wanted to keep Solomon's baby."

Traci wanted to talk about what happened, so after work they decided to head to Friday's for happy hour. All the tables were taken, so they ate at the bar.

"Can you believe that?"

Sharlana concentrated on a tall black man with an expensive black suit who watched the basketball game on the big screen.

"Did you hear what I just said?"

Sharlana pulled her hair to the back and redid her ponytail as she continued to stare. "I heard what you just said."

"Well?"

"Honestly, T, you're messing this one up all on your own." Sharlana lifted her right hand toward the sky and laughed. "God forgive me for saying this, but I'm on Jordan's side this time."

Traci continued to twirl spaghetti. After sucking down the last of it, she wiped her mouth, pushed her plate away, and stated firmly, "I'm going on Friday!"

Sharlana stirred her drink and continued to stare at the suit man. "To where?"

"To meet Solomon at the Hilton in downtown D.C. and tell him that I'm happy and it's time for him to move on."

"You can just call him on the phone and say that."

"I can't. This is one of the demons of my past that I have to lay to rest. Not to mention, I promised to meet him if he returned the furniture."

"Tell him you'll meet him after you get the furniture back!"

"He said his guys couldn't deliver it until Saturday."

"Gotta give it to him, he is a slick SOB. You gonna tell Jordan?"

A wave of people passed and the noise level raised another notch. A large white woman with cheap perfume and a hideous overbite slid between Traci and Sharlana without an apology. She ordered a Bloody Mary, and then turned to face the crowd.

Sharlana grew tired of looking around the lady to have a conversation. "Excuse you!" she barked.

The lady sized up Sharlana, issued a generic apology, and stepped to the side.

"Are you going to tell Jordan?" Sharlana repeated.

Traci slid her stool closer. "I don't know."

"Don't you think you should be up front about things before they blow up in your face?"

Traci reminded her she had everything under control. She just needed a little more time.

"I don't understand you, T. You're telling me one thing, but acting another way. For five minutes, please be honest with me and with yourself."

Traci's head hung low, her pride shot to shit and her cover blown. She wanted to be honest and confront her feelings head-on, but something was holding her back.

Her breath was short. "Solomon is the man I have been in love with all my life. I loved him before I met him. Loved him when I met him. I loved him at that party. Loved him when he shit on me for so many years." A tear streamed down her cheeks, but she didn't bother wiping it away. Sharlana watched as Traci opened wounds that had never healed.

Sharlana consoled, "I know it's hard, T."

"And the funny thing about it all," she said, pausing to blow her nose, "was that I found something in Jordan that helped me replace Solomon. Jordan was my rock, my savior, and my man. But like you said, they are just alike. I don't want him to be a substitute for Solomon. I want to know that I can walk away from Solomon because I don't want him. But what's so funny is that while I'm trying to clear my conscience by myself, I might end up alone. I mean, I told Jordan that I had trust issues because of that Monica chick, but she was only an excuse lately for me to be comfortable enough to talk to Solomon. Sharlana, I don't know what to do."

Sharlana hugged Traci and whispered, "Yes, you do! You're halfway there now. Knowing the problem is half the battle. Whatever you choose, I'm here for you." She smiled and gave Traci a hug. "Next time, just pick a white man and we won't be having all these problems."

They both left for the bathroom to freshen up. When they got back to their seats, the bartender approached Traci and slid her another drink. "Compliments of the lady in the black dress over there," he said pointing to the opposite end of the bar.

Traci searched for the lady in the black dress. She looked around a few people that stood in front, but still couldn't get a good view of her mystery person. Traci pulled the drink close and took a whiff of it.

"What's that?" Sharlana asked.

Traci wrinkled her nose and fiddled with the straw. "A cosmopolitan, I guess."

Sharlana joined Traci's quest to find the origin of the hand that flailed widely in the air. After taking a few steps to her left, Traci spotted her mystery buyer.

Sharlana's face wrinkled. "Who's that?"

Traci pushed the drink to the side. "Deanna."

"Who?"

"Jordan's secretary."

Sharlana looked back at Deanna and brought the drink to her nose. "And what did she decide to put in your little drink here?"

Traci searched the glass for foreign objects. "I don't know, but I wouldn't be caught dead drinking it!"

She watched Deanna from across the bar. She didn't look as cute as she did before. Her hair was frizzed, her shirt wrinkled, and eyes subdued. Traci thought about Deanna and the t-shirt and had to calm herself down. She wanted to put her in her place, but she knew it was a dead issue.

Traci snapped her fingers to get the bartender's attention. He rushed over. She jotted something on a piece of paper, wrapped it around the glass, and asked the bartender to return the drink to Deanna.

"What did you write?" Sharlana asked.

"I told her to leave it alone."

After receiving the drink, Deanna unwrapped the note, read it, smirked, and rose slowly. She adjusted her hair before heading their way.

Sharlana rolled up her sleeves. "Want me to handle this?"

Traci grabbed her arm and assured her, "I got this."

Traci waited for Deanna to walk halfway before she got up to meet and greet her properly. Her palms began to sweat. She wiggled her fingers in anticipation.

As Deanna neared, an older black gentleman wearing a green short set and matching alligator shoes grabbed her arm. "Want something to drink?" he asked.

Deanna's voice was irate. She snatched her hand away. "Excuse you?"

He confidently twirled his unlit cigar and relinquished his grip. "Just wanted to buy you a drink," he said.

Deanna declined and continued her journey.

Traci walked up to Deanna and without waiting for eye contact, shouted, "Thanks, but no thanks."

Deanna's intensity matched Traci's. The tone of her voice rivaled that of her counterpart. "Is there a problem, Traci?"

Traci glared at Deanna, wanting to strangle her, but better judgment wouldn't allow her to do something stupid. "Maybe."

A waiter slid between them carrying a tray of fresh mozzarella sticks. The aroma danced around Traci's nostrils and reminded her that she hadn't had enough to eat. Deanna stepped aside and continued her frigid stare. "Listen Traci, I'm not here to start a fight. It was a good-natured gesture to ease the tension."

Traci's eyes harbored resentment. "I don't need any more friends!" Traci, angered by Deanna's weak attempt at friendship, turned around and began counting her steps back to Sharlana.

"I heard you talking about Jordan," Deanna shouted.

Traci's feet, heart and breathing stopped simultaneously. Heat flashes caused dizziness as she barely managed to turn fully around. Her head tilted toward the left, she squinted, and walked slowly toward Deanna. She gritted her teeth and asked, "What did you just say?"

Deanna drew a deep breath and her eyes shifted from left to right before looking directly at Traci. Her words were chosen carefully.

"I was just saying, I heard you talking about Jordan and-"

"When?"

"About fifteen minutes ago. I was at the table directly behind you," she explained pointing in the direction of Sharlana. Traci turned and saw a table, but could only make out the back of a man's head.

Traci's recollection of her conversation was vague at best. She couldn't recall what she was talking about. "What did you hear about Jordan?"

Deanna's laugh was perturbed. She did a shoddy job of concealing her true feelings, as she looked everywhere but at Traci. She clasped her hands together and smiled. "I just heard his name and not too many people around here have a name like that." Her demeanor changed. "I didn't recognize you at first, and when I realized who you were, I didn't want to interrupt your dinner. I just heard his name and popped my head up. And for the misunderstanding we had at his house, I just wanted to buy you a drink."

Traci was cautious but happy Deanna hadn't heard too much. Happy that she could make this entire misunderstanding blow over in a matter of minutes. Traci extended her hand and gave an artificial smile.

"I'm sorry, Deanna. I'm trying to get through so much right now and I'll admit that I am getting a little jumpy." She tried to read Deanna's thoughts, but couldn't quite get a handle on them. She didn't want to add fuel to the fire, so she decided to smooth things over and get back to her seat. "Can I buy you a drink?"

Deanna smiled and politely declined. "I ordered an appetizer and it should be up soon." She accepted Traci's hand. "But the next time I offer to buy you a drink, you have to promise to accept."

Traci's smile was genuine. "I promise. You sure you don't want to stay for a bit?"

"I got a date." They gave each other respectful nods and went their separate ways.

On her way back, Traci thought about Deanna and Jordan's relationship and the nature of her own relationship with Solomon. She hoped they had nothing similar to her and Solomon's relationship. She was going to do everything in her power to make the situation right. She knew what came around, went around.

"What happened?" Sharlana quizzed as soon as Traci hit the seat.

Traci ignored the question and watched Deanna walk back to her seat, finish her drink, and call for the bartender. She turned to Sharlana and whispered, "I don't know what happened. She said she was sitting at the table in back of us."

Sharlana's forehead wrinkled in disbelief. "In back of us where?"

Traci turned and pointed to the table a foot away.

"Did she hear us?"

"She said she heard his name, but that's it."

"Damn!"

Traci turned her attention back to Deanna. She watched her speak to the bartender, point in their direction, and smile.

"She said she didn't hear anything. Did I say something stupid?" Traci's facial expression showed hope, but her body language showed despair.

Sharlana rubbed her chin to jog her memory. "You were talking about going to visit Solomon."

Traci's hand flew to her opened mouth. "Oh shit! I was!"

Sharlana added, "But she said she didn't hear anything, right?"

Traci's wavering nod wasn't convincing.

The bartender returned with a huge bottle of Moet inside a bucket filled with ice and two champagne glasses. "The lady across the way said you promised."

Traci shot Sharlana a quick glance before looking in Deanna's direction. She had a similar bottle of Moet in front of her. She raised her empty champagne glass in the air to toast. The bartender continued to wait for confirmation.

"I did promise," she said to him. He left and Sharlana slapped Traci playfully on the arm.

"I told you not to worry."

Traci bothered by her fooled assumption, put her glass up for a mock toast with Deanna. After toasting, Deanna grabbed her appetizer and bottle of Moet, and headed for the door.

Traci's body sank into the high back chair at the bar. *After Friday, it'll all be over..* Deanna's presence reaffirmed that something had to be done before all hell broke loose.

Traci wiped fake sweat from her brow before wiping it on Sharlana, joking, "That was a close one."

"What are you going to do with all that champagne?"

"Call Jordan and have a much needed date!"

Sharlana guzzled down the rest of her drink. "Want me to wait for you?"

Traci inspected the huge bottle, smiled, and said, "I'm good. Thanks for keeping me company."

They hugged, Sharlana split, and Traci snapped for the bartender.

He smiled, slammed the bill upside down on the bar, and cleared away a few glasses in front of him.

"Three hundred and twenty-two dollars!"

Chapter 28

JORDAN

"Who is it?" I yelled.

No one answered.

I yelled again, "Who?" It was ten thirty in the evening, and someone was about to be screamed on.

The bell continued to chime, and no one continued to answer. Kendal was in his room asleep, and I was lying on the couch switching from sleep to the basketball game. I counted to three and pushed myself off the couch. Whoever it was should have the decency to answer when ringing somebody's bell. On the way to the door I tried to hold back a yawn, but it hurt my nose and jaw, so I let it ease out while I stretched my arms and arched my back. My forefinger and thumb touched the outside of both eyes, and after a long, slow wipe, met at the bridge of my nose.

The bell chimed again.

My voice matched my aggravated mood. "Who?"

I looked through the peephole and saw a few cars parked in front. Hesitantly I opened the door. *What the hell is this?* I looked down and noticed a huge bottle of Moet with a note and card key attached to it.

Meet me at the Hilton at midnight!

Room 515

****

I parked, checked my pocket for the key and entered the front door of the Hilton. For a Wednesday evening, there was a lot of action going on. They were having some sort of party in the ballroom, where people filtered into the lounge area. Under the archway that separated the lounge from the hotel's front desk area was a white man wearing black leather pants, groping the ass of a tall slender black man wearing an oversized black three-piece suit. They stopped as I walked by, gave me a nod, and continued as I passed. The closer I got to the elevators, the more men spilled out into all parts of the lounge area. There were a couple of Asian men dancing erotically against a window while three white men danced together, puffing on cigarettes near the side door.

I got to the elevators and waited for one to arrive.

"You've got a pretty big one," a man said.

I turned around and noticed a gangly man in his forties that looked like Mr. Amsterdam. He leaned against the wall and continued to press the up and down buttons.

He smiled and nodded toward the bottle of Moet. "I meant the bottle," he said. "Looking for someone?"

I turned back around and continued to watch the elevator numbers descend. "I'm good!"

His finger paused on the down button. "You going up or down?"

My fist clenched, temple throbbed, and I slowly counted to ten. His hand continued to click the down button as he cleared his throat. I turned and walked toward the stairs.

Five flights later, I was out of breath, but closer to my baby!

I walked down the quiet hallway and searched for room 515. There was not a sound to be heard as I followed the arrows toward the room. I pulled the white plastic key from my inner jacket pocket and twirled it between my fingers as I walked closer to my destination.

Half of me was nervous, while the other half remained ready for anything and everything. The closer I got to the door, the crazier my thoughts became. What if Solomon was the one that left the bottle and he wanted me to hear him and Traci in the room? What if Traci wanted to explain that it was over? What if that guy at the elevator actually left the note at the house? My head hurt. I thought of the mystery bottle and the key, and there I was, going somewhere to deal with something.

I pressed my ear to the door and heard pianos playing lightly in the background. After three deep breaths, I slid the key into the lock, pulled it out, and watched the clear light change to green.

I pushed the door open, entered the dimly lit room, and waited for the guillotine to swing and chop off my head. *Phew!* The suite was large and desolate, but warm and inviting at the same time. I looked to my left and saw a half-kitchen. I tiptoed by and entered the living room where a trail of smoke clouded the ceiling and jasmine incense blessed the air.

The large living room was decorated with a honey leather sofa and chair. A fake plant hung near the window and three framed paintings hung on the walls. Kinda looked like old-fashioned paintings of a man fishing, a man relaxing underneath a tent, and of a man hugging a child. Made me think of Kendal.

I rested the bottle of Moet on the coffee table.

"Hello?" I yelled. I was getting uncomfortable with the silence and the Houdini trick Traci was playing. Pianos continued to fill the room with a different soul sound as the smell of jasmine did nothing to relax me. I snatched the bottle from the table. I was angered by her disappearing act. I wasn't one for surprises. "I'm out," I yelled.

Warm colors brightened a small section of the rug near the bedroom door.

"Don't leave."

The Moet bottle came crashing to the floor. Champagne hit the floor, bounced off the wall, and saturated the leg of my jeans. I didn't move.

I squinted and whispered, "Deanna?"

She ignored the broken bottle and moved close to me. She wore a long blue nightgown that opened up and showed everything. I took a step toward the door as she took a step closer. Our eyes met. Mine showed contempt, confusion, and shock. Hers revealed passion, wonder, and awe. She reached for my hand. I pulled away, looking down at the broken bottle of Moet. I couldn't force myself to look at her. I didn't budge.

"Don't move," she instructed as she bent to pick up glass particles that lay on the carpet.

I closed my eyes, clicked my heels, and opened them again. Deanna was still on the ground picking up glass and I was still in the hotel room. *Where the hell was Traci?*

After picking up the last pieces of glass, Deanna stood and faced me. A meek expression covered her face. "Let me explain, Jordan."

I tried to wipe confusion from my forehead, but was unsuccessful. My head throbbed, my heart continued to flutter with wild abandon, and Deanna remained.

I tried to put the pieces together, but remembered I hated puzzles. *Get the hell out now, Styles!* Deanna looked at me and held her hand out. I declined with a simple nod. She walked to the couch, blew the candles out, and turned the music off.

She sat on the couch and crossed her legs. "Can you sit down for a second?"

I declined again. I couldn't believe she had the audacity to think I would entertain the thought of staying. I retrieved the door key from my jacket pocket, walked to the kitchen counter, and slammed it down.

Deanna continued to sit and pat the couch in a gesture for me to sit down.

"Let's just forget this ever happened, okay?" I grumbled.

She continued to call, but my mind was made up. I wanted no part of her. I wanted to get out of a bad situation before things got worse.

I spun around and walked toward the door. With every step I could feel my left pant leg stiffen. Champagne soaked through my jeans causing a slight discomfort when I walked. I cuffed my pants leg until it reached just below my kneecap and continued to the door. "Later!"

"Traci told me about Solomon!"

My hand froze on the cold silver handle. My wrist wanted to continue the corkscrew motion to pry myself out, but my mind wouldn't allow it. My emotions were on the same page with my body. *She's full of shit!* My hand twisted the handle and eased the door open. I heard Deanna get up and walk in my direction. I didn't want to hear any more, didn't want to see any more, and didn't want her being the bearer of my personal bad news.

I remained at the door with evil thoughts flying through my head. A beam of light slid through the door and lit my ashy calf. Chitchatting could be heard down the hall, but in here it was as silent as a confessional booth with two whores and a priest. I wanted to say fuck it to everyone, but my heart wouldn't let me walk away. I had to have answers, but didn't want them. My hand jerked the door open and I walked out.

The cool lights from the hallway temporarily blinded me. I shook my head to adjust, but my vision didn't clear right away. In the distance, I could see men laughing hysterically while waiting on the elevator. That was an elevator ride I didn't want.

Deanna's voice, which was a little more aggressive, followed me into the hallway. "Traci told me about Solomon!" she repeated.

Damn it! I tried to keep going, but couldn't help myself. I needed her mind. Needed to find out what it knew. Telepathy wasn't working, so I turned around. She leaned against the doorway. Her head was in her cupped hand as she cried silently. Her nightgown remained opened at the top and her cleavage held her arms steady as she continued to feel my pain. I was confused about a plan of action.

Traci told her about Solomon? It was hard for me to fathom that Traci would tell Deanna anything. I had to figure out what the hell she was talking about. I walked back toward Deanna and stood in front of her. I didn't know whether I should console her or kick her fucking ass for pulling this on me. I grew more confused with each passing minute.

Nervous, I bit the sides of my cheek. "What did she tell you about Solomon?"

"I can't talk out here," she said weakly. "Can we talk inside?"

Hell, no! I didn't want to feed into any of her bullshit. I wanted to leave, but how could she know Solomon's name? My interest was piqued. I needed confirmation about something, so I agreed to come back into the room.

I followed Deanna to the couch and sat beside her. For a minute, she said nothing. The lights were still off in the living room, but the lone light in the kitchen lit up enough to where we didn't have a romantic setting.

"Go ahead and tell me about this Traci and Solomon thing," I coaxed.

"You want something to drink?"

I shook my head. I wanted to get this over with.

"I don't know if I should be telling you this, Jordan." Her voice showed concern, but I had seen her in action and couldn't believe anything I heard.

"You should be telling me this because you brought it up," I reminded her.

She breathed in deeply and held it in for a few seconds before releasing. "I was at Friday's and happened to see Traci and her friend." She shook her head as if she was wrong for telling me, but she gathered courage and continued. "She remembered who I was and I sent her a complimentary drink. After that, she decided to come over and talk."

"She decided to talk to you?" I asked suspiciously. I could never picture Traci burying the hatchet so easily. I needed more proof that they actually spoke. "And?"

Deanna got up to get a glass of water and sat in the chair opposite me. Her nightgown remained open near her breasts.

"I feel bad for you, Jordan. You really are a good guy."

I was tired of the sugar coating. I wanted it raw and uncut. "Let's cut the BS, Deanna! What did she tell you?"

She grimaced and blurted, "She said that she was still in love with Solomon and that you were some kind of substitute until he came back!" She turned her face away in embarrassment.

In love? Substitute? "Yeah, right!" I laughed off her comment.

"You don't believe me?"

"I don't believe you heard that. Maybe you got her confused with someone else."

"Did he take some kind of furniture from her house?"

Huh? "Huh?"

She repeated, "Did he take some kind of furniture from her house?"

"Why would you ask that?"

"Because she said she was meeting him on Friday so he could bring the furniture back. She mentioned something about not wanting to bring it to a physical level, but if that's what it was going to take to get you back, she was willing."

Anger crept slowly up the back of my neck like a venomous snake in the jungle. She had too much information to be bullshitting! Tears of anger streamed down my cheek as I sprung up and began to pace frantically. The calm of the night didn't match the fury in my soul. I didn't care if Deanna saw that I cried. Didn't care if she told anyone, either. My body slumped back onto the couch. My head found a home on the pillows behind me, and my tears cleansed my soul.

Deanna watched me from the other side of the room. She wasn't sure what I wanted or how to comfort me. With all the information she possessed, I still needed more confirmation.

"Deanna, I need some privacy, okay?"

She walked over, grabbed my hand and whispered, "If you need me, I'll be in the bedroom." She kissed my cheek, and covered her exposed nipples.

Call her! I picked up the receiver, only to slam it down again. I couldn't bring myself to make the call and find out the truth. It was easier to remain in the dark about everything. I could walk away, pretend Deanna lied, and leave the relationship still loving her, or I could call and find things out for myself.

Part of me wished I never gave Traci the ultimatum of speaking with him again. I was too stubborn to go back on it.

She picked up on the third ring.

I faked like I was half-asleep. "Hey, Traci," I said groggily.

"Jordan?"

"Yeah, it's me." My voice was strained. I didn't want Deanna in my business any more than she already was.

"What are you doing up so late? Don't you have to work tomorrow?" she asked.

"Yeah, but I woke up thinking about you. What are you doing up?"

"Me and Sharlana went out to eat after work."

"Where?"

"Friday's."

I remained silent, hoping she would offer some information. My heart hurt as the silence continued to linger. I decided to ask questions. "That's good. How was the crowd?"

"It was okay, I guess," she said nonchalantly. "What did you do?"

"I worked on some projects for the job."

"Oh."

"What are you doing on Friday?"

"I gotta check my schedule," she said. "I think I have something planned."

"How about going to the movies with me on Friday?"

She fell silent again. She cleared her throat and hemmed and hawed. She asked for a second and flipped through some papers. "I think we got this children's function at the daycare Friday evening."

"What about earlier?"

"I'm tired, Jordan! Can we talk about this in the morning?"

"I'd rather get it over with now so I can plan my day tomorrow."

"What about Saturday?"

"I'm busy on Saturday. I want to see you on Friday."

"I have to get back to you on that."

Without giving a response, I slammed down the phone.

Chapter 29

TRACI

"It's twelve-thirty in the morning," Sharlana screamed.

Traci pleaded, "But I have to talk to you!"

"It can't wait until the morning?"

"Not really."

Sharlana asked for a few minutes to gather herself.

Five minutes later, Traci's phone rang. She picked up on the first ring. "Lana?"

"Yeah. What's going on that you had to call me at twelve-thirty?"

"I was going to wait until the morning, but I couldn't after Jordan called and woke me up."

"He called you this late, too?"

"Yes!"

"You guys need to get off the vampire schedule and talk during regular hours like normal people."

"Never mind that. Remember today when we saw Deanna at the bar?"

Sharlana tried to recollect the evening as quickly as possible. "Jordan's secretary, right?"

"Yep! Remember she sent a bottle of Moet over to us?"

"Yeah."

"She put the bottle of Moet she sent to us and the bottle she had on my bill!"

Sharlana's laugh wasn't a pleasant one. "She did what?"

"She put it on my bill. Remember when the bartender asked about a promise?"

"Yeah."

"Deanna told me to promise that the next time she offered a drink, I would accept."

"Okay."

"But what she did was, tell the bartender I promised to buy her whatever she wanted to drink. That's why he came over and asked did I promise. Like a dumb ass I thought she was buying it for me. She got her appetizer and free champagne, and left."

"Get the hell out of here!"

"I was pissed about that, but then Jordan called and started asking tons of questions."

"Like what?"

"Like what was I doing this Friday and could we go to the movies?"

"What's wrong with that?"

"Nothing, if he liked the movies."

"Isn't that movie with Denzel playing? Maybe he wants to see that?"

Traci gave the idea some thought and agreed. "Maybe I am acting a little paranoid."

"The question is, how are you going to get Deanna for pulling that stunt? I say we find the bitch, iron her shirt, rip that weave out her hair, and leave her for dead!" Sharlana suggested.

"I thought about all of that, but I can't find her. I can't ask Jordan for her information because he might get suspicious, and if I did find her, she might start recollecting our conversation."

"You don't think she's that smart?"

"She got a free bottle of Moet, didn't she?"

Chapter 30

JORDAN

"Sir, you're here!"

Damn! My head was spinning. I tried to open my eyes, but as soon as light hit, a pain shot through my forehead and landed in the back of my skull.

"Sir, you're here!"

Sir, you're here! Who in the hell? I covered my face with my hands and rubbed my eyes with the bottom of my palms. My stomach bubbled and bile crept to the back of my throat. Still unable to see, I reached for something to let me out. I grabbed a long handle and heard the man's voice again.

"You need help?" His tone reflected agitation at my lack of speed.

My words were hoarse and scratchy. "I'm fine." I covered my face with my hand and tried to peek around the light. "Where am I?"

"In America," he sarcastically joked. I could tell he was from Pakistan by his accent. I just couldn't pick up why I was where I was.

My eyes slowly adjusted to the light. My stomach gurgled and the nasty taste in my mouth refused to go down. I swallowed and pain shot to my head again as I moved to the left. "Where am I?" I repeated.

"You live at Thames Mead Court, right?"

I nodded. I looked down and saw how disheveled I was. The top three buttons of my open-collared white shirt were undone, my left pant leg was high above my calf and I reeked of alcohol. My stomach bubbled and my head jerked. My hand flew to my mouth as I reached for the door.

"You all right back there?"

My head continued to jerk as horrible tasting fluid rushed my throat. After unsuccessfully opening the door, the dam of my hand began to give way. Three more jerks of my stomach muscles caused my body to lean forward. I tried to swallow, but fluid kept rising. My free hand pounded the seat in front of me to get help. I could see that whoever was in front was wearing a turban and still hadn't turned around.

I tightened my stomach muscles to stop the jerking and held my hand tight against my mouth as I doubled over. Fluid began seeping through my nose and hand that held it altogether.

Turban turned around and yelled, "Not in my cab!" He rushed out and opened the door, but it was too late.

My eyes watered as I spewed the remaining fluid out with a loud hacking cough. I looked down and saw a puddle of greenish looking fluid surrounding my foot. My pants were covered and the smell was repugnant. I lifted my leg out the cab and heard a sloshing sound as my other foot slammed into the puddle. The cold air from the outside did little to hide the chitterlings and bacon smell.

"How much do I owe you?" My breath tasted worse than the smell. I attempted to wipe the few specks from my shirt, but only smeared it deeper. My pants were undone and shoes were untied.

Turban looked inside and shook his head. "Look what you done to my cab."

I didn't bother to turn around. I coughed, squinted, and walked toward him. "How much do I owe?"

"The young lady at the hotel paid for it."

"The young lady at the-" *Deanna! The hotel!* If memory served me correctly, I was going to die a slow death.

"Hey! You forgot your empty bottle of Moet in the back."

Just the sound of the word Moet had my head spinning again.

****

Tony laughed hysterically. Doubled over in pain, he attempted to sit up, but couldn't.

I massaged my temples and told him to keep it down.

"Kendal knows your ass was drunk," he said.

"No, he doesn't! I told him I was at a party last night and they were playing loud music."

"That boy knows you were drunk. He ain't six-years-old."

Tony had a point. No sense in lying about it, but I didn't want to broadcast it either.

"So, you don't even remember if you slept with her?"

I slammed a pillow against my face to block the light that crept from the living room window. "I would know if I slept with her."

"But you don't remember getting in a cab?"

"Right!"

"Start from the beginning. You can't just start in the middle."

I hated to be the butt of the jokes, but I had to hear it from my own mouth to believe it. I removed the pillow from my face and turned over to face him. "I went over there because-"

"You thought Traci left the bottle of Moet, right?" Tony interrupted.

Annoyed, I asked, "Am I telling the story or you?"

A series of guffaws and snickers erupted from him.

I gave him a stern look to insinuate that I wouldn't continue. "Okay, my bad."

"I went there and she told me about seeing Traci and Sharlana at the bar. I already told you what she said they said. Then I called Traci and asked her about Friday, and she acted like her day was top secret, so I drew my own conclusion."

He waved his hand as if to say, come on. "And?"

"Tone, I was heated. Tears started to come, but I fought them off. You know I can't be crying like no little girl, right?" He nodded. I continued, "I was so mad that I had to have something to drink, but I didn't want to go to the gay bar, so she went down and bought us a bottle of Moet."

"After the other one broke, right?"

"Yeah. Man, we drank the whole bottle and ended up downstairs at the gay spot for more drinks."

Tony continued to snicker.

"I think I had about three shots of Hennessey, then we went back upstairs. Next thing you know, she changed back into her nightgown and showed me everything."

Tony's eyes got big as he scooted to the edge of the loveseat. "Word?"

"Word! But get this, she closed up her nightgown and apologized for taking advantage of the situation. Hell, by that time I wasn't worried about a situation. My girl was planning on meeting her ex, and I was drunk and ready to fuck!"

"And you didn't?"

"I tried like hell to fight off the Hennessey, but that shit beat a brotha down. Me and Deanna must've danced three slow songs to some damn piano music."

"Piano?"

"Yeah, piano. She is so sexy that I would've danced to bagpipe music," I joked.

"Then what?"

"I remember resting on the couch, and next thing you know, everything went blank. I don't remember a thing."

"What are you going to do about Traci?"

"I guess I'll know tomorrow."

"You're a better man than me because after all that, I would've been trying to do something else on Friday. If you need me, give me a ring. Keep your head up."

Tony left and Kendal crept out his room.

"You okay, Dad?"

Oh boy! "I'm okay, son. Why?"

"Because you look like sh-" My head flew up to meet his next word. "Crap. You look like crap, Dad."

My body slumped back into the couch. I swung my feet off the couch and waved for him to sit next to me.

"Want something to drink?" he asked.

Just hearing the word drink made me cringe. "Nope!"

He poured himself a glass of Kool-Aid and plopped down next to me.

We both listened to each other breathe for a few minutes. I debated on whether to tell him about what was going on, but decided he wasn't old enough to handle everything.

"You ever drink?" I asked.

"Nope!"

"Ever smoke?"

"Nope!"

"Ever want a girlfriend?"

"Nope!"

"Ever thought about love?"

"Nope!"

I turned on the television to Springer and rubbed his head playfully. "That's my boy! Keep it that way for as long as possible."

Chapter 31

TRACI

Traci looked into her full-length mirror and sighed. It was six twenty and she was supposed to meet Solomon in forty minutes. Jordan had left three messages for her at work to call him, but she didn't want to speak to anyone. Today was her Day of Atonement. She was going to lay her demons to rest for good.

She zipped up her black dress, sprayed perfume on, and stared into the mirror.

What the hell am I doing?

She wondered what Jordan was doing. She wondered if, after tonight, Solomon would leave her alone for good. She wondered why she had to see him face-to-face. So many questions filtered through her mind, and she had no answer for any of them. What she did know was that she truly loved Jordan. She knew she risked losing the man she loved because of something she needed to do. Jordan was right in the part that he shouldn't have to hear about Solomon so much, but she couldn't understand how come he didn't respect what she had to do. If the shoe was on the other foot, she realized she would probably do the same thing he did.

It was six forty. She picked up the phone to dial Sharlana, but quickly placed the phone back on the hook. Too many times in life she leaned on her friends and family to help her, but after her decision was made, she had to live with it.

Traci got into her car, slid a CD in, and listened to Keith Sweat sing about making it last forever. She needed a love like that. Needed a love that lasted forever. A love that made her body tingle. Her toes curl. She reached up, opened the sunroof, and let damp air cool her off. For it to be only seventy-two degrees, it felt like the summertime as she drove toward downtown.

With one hand locked around the wheel, the other hand held onto her cell phone just in case. She wanted to call Jordan and tell him to meet her there, but remembered if he found out she went, there wouldn't be a tomorrow. There would be no more smiles, hugs, laughs, or them. She couldn't risk Solomon not giving back her stuff, couldn't risk Solomon popping in and out of her life, and couldn't risk not knowing the truth.

She pulled into the Hilton Hotel and a young black valet approached her car.

"Keys, please?"

Traci sat in her car and thought about continuing her journey, or just forgetting about everything. Was Jordan really Solomon's substitute? Could she ever trust Jordan? Had Solomon really changed? These three questions allowed her key to stay in the ignition a little longer. Made her think a little harder and made her heart ache even more. Secretly, she wished one of them would have made the decision easier for her, but neither did.

She reached for the tissue box, hesitated, and handed the valet the key. Reluctantly, she pulled a few papery wipes from the box. *What the hell!* If she cried, she cried.

"Thank you. You here for Mr. Jackson's unveiling?"

She nodded, accepted his hand, and got out of the car.

"It's right around the corner, Room 5." He held her hand until she stepped over the curb. "You okay, Miss?"

Traci wiped a tear from the corner of her eye and whispered, "I'll be okay."

Traci followed the noise to Room 5. She wanted to turn around and leave, but knew it had to be done. Knew it was her last shot at closure. Knew she couldn't move forward without taking a step back and closing up all the holes in her heart. Her blood pressure had to be near stroke level. Either way, she was sure a stroke would come.

Before she reached the room, she took out her compact and checked her make-up. She took a deep breath before walking through the double doors.

"Is your name on the list?" the older gentleman at the podium asked.

"I guess so," Traci said quietly. She looked into the room and everyone, minus a few, was dressed up. There were businessmen, ladies in suits, and a few people dressed in casual clothes networking. The tables were all decorated in black and white with streamers across the room. A huge colorful banner sat above the table in front reading, "Congratulations Solomon."

She cleared her throat. "My name is Traci Johnson."

The man looked up and smiled as if he knew her. "So you're Traci Johnson! Let me take a look at you," he said, adjusting his glasses. "I've heard so much about you."

Traci clutched her pocketbook and a startled look crossed her face. "And you are-"

He covered his mouth and laughed. "Oh, I'm James." He put his arm around her and squeezed tightly. "But you can call me, Uncle Jimmy."

"Okay-" she paused and smiled, "Uncle Jimmy."

He quickly reached in his pocket and took out his cell phone. "She's here, AJ."

He guided her to the side. "Hold tight." He perused the list for a lady that stood in back of Traci.

Traci looked around and marveled at all the people Solomon knew. He said he was making moves, but this was unbelievable. She felt a tugging at her hand.

"You are looking good!" The smell was familiar and the voice matched.

Traci turned around and saw Solomon dressed in a black and white tuxedo. He smiled that infectious smile of his as he bent down and scooped her up in his arms.

"I'm so glad you could make it."

Traci felt like crying. She wanted this for so long, but now it wasn't the same. She had changed over the past year and a half. He could no longer walk away and come back to the same Traci, like he used to. He could not put on the charm and get her to melt in his arms. She had someone that would never walk away like she meant nothing. As they continued to embrace, Traci looked at all the smiling faces that walked around the room. Maybe some of their smiles were artificial like hers. Maybe some settled for someone because they had to. It didn't take this function to make Traci realize what she wanted. It took this place to make her realize what she didn't want. She didn't want to be treated like a sex object. She didn't want to be the good one the men kept at home. She wanted to be everything to one man. Jordan wasn't the substitute for Solomon, instead he was the answer to the question she had asked herself all of these years. Can a man love me unconditionally?

Traci released her grip from him and looked him in the eye. "I held up my end of the bargain, now could you hold up yours?"

"Stay a little while longer," he begged.

"I can't."

"You have to," he pleaded.

"I shouldn't have come here now, but I had to. Are you going to hold up to your end of the deal?" she repeated.

Solomon smiled, grabbed Traci's hand and led her to the door.

"I just want you to see what I'm doing. See where I'm going. Understand that I can take care of you now."

"But I don't want this. I'm happy where I am. Happy with the direction my life is going, and happy that I've gotten over you."

A few people to their immediate left began eyeing Solomon and Traci. Solomon grabbed her hand and pulled her to the side.

"Baby, I never meant to hurt you, but I wanted to do something to hurt him and make that nigga go away."

"Well, you almost did that. I got in so much shit because of you coming to the poetry spot and-"

"Its a free country. I love the written word just like the next man."

"Whatever! You almost ruined what took me so long to get. A real relationship that I've wanted all my life. Some normalcy."

He turned her toward the crowd of people. "I've got normalcy. Hell, I just sold the construction business and I'm moving into something else."

"What?"

"A catering business. You know how much I love to cook. Someone offered me great money for the business and I wanted out. I wanted to try something new and have you by my side. We can move an hour from here and start all over."

Traci cried as she tried to break away from Solomon's grip. "I can't. I don't love you like that anymore."

Solomon couldn't understand why Traci didn't want him. Didn't want to see the truth. His face became intense. "You gotta give me another chance."

"Why?"

"Because I've got so much to offer."

"I don't need anything from you but my furniture."

"Please."

"Let it go."

"One more try?"

"No, Solomon."

Traci snatched her hand away as tears poured from her eyes. She sought an escape. She fled the room.

Solomon caught up and held her tight. Traci fell into his arms and cried for Jordan. She cried for Solomon. She cried for her unborn baby. She cried for freedom.

"I gotta go, Solomon."

They walked in silence. His arm was around her for the last time. Neither wanted to say goodbye forever, but both knew it had to be done.

Solomon made a gesture for the valet to retrieve her car.

He pulled her close and held her tight. Traci's head fell to his neck and she inhaled his cologne one final time. She wanted to remember what he smelled like. She wanted to take it all in because this was her final goodbye.

Solomon wrapped his arms around her. "I love you."

Her head remained buried in the hollow of his chest. "Why didn't you tell me this a year and a half ago?"

"I was growing." He bent down and kissed Traci on the cheek before relinquishing his grip. "I will always love you."

Traci wiped her face and whispered, "I will always love you, too!" She slid into her car and snapped on her seatbelt.

Solomon stood over her and smiled, "What are you going to do now that you're all dressed up with nowhere to go?"

Traci popped Keith Sweat back in and said, "I'm going to the movies."

Cell phone in hand, she sped off without looking behind her. As she neared the exit to the hotel, she noticed a note on her windshield.

The letters were large and black. "Turn around!"

Chapter 32

JORDAN

$\mathcal{I}$ couldn't believe what I was seeing. Solomon's hand glided down the back of Traci's dress as he whispered something into her ear.

Go bust his ass! It wasn't his fault. I watched them talk for a few moments and then embrace for a few. My heart ached and body went numb when his lips touched her cheek. If I was going to throw up this time, it wasn't due to alcohol. I turned the music down and watched it as though I were watching a movie. I didn't want to be there, but I had to see things for myself.

Traci pulled off, reached around to get the note from her windshield, and came to a screeching halt.

Fifteen yards separated us. Solomon stood in between both of us, his eyes transfixed on her. I inched closer to the windshield wanting to see her eyes. Wanting her to see me.

She read the note and her eyes instantly scanned her rearview mirror.

My heart thumped so loud I could hear every throb, feel every ounce of blood running through my veins. My eyes were glossed, ego shattered, and feelings hurt.

Solomon, who watched her pull off, thought she was stopping for him. A grin replaced his smug look as he walked toward her. He raised his hands in the air as if he knew she would come back.

I quietly exited my car and followed their trail.

Through her rearview mirror, Traci could see Solomon walking toward her and me toward him. Solomon continued his vibrant strides her way with me doing my ninja thing in back. My blood pressure bubbled and my heart raced. Visions of their embrace had me blacking out. I lost control. I wanted Traci, but at the same time I was through with her. I saw what I had come to see. Now it was time to do what I had to do. Fuck a ramification. I just witnessed my woman hugging the man that wreaked havoc on my life and my relationship for the past four months. If it wasn't him, it might've been someone else. I didn't want to think about that either, so I concentrated on their lips locking, his hands cradling her back, and the smile on her face.

Traci didn't drive off or get out. She watched the movie play out in her rearview mirror. I didn't know whether her proof that she was on my side was not telling him I was coming or if she was simply stunned. Regardless, he continued to walk, and I continued to stalk. I was gonna be king of this damn jungle! I realized that I wanted a piece of him and no piece of her.

Solomon yelled, "I knew you couldn't leave me."

I was two steps away as he neared Traci.

"I knew you would come back," he said confidently. He stood above her car, hands on her hood, smiling. Traci didn't respond as he watched her glare into her rearview mirror. He saw the horrid look on her face and as soon as he looked up, a large thump blessed the air. With blood oozing from his left temple, Solomon lay on the sidewalk, out cold.

Traci jumped out of her car. "Jordan?"

As she reached her fallen soldier, I took a few steps backwards and yelled, "He never played fair either!"

As she tried to revive him, she yelled, "I love you, Jordan."

I wiped my eyes and knew my knuckle was broken this time as I continued to walk backwards and watch her try to revive Solomon. As she watched me, she stood and walked the opposite direction as I, leaving Solomon in a mangled position. It was like an exit from a horrible love story. My steps were heavy. My eyes glazed and my body shook. I could see Traci sliding into her car. Her head never went forward . Her eyes said she wanted to stop me, but in her heart she knew it was over. Knew that too much damage was done. Knew I would never come back.

I jumped in the passenger's side of the car and seconds later the wind trailed up my sleeve, cooling my burning knuckle, subduing my burning desire to go back and finish the job. My mind was finally at peace.

"Where do you wanna go?"

"Take me anywhere, Deanna. Take me anywhere."

Her tires screamed. The sun peaked out from underneath the tunnel ahead.

Visions of the kiss, his elbow, the furniture, the poetry, the lovemaking, her child, my son, and our future quickly ran through my head. It was like a good movie with a few bad scenes.

"Wait!" My hands slammed against the dashboard.

Deanna hit the brakes.

I jumped out.

I walked near the sliver of sunlight that Traci sat near.

Solomon rolled toward darker shades of the concrete.

I stepped over.

Traci continued to watch through the rearview mirror.

I opened my arms. A piece of sunlight hit my wrist and glistened in the light.

Her door cracked.

We embraced.

I whispered, "No more ultimatums, baby."

ALSO AVAILABLE FROM
Q-BORO
B O O K S

DOGISM
$14.95
ISBN 097530660X

MY WOMAN, HIS WIFE
$14.95
ISBN 0975306626

STREETS OF NEW YORK, V. 1
14.95
ISBN 0975306618

GHETTO HEAVEN
14.95
ISBN 0975306634

KING OF SPADES
14.95
ISBN 0975306642

BRAZEN
14.95
ISBN 0975306650

MONEY POWER RESPECT
14.95
ISBN 0975306677

SHAMELESS
14.95
ISBN 0975306669

Attention Writers:

Writers looking to get their books published can view our submission guidelines by visiting our website at:
www.QBOROBOOKS.com

Or by mailing us at:
Q-Boro Books
Attn: Submissions
110-64 Queens Blvd., Ste. 191
Forest Hills, NY 11375

(Please check our website for any address changes.)